ENDLESSLY

PRAISE FOR
THE PARANORMALCY TRILOGY

"The most imaginative
vampire/werewolf/supernatural series going."
—*Newsday*

"Strong characters, a clever premise, and a hilarious voice
all team up to make *Paranormalcy* the most refreshing
paranormal debut of the year."
(((((LISA McMANN)))))
New York Times bestselling
author of the Wake trilogy

"A fast, flirty roller coaster of a ride. This story was everything
I hoped for—sassy, light-hearted and downright scary.
Oh, bleep! I'm in love!"
(((((BECCA FITZPATRICK)))))
New York Times bestselling
author of *Hush, Hush*

"*Paranormalcy* seduced me. The two sexy paranormals who
vie for Evie's affections each had their own victory; one won
Evie's heart and the other won mine."
(((((APRILYNNE PIKE)))))
#1 *New York Times* bestselling
author of *Wings*

Also by Kiersten White

PARANORMALCY
SUPERNATURALLY

ENDLESSLY

KIERSTEN WHITE

HarperCollins *Children's Books*

First published in the USA by HarperCollins *Publishers* Inc. in 2012
First published in paperback in Great Britain by HarperCollins *Children's Books* in 2012
HarperCollins *Children's Books* is a division of HarperCollins*Publishers* Ltd,
77-85 Fulham Palace Road, Hammersmith, London, W6 8JB.

www.harpercollins.co.uk

1

ENDLESSLY
Copyright © Kiersten Brazier 2012
All rights reserved

ISBN 978-0-00-739017-5

Printed and bound in England by Clays Ltd, St Ives plc.
Typography by Michelle Taormina

MIX
Paper from
responsible sources
FSC
www.fsc.org
FSC® C007454

FSC™ is a non-profit international organisation established to promote
the responsible management of the world's forests. Products carrying the
FSC label are independently certified to assure consumers that they come
from forests that are managed to meet the social, economic and
ecological needs of present and future generations,
and other controlled sources.

Find out more about HarperCollins and the environment at
www.harpercollins.co.uk/green

FOR ELENA AND JONAH
MY LIFE, MY JOY, MY TWO LITTLE WONDERS

PINK GOES WITH EVERYTHING

$\mathcal{H}$ere's the thing about dragons: I know absolutely nothing whatsoever about them.

Which made my task to scare raccoons out of the alley behind the diner much more complicated. Instead of the mini masked bandits, I was greeted by a pale, serpentine body with feathers raised like spikes along its spine and shoulders. Its face was almost wolfish, a long snout cut by two thick tusks jutting out and curling up over the lips. Oh, and claws. Sharp claws. "You are not a raccoon," I whispered.

"Nae, child, I am no wee beast." The air tasted like

charcoal as its voice slid out, high and smooth and age-less, momentarily shocking me even more than the fact that there was a dragon hanging around behind the trash cans. *It talked*. Well, of course it talked, Evie. Because really, what kind of self-respecting, trash can–scrabbling mythical dragon wouldn't talk? I was equal parts terrified and annoyed. But at least the dragon didn't smell as bad as unicorns.

Then again, unicorns were herbivores.

It breathed in deeply, a golden glow growing in its chest. For once I didn't think that light was related to its soul. Not soul; definitely fire. I didn't have time to dash back through the door and close it before being roasted—nor did I like the door's odds against a dragon. I could make a break for it down the alley, but I had no idea how fast this creature was. I decided on honesty. "Are you going to eat me?" I asked.

"Is that your desire?"

"Not really, no. The Winter Formal is coming up, and it's not going to plan itself, so this is kind of a bad time for me. Can we reschedule?" I took a step back. People used to fight dragons, right? I could do this. All I needed was a full suit of armor. And a sword. Or a mace. Or *some* Mace.

The door opened behind me, flooding the alley with light from the kitchen, and I yelped in relief.

"There you are," Nona said. She nodded to the dragon.

"You two know each other?" Why did this surprise me? Of course the resident tree spirit would know the talking dragon hanging out in the alley, just like she knew every other weird paranormal recently lurking about town. And I had no doubt that this meeting, too, would go entirely unexplained.

I so needed to get a new job.

"Evelyn, I have served your friends milk shakes. Please enjoy your evening." Smiling placidly at me, Nona walked out past the dragon toward the end of the alley where the forest pushed up against the town. The dragon fixed one gleaming, dark pink eye on me, then winked.

Forget a new job. I needed to get a new town.

A breeze blew past me in a massive gust, flinging my hair into my mouth. The dragon took a few graceful hops, then slid like a snake through the air after Nona.

"Fabulous," I muttered, going into the kitchen and shutting—then locking—the door. "Glad Nona has another new friend." Taking a deep breath to clear my sinuses of the lingering smell of smoke, I squared my shoulders and walked into the main part of the diner. I just faced off against a dragon and came away char free. I was ready to fight.

"Now," I said, sitting down at the corner booth and glaring at the five other teenagers there, "who says pink isn't a good color scheme for this dance?"

I threw my binder of materials down on our apartment's tired floral couch. "Seriously, pink *is* a neutral color! And what's elegant about navy blue? No one ever says, 'Hey, you know what's elegant? The Navy!'"

Arianna rolled her dead eyes. "There is nothing neutral about pink. They need a color that looks good as a background to any shade of dress."

"What color clashes with pink?"

"Orange?"

"Well, if anyone shows up in an orange dress, she deserves to clash. Yuck."

"Chill out. You can do a lot with navy."

I sank down into the couch next to her. "I guess. I could do navy with silver accents. Stars?"

"Yawn."

"Snowflakes?"

"Gee, now you're getting creative for a *winter* formal."

I ignored her tone, as usual. I was just glad she was here. She'd been gone a lot lately. "Hmm . . . maybe something softer. Like a water and mist theme?" I asked.

"I . . . actually kind of like that."

"Wanna help me with the sketches?"

She leaned forward and turned on *Easton Heights*. "Decorating a stupid dance is all yours. You're the one who decided to be more involved in your 'normal' life. I'd prefer to be sleeping eternally six feet under."

"This is probably a bad time to mention I also might have signed up to help with costumes for the spring play. And since I know nothing about sewing, I kind of maybe signed you up as a volunteer aide."

She sighed, running one glamoured corpse hand through her spiky red and black hair. "I am going to kill you in your sleep."

"As long as it doesn't hurt."

We hummed along to the opening theme, which ended when the door banged open and my boyfriend walked through, shrugging out of his coat and beaming as he dropped a duffel bag. "Free! What did I miss?" Lend asked, his cheeks rosy from the cold and his smile lighting up his water eyes beneath his dark glamour ones.

"I lost the vote on color schemes for the dance, the last episode of *Easton Heights* before they go into reruns is back on in three minutes, and Arianna is going to murder me in my sleep."

"As long as it doesn't hurt."

"That's what I said!"

Lend scooped me into his arms, turning around and sitting back down on the couch with me in his lap. This Christmas break of his couldn't have come soon enough. After the crazy events of last month—including but not limited to finding out that my father was a faerie, being abandoned in the Faerie Paths by a vengeful Jack, and finally finding my way back to Lend—we needed some time together to relax. I'd figured out that *this* was the only answer I needed about my life. No more worrying about how much time I'd have, no more fretting over what I was or wasn't. What I *was* was here, now. And happy.

"Anything else?" he asked, playing with my hair.

"Oh, yeah, there's a dragon in the alley behind the diner, hanging out with Nona."

Lend frowned at me, his warm fingers lingering on the back of my neck. "And this gets a mention *after* the color scheme for a dance and a new episode of a teen soap?"

"Priorities, Lend. Priorities."

My IPCA communicator beeped from the coffee table during a commercial, earning me an icy glare from Arianna. "If it goes off during dialogue, I will smash it to pieces."

"Sorry! I told Raquel to call on my actual cell. The one that is cute and pink and has a cool ringtone instead of an annoying beep. Not like I can do anything for IPCA now anyway."

"That whole lack-of-faerie-transportation thing does kind of make it pointless." Lend tried not to sound too happy about it, but I knew he was secretly thrilled.

I wasn't sure how to feel. It had been nice to be involved with Raquel again, and I didn't mind helping out in the ways that *I* wanted to with IPCA. But I wouldn't travel anywhere with a faerie. A very small part of me was curious to see if I could use the Faerie Paths on my own now. But that part was very, *very* small, and all the other parts of me thought that part was crazy and wanted to beat it up. I was never going back into that inky, empty darkness.

My communicator beeped again, and Arianna gave it such a death look that I snatched it from the table and ran back to my room before she could put it into early retirement.

"Raquel, honestly! Just call on my cell!" I answered.

"Evelyn," a strong voice that was definitely not Raquel said.

"I— Who is this?"

"Anne-Laurie LeFevre, Supervisor. Raquel's no longer over you; you will report to me."

"I'll *what*?"

"From now on I will be your supervising authority with IPCA. We need to discuss your schedule and reform the current arrangement. There are several infractions that need to be addressed as well."

"Whoa—first things first, I'm not *with* IPCA. So you are not my Supervisor or my authority or whatever. Second of all, I work with Raquel. Only Raquel. Does she know about this? I want to talk to her."

"Raquel isn't available; she's been reassigned."

"Well, so have I. To my life. So thanks but no thanks, and don't call back." I disconnected and glared at my communicator. Which beeped—again. I ignored the incoming line and dialed Raquel, but the call didn't go through; maybe she was busy with her reassignment, whatever that meant. I'd have to get ahold of her to find out what the crap was up with IPCA. When I went back to work for them, we all agreed it was on a contract basis and I could leave whenever I wanted. Apparently someone hadn't gotten the memo. Raquel would take care of it, though.

"Evie! Commercial is over!" Arianna yelled. Frowning, I shoved my communicator into my trusty sock drawer.

Lend stood up, shouldering his duffel bag, as I walked back into the living room. "Where do you think you're going?" I snatched his coat away and held it. He just got here. There was no way I was letting him go anywhere else.

"I happen to have very important things to do."

"What on earth is more important than watching *Easton Heights*?"

"Christmas shopping for you?"

I dropped the coat into his arms and opened the door. "Take your time."

"Glad to know I'll be missed."

"Have fun!" I leaned up and kissed him hard, then shoved him out and sat back on the couch with a sloppy smile on my face. "Best boyfriend ever."

"Shut. Up. Now." Arianna didn't move, eyes fixed on the television. A firm knock sounded on the door. "And tell Lend he can just walk in already!"

"Did you forget something?" I said as I opened the door, surprised to see a short black woman in a suit. And not Lend pretending to be one, either. Definitely just a woman, no glamour. "Umm, hi?" That was when I noticed the man standing to the side behind her. The man who, beneath the glamour, was a faerie.

"Evelyn," the woman said, in a voice I instantly recognized from our phone conversation. Oh, bleep no. Not here, not now, not with my best vampire friend sitting right there on the couch. This was the last place I wanted anyone from IPCA other than Raquel.

I straightened my shoulders and fixed Anne-Whatever Whatever with an icy glare. "I'm sorry, did I say it was okay for you to come here? Because last time I checked, I don't work for you anymore. In fact, wait."

I stalked back to my room and grabbed my communicator. "Here," I said, shoving it into her hands. "I won't be needing this. When I said I will only talk to Raquel, I meant, *I will only talk to Raquel.* Feel free to pass that along. And if you ever use a faerie to come to my home again, I will tase you both."

I slammed the door in her face, then put both hands over my mouth in panic. IPCA. Here. Pretty much the epicenter of free paranormals in the United States. Regardless of the reforms they'd undergone, I did not want them paying any attention whatsoever to my town. Or to my swarming-with-paranormals diner. How did they know where I was? Raquel wouldn't have told them. Would she? No. *Never.* I needed to call David right now. I needed to talk to Raquel to figure out what the bleep was going on. And I needed to make sure that Arianna *never* got fitted with an ankle tag.

"What did she want?" Arianna's tough voice betrayed a hint of fear.

"I don't know," I whispered, my heart still racing as I stared at the closed door and willed it to stay that way.

BARKING MAD

Pouting again?" Vivian and I sat on our usual dark hillside, but it seemed darker than normal, the stars winking out one by one as I watched.

"Hmm? Oh, no. Just worried about the usual. Weird stuff going on with paranormals. IPCA being obnoxious. Did you know dragons are real?"

She snorted. "You really should give the whole coma thing a shot. It makes life much less complicated. In fact, the only complicated thing here is you."

"As tempting as a coma sounds, I'd miss out on all the snuggling parts of life. I like those."

"Fine," she said, sighing. "It's lonely here between visits, though."

I leaned my head on her shoulder. "I know. What's up with the stars?"

"I haven't the foggiest. Does it feel warmer to you?"

The last star winked out.

The Vivian dream faded to blackness.

The next morning, disappointed I hadn't had a chance to recap the most recent episodes of *Easton Heights* for my comatose sister, I snuck out past Lend. He was asleep on the floral couch, having passed out sometime in the wee hours of the morning. He'd insisted on staying the night and keeping watch in case anyone from IPCA showed up again. Tasey, my hot pink and rhinestone-covered Taser, looked kind of ridiculous still clutched in his hands. We'd have to get him a matching one, maybe in electric blue.

I didn't think that a midnight attack was IPCA's style; it was weird for them to show up here, yeah, but they weren't the sneak-around-in-the-night type. They were the slowly-suck-the-soul-from-you-with-the-bureaucracy type. Even if they were restructuring again (which wouldn't be shocking, given that they'd lost most of the senior members during Reth's postfreedom revenge spree), it'd be a while before anything actually happened policywise. I've been around long enough to understand how international government agencies work. It doesn't matter if they're regulating the transportation of goods like socks or the transportation of mythical creatures like pixies. Papers, more papers, forms, documents, signatures, lawyers—trust me, the whole thing is scarier than a vampire with a slicked-back widow's peak.

Which wasn't to say that I didn't feel a little bit nervous, but Raquel would know what was going on. She'd fix it.

David had just forwarded me a text from her saying she would meet me at our café in thirty minutes. He didn't have more specifics, and I figured she meant the Jitterbug Café we talked in after my troll encounter this October. How David had gotten ahold of her I didn't know. Since when were they texting buddies?

It'd take me at least forty-five minutes to get to the café, assuming I made the next bus. Lend would give me a ride if I woke him up and asked, but he'd gotten so little sleep last night, and I didn't think I could deal with his attitude toward Raquel on top of all the other worries. They never got along.

I resisted the urge to sit and stare at Lend while he slept; when he dreamed, instead of his eyes moving behind his eyelids, his whole glamour shifted appearances like a stop-motion film. It was fascinating and wildly entertaining sometimes—also a bit freaky considering I showed up constantly.

I nearly ran over Grnlllll as I burst through the door into the diner. "What are you still doing here?" I asked, before seeing Nona swishing around the red tables, which were populated by several paranormals, including Kari and Donna, the resident selkies. "You were supposed to evacuate!"

When I told David about my non-Raquel IPCA visitor last night, he had made a snap decision to get all the paranormals out of town. I supported this, although it was harder than I'd expected to motivate Arianna to pack and leave. Finally she said she'd go to David's secluded house, wanting to be around in case we needed help. But these paranormals had no reason to be here.

"Nona, you all need to leave! IPCA knows I'm here, which means they might know you're all here, too!"

Nona smiled at me, waving a hand like a branch disturbed by the wind. "IPCA poses no threat to us."

I ran my fingers through my ponytail, torn. I needed to book it to meet Raquel in time, but I needed to convince them to leave, too. I had no idea what IPCA would do taggingwise with a huldra, a gnome, two selkies, and, well, whatever those three mournfully beautiful but kind of scary-looking women with long black hair sitting— floating?—in the corner were.

"No, really, they might be a problem. Just go somewhere else until we figure out what's up with IPCA. It's probably nothing. Hopefully it's nothing. But until we know for sure, I need to know you're all safe."

"Dear child," Nona said, smiling warmly and taking my face in both her hands. She leaned forward and brushed my forehead with her moss-green lips. "Soon."

She backed away and I frowned, adding her affection to the ever-growing list of Suspicious Things Nona Does, then pulled out my phone and looked at the time. "Crap! I missed the bus."

Kari fixed her impossibly big, round brown eyes on me. "Do you want a ride? We can give you a ride! Anywhere! Fast!"

"You have a car?"

She and Donna barked their matching laughs. Torn, I looked back at Nona, who was calmly wiping the long barstool-lined counter. "We'll talk more when I get back."

I followed the selkies outside to a classic VW Beetle parked along the street. It was a sparkly midnight-blue convertible with white leather seats. "Seriously?" I asked. How did two creatures who spent the better part of the last few centuries as seals have a car this cool? And how pathetic did that make me that I still didn't have one?

I slid past the passenger seat into the back, and Kari sat behind the wheel.

"How did you get a driver's license?" I asked, curious. I was going to take a driver's ed course in the spring, but maybe they could hook me up with an easier class.

"What's a driver's license?" Kari answered, before peeling out into the middle of the street.

Oh, *bleep*.

My eyes were squeezed shut, my fingers in a death grip

around my seat belt, when the chorus of my latest favorite song played, muffled by my purse. I pried my hand free and dug out my cell. Kari took another curve at blinding speed, centrifugal force smashing me against the window.

"Slow down!" I screamed, putting the phone up to my ear. "What! I mean, hi!"

"Where are you?" Lend asked. I could hear the panic in his voice. Ah, crud, should have left him a note.

"I'm on my way to meet Raquel at the Jitterbug Café. Kari, *tree*!" We swerved violently and the car lifted completely off the right-side wheels before bumping back down. "Trees do not move for cars! Cars *avoid trees*!"

Donna's barking laughter rang through the tiny space as she clapped her hands, delighted.

"What are you doing? Are you safe?" Lend asked, shouting over the background noise coming through my end.

"Not right now, no. Red light! *Red light!*" We sailed through anyway, an SUV coming so close to clipping our bumper I could have counted the other driver's teeth, all of which were showing in a grimace of terror. "Pull over! I'm getting out!"

"But we're not there yet," Kari said, turning all the way back to fix her round, watery eyes on me.

"Eyes on the road! The road! Stop stop stop *stop stop stop* STOP!"

Kari blinked, then turned around and slammed her foot all the way down on the brakes. I flew forward as the seat belt locked and dug into my collarbone so hard I was sure I'd be bruised. A screeching sound echoed through the Beetle, and the acrid smell of burning rubber filled my nose as we came to a complete stop in the middle of the road.

"I'm gonna call you back," I said, my voice trembling, then I hung up.

Donna jumped out and flipped her seat forward, smiling helpfully as I fell out of the car and scooted on my hands and knees to the sidewalk, resting my forehead gratefully against the freezing cement.

Okay, maybe there *were* some forms of transportation worse than holding a faerie's hand.

Donna patted me on the back, her hand coming down too hard. "That was fun!" she said. "Where should we go next?"

"Nowhere with you two, ever again."

I turned and sat down. Kari had left the car where it stopped and walked over to us. She raised her eyebrows quizzically at me. "Are you okay, Evie?"

"No! You almost killed me!"

She shook her head vehemently. "No! We're here to keep you safe. Always safe. We're in charge of you." She smiled proudly.

"You aren't—" I paused and forced my face into a calm smile. The selkies lacked any artifice or pretense. Nona dodged my questions, but maybe they wouldn't know they needed to. "Yeah. Of course! Remind me who put you in charge of keeping me safe?"

"Nona!"

Donna nodded in agreement. "And the shiny man."

"The shiny man?" I asked. "You mean Lend?"

"No, the shiny man with hair and eyes like sunshine."

I held my smile firmly in place. "Reth? The faerie?"

"Faerie, yes! That's not his name though; he'll never tell. He's shiny. And pretty. I like it when he talks to me." Donna reached up and smoothed her luxurious walnut-brown hair, smiling dreamily.

"I knew it! I knew Nona was working with Reth!" I stood, shaking with fury. Despite David's insistence that we could trust that wicked tree spirit, I'd known something was up with her for months. And now she was assigning the selkies to keep tabs on me for Reth?

"Are you angry?" Kari asked, concern pooling in her eyes like tears. "Did we do something wrong?"

I took a deep breath, the bitingly cold air filling my lungs and stinging my throat. This wasn't their fault. The selkies were as innocent and happy as seals playing in the waves, their immortal lives nothing but an eternal game. They were just doing what they were told—what they thought was best. "No, you didn't do anything wrong. Thanks."

"Okay! Let's drive more, then!"

"NO! I mean, umm, I want to walk the rest of the way to the café, since we're almost there. But you two can go.

Lend is going to come and get me, and I'm always safe with him."

Donna frowned dubiously. "Are you sure? We can stay. I'll braid your hair!"

"And I have nail polish in the car!" Kari said, already bouncing in anticipation.

"No, you should go tell Nona that I'm safe. She might be worried."

"Should we wait where you can't see us, like we do when you're in school?"

I froze my face into a mask of a smile, but the veins in my neck felt like they were going to explode they were pounding so hard with fury. I didn't get out of IPCA's controlling grasp to be spied on and monitored by a tree spirit and my crazy faerie ex. "You don't need to. I talked to Nona today and she said it was okay for you two to leave me."

Kari's eyes narrowed, cutting their shape from near-perfect circles to almonds. "Are you sure she said that?"

"Absolutely."

She held my gaze for another moment, then shrugged, smile bouncing back into place. "Okay then! See you later!"

Donna waved cheerily and they both got into the car, squealing away. I watched until they turned the corner, then ran as fast as I could toward the café. When I got there, I collapsed against the dark brick exterior, my breath fogging out in pants.

How long had they been tailing me? Which other

paranormals were in on it? Nona and Grnlllll for sure, but them I already suspected. Those three weird women this morning—I'd seen them once before talking to Nona. The dragon? Did she have a dragon tailing me? I looked up at the sky, paranoid, but didn't see any white monsters snaking through the sparse clouds.

What about . . . Arianna? I bit my lip. She lived with me, after all. Who better to watch me than my roommate? I put my head back against the rough, uneven bricks. I wanted Lish back. I'd never, ever had to doubt her or question her motives. I knew she was my friend no matter what. It had been the two of us against the world, and sometimes I didn't know where my place was without her to talk to.

Arianna wasn't the friend Lish had been. She was cranky and rude, and sometimes it seemed like she hated me more than she liked me. But then again, Arianna really wasn't the same type of paranormal as Nona and her ilk. They came that way. Arianna was forced into the paranormal realm against her will.

Besides, surely anyone trying to spy on me and get in my good graces wouldn't leave so many sopping wet towels on the carpet.

No, I trusted Arianna. Arianna, Lend, David, and Raquel. I sighed heavily, then pulled out my phone to check the time. I was still a couple minutes early. I'd missed three calls from Lend and had a new text from Carlee, my one normal friend. I'd kill to go get a pedicure with her today and debate the merits of the boys' basketball team versus the soccer team. While I personally found shape-shifting artists superior in all ways, I did admire soccer player legs.

Alas. My fingers were too cold to type anyway. Ignoring the text, I hit dial and Lend picked up on the first ring.

"I need you to come pick me up after I talk to Raquel," I said. "And I need to move out of the diner apartment."

"Done and done. I was going to make you come to my dad's place tonight anyway. And I assume you're going to tell me what's going on?"

"As much as I know." My voice was as glum as I felt. Because, as usual, as much as I knew wasn't nearly enough. At least Raquel would have some answers for me.

THE SHORTEST DAY OF
THE YEAR

Thirty minutes later my knees were bouncing uncontrollably. Partly from nerves—where was she?—but mostly because I was on vanilla Coke number four. Caffeine and I had always been a bad combination, now made worse by the nervous energy I could feel constantly flowing through me from the part of Uber-vamp's soul I'd taken when he attacked me on Halloween.

I checked my phone every thirty seconds, but I hadn't missed any calls and there were no new texts from David. Did I get the café wrong? This was the one we met at last October. But maybe she was thinking of another place? I needed her to tell me everything was fine.

The door chimed, and I looked up into Raquel's face. "Thank goodness!" I said, almost knocking my glass over as I stood up.

She rushed over to me. "Evie, I'm so sorry. This is the only chance I've had to get away, and—" The door chimed again, and Raquel watched as two men in itchy-looking wool coats walked in and stared at the menu. She turned back to me, her face smooth. "Sit down, please."

"Yeah, sure."

She sat across from me and put her hands up on the table, crossing and uncrossing her fingers like she couldn't get them to fit together quite right.

"What's going on? Who is this Anne-Whatever Whatever woman? Why is IPCA contacting me through someone other than you?"

Raquel took a deep breath. "I'm here to ask you to come back to IPCA in a formal capacity."

"You're *what*?"

"It's been determined that this experiment"—she closed her eyes briefly at that word, then quickly opened them and moved on—"isn't effective. You're being asked to return to your position at the Center. With full employee rights and salary, of course. They will also grant you conditional clemency for rule violations."

I sat back, stunned. "You're the one who helped me get out in the first place. You know I can't—I *won't*—go back!

Besides, there's no point. I won't travel with a faerie, which makes me pretty much worthless. And even if I was willing to work with faeries, there's no way I'd go back to living in the Center! What are they thinking?"

She bit her lip. It was then that I realized she hadn't uttered a single sigh. Weird, and very un-Raquel. "Evie, I really think you should consider this offer. Or at least be open to negotiating the terms of your employment." She glanced over her shoulder, then leaned forward. "Please tell me you will consider it."

"What the bleep are you smoking? I—"

Her eyes flashed, her brows knit together, and she leaned even farther forward, shaking her head in an almost imperceptible motion. "Evie! *Please. Tell me you will consider this.*"

Something was very wrong here. I trusted Raquel, I knew I could. "I—yeah, sure. I'll consider it."

She didn't look relieved; if anything, she looked more agitated than ever. "Thank you. I will give you a couple of days to think things over." She reached out and took one of my hands in hers, squeezing it way too tight.

"Maybe switch to decaf," I muttered, scowling. "Now can you tell me what's going on? And what about the town, are the para—"

"Thank you, yes, I must be going." She stood up, smoothing out her charcoal-gray skirt. "I'll speak with you at the end of the week when we've finished making the arrangements."

"I didn't say— Raquel!" I stood up as she turned on her heel and marched out.

Lend tapped his fingers on the steering wheel, frowning thoughtfully. "So, we know for sure Nona is keeping tabs on you. But she's told us before she wants you to be safe."

"Still, creepy. She's having me followed by her little seal cronies. And what about Reth?"

"Are you sure it was Reth?"

I traced my finger through the condensation on the window, watching the leafless trees fly by. There wasn't any snow out, which just made everything dead and flat and cold and brown.

I hate brown.

"Pretty sure. We know they're in contact. But even if it isn't him specifically, it's a faerie."

"Alright. No more Nona. You can stay with my dad more permanently than we had planned. Plus, it's safer there if IPCA decides to come knocking with their pet faeries."

"Too bad your dad is my legal guardian. Otherwise there wouldn't be any way to find me through him." My stomach dropped. "Oh my gosh, Lend. They can find him if they look, which means they'll know that he's not dead, either." David had faked his own death almost twenty years before when he was an employee of the American Paranormal Containment Agency. Falling in love with a water elemental wasn't exactly conducive to working for them anymore.

Lend shrugged dismissively, resting his right hand on my knee. "My dad's been doing this a long time, Ev. He'll be fine. Don't worry about him. I'm just pissed Raquel is still IPCA's lapdog and didn't tell you what was really going on."

I scowled, wiping away the hearts I'd traced along the window. "It wasn't like that. Something was up—something weird. She's definitely not acting like herself. I think she's scared about something, or . . . I don't know. It was like she *couldn't* tell me anything. Maybe she's trying to protect me by bringing me back in. Remember I told you I read all their documents about elemental paranormals going missing?"

He nodded grudgingly. "We still haven't heard from my mom in months. But she usually doesn't come out in winter anyway because of the ice."

"It could be connected. Nona's getting weirder by the day; now she's having me followed. There could be something going on that Raquel knows about."

"Why didn't she tell you what it is, then?"

"I don't know. But Raquel has my back. Always."

"*I* have your back."

I smiled and wove my hand through his elbow, leaning

over to put my head on his shoulder. "I know."

"Good. That settled, I hereby declare a moratorium on any and all talk of IPCA or paranormals stalking you."

"Ooh, breaking out the fancy language. Why?"

"Because today is about fun."

"I like fun days!"

"This is a special one."

"It is?" Had I forgotten some sort of anniversary?

His face split into a sly grin. "It's your birthday."

"No, it's not," I answered, confused. "I mean, I guess it could be, but since we didn't know when it was for sure we always said I was a year older on New Year's."

"Ah, but when was the last time you checked your birth certificate?"

I laughed. "You mean the fake document your dad had Arianna compel the county records office into making?"

"Yup. You never noticed the date we put on it?"

"No . . ."

"December twenty-first. Which is today." He pulled into the mall and parked. "Happy birthday, Evie," he said, leaning in and kissing me with his perfectly soft lips. I smiled under his mouth, letting everything else slip away. Best fake birthday ever.

"Okay, I never thought I'd say this, but I'm tired of the mall." I sat on a bench, feet aching but heart happy. Lend had dragged me through the entire thing, even insisting I get a manicure and surprising me with a scheduled make-over appointment at one of the high-end salons. My hair twisted and curled just so, along with dramatic eyeliner, looked a little odd with normal clothes, but I felt special.

Lend finished texting someone and slipped his phone into his back pocket, then stood up. I'd never paid much attention to guys' jeans before (not for lack of desire, but rather lack of opportunity in the Center), but in the past few months I'd come to realize that most guys' jeans are really, truly horrendous. Too baggy, too tight, too low, etc. It's like guys don't realize that they can look great in a good pair of jeans. Shockingly enough girls, too, enjoy a well-framed butt.

Another area Lend was perfect in. His jeans choice, I mean. Well, his butt, too.

I smiled and stared at his face, watching his two profiles—the glamour one, which fit snugly over his real one. He looked down and caught me staring.

"Evie?"

"You, my dear boyfriend, are kind of beautiful, you know that?"

"That's what all the old ladies tell me before pinching my cheek."

"Which cheek?" I reached out and goosed him. He jumped and swatted my hand away, laughing.

"Okay, we're going to meet Arianna and my dad at the

house; they made a big dinner and cake. Then a movie?"

I shrugged, happy. "Sounds good to me." It wasn't huge or over-the-top, but that was never Lend's style. I was glad that this wasn't when I usually had my birthday. New Year's would remind me how I used to celebrate. Every year I was in the Center, I figured out a way to sneak a ladder into Central Processing, climb the side of Lish's tank, and cannonball in. It was my favorite tradition.

Maybe I could talk Arianna and Lend into a polar bear plunge as a memorial.

My phone buzzed with a text and I pulled it out. Carlee. I smiled as I read, "OMG BRATTT U DIDNT TELL ME ITS UR BDAY. Girls nite friday?"

I texted back a yes, touched she cared about my pretend birthday. "Did you tell Carlee it was my birthday?" I asked Lend as we wriggled into our coats, held hands, and braced ourselves against the bitter chill of twilight that slammed into us when we walked outside.

"Guilty."

I smiled, then shivered. "It's dark so early these days."

"Today's Winter Solstice—shortest day of the year."

"Gee, thanks a lot. Way to pick the shortest day of the bleeping year for my birthday."

He laughed and put his arms around me. "Ah, but the longest night . . ."

"Scandalous!"

He blinked innocently at me. "What? More time for movies, right?"

"Sure . . ."

We drove through the town and into the trees toward his house, finally turning onto the long, winding drive. Just before we passed the last curve of the driveway he stopped the car and turned it off. I smiled wickedly, remembering how many times we'd sneaked off into the forest for a little post-date making out. Alone was really the only time he could melt off his glamour and be himself with me. Even around his dad and Arianna it made him too self-conscious. I reached out to open my door, but he leaned over and pulled it shut.

"Too cold?" I asked.

"You have to wait here for a minute, okay?" His look was brimming with excitement and mischief and I wondered what he had for me. Maybe some sweet present, like my necklace. I fingered the iron heart pendant, warm from being against my chest.

I bounced impatiently in my seat, watching as he ran up the drive and around the curve. In the dark I pulled open the neck of my shirt and peered down at the skin over my heart, doing my nightly soul check. No visible difference, just that same faint glow with a spark or two. Not gonna die today. Another thing to add to the happy list.

A couple of minutes later I was surprised when the figure that came back was . . . not him. It was Arianna, holding something bulky draped over her arm.

She opened my door, and I got out. "Where's Lend? I'm supposed to wait for him."

"Nope." She smiled bigger than I'd ever seen her smile before, and suddenly I was a touch nervous. What if she *was* working with Nona and the faeries? "You were waiting for me. Now, strip."

"I— What?"

"You heard me. Strip. Take off your coat, shirt, and pants. You can leave your bra, for all the good it does you."

I noticed then that the bulky thing over her arm was a garment bag. Aha! "Ar, listen, I don't feel that way about you. You're not my type."

"Oh, shut up, take your clothes off, and close your eyes."

"Again, not something I was hoping to hear from *you* tonight."

Her smile was replaced by an annoyed scowl. "DO IT NOW."

I laughed, confused but figuring this was her present to me. She had been in fashion school before she died and was an amazing seamstress. I closed my eyes and peeled my clothes off, goose bumpy and shivering in the frigid air. "Hurry, hurry."

"Lift your arms up."

I did and tried not to squirm as she pulled what felt like a hundred layers of fabric over my head. A zipper went up my back, then she tugged and twisted and smoothed. From what I could tell it was a dress—nothing on my arms, but material swishing against my legs. "Perfect. Of course." She sounded smug. "Foot," she said, taking one and pulling off my boot before putting a much higher heeled shoe on, then repeating the process.

"Can I open my eyes yet?"

"No. Take my arm."

I did and let her walk me around the corner. Behind my closed eyes I could tell there was light—a lot of light, way more than there should have been.

"Hold still," she said, slipping something carefully past my hair and putting it in place over my eyes and the top of my nose. "And keep your eyes closed!"

"Hmph."

"Brat." She let go of my arm, then put both of hers around me and gave me a quick hug. "Have fun."

Another hand took my elbow, one I instantly recognized by its perfectly smooth skin. "Can I open my eyes yet?"

"Yes," Lend said, and I opened them to see him, in a tux with a gorgeous midnight-blue and silver mask. Okay, maybe it was a good color scheme, after all. I looked down and my breath caught at what was quite possibly the most beautiful dress I'd ever seen in my life. Layers of sheer fabric cascaded from my waist with impossibly intricate pleating and ruffle accents. Flowers trailed from my shoulders down to the bodice, and it was a rich, perfect plum color. It felt like I was wearing a dream.

Beaming, I put a hand up to feel my own masquerade mask. I couldn't believe Lend had done this for me. Then I turned to see the entire house lit up with twinkle lights, and what looked to be half the senior class on the wraparound porch, Carlee at the front, all wearing formals and masks.

"*Surprise!*" they shouted.

It definitely was.

GLAMOUROUS PARTIES

Lend twirled me to the beat in the furniture-free living room and I laughed, my dress spinning around me. They'd draped the walls with swaths of shimmery material in purples and violets, and covered the overhead lights so that even the lighting was filtered and soft. I didn't know what it was about putting on masks and fancy clothes, but the people I saw every day in the halls seemed prettier, more mysterious, older. *Easton Heights* totally had this one right after all.

I spun back into Lend's arms and rested my head on his shoulder. "This is the most amazing thing anyone has ever done for me." The amount of time and preparation he must have put into this—it boggled my mind.

He squeezed my hand in his. "Had to make up for prom, right?"

Reth kidnapping me, confronting Vivian and almost killing her, nearly sucking the soul out of Lend . . . yeah, prom hadn't been quite what I'd hoped. "Let's not mention that dance. Where did everyone get the masks?"

Each mask was individual, with different flourishes and details; everything from sequins to feathers to what looked like gold leaf. They were breathtaking. Definitely not something from a cheap party store.

"I designed most of them and Arianna made them. A little mystery that *you* can't see through—and you don't have to. Just a magical normal night."

"It's amazing."

He dipped me down, then leaned forward and nuzzled into my arched neck. "So are you."

When the dance music sped up, Carlee found me amid the crush of people. She looked hot in a deep green strapless mini, dark brown hair stick straight and loose, her mask blue and green with peacock feathers trailing down either side.

"Happy birthday!" she shouted, throwing her arms around me, and I hugged her back, giddy.

"Thank you!"

"Is this not the best freaking party ever?"

"Totally!"

She beamed. "Lend's been working on it for like a month. I've been here all day setting up."

"You were in on it?"

"Psh, of course I was, girl. Who do you think did invites and forced the idiot boys from school to actually dress nice?"

"Carlee, I'm so glad you're my friend," I said, blinking back any hint of tears because I was so not messing up my makeup.

"Me, too. And I'm glad Lend finally manned up and threw a decent party."

"I'm right here, you know," he said, leaning over my shoulder. "So let's not go too heavy on the manning up talk."

My stomach growled. "Food?" I asked.

"In the kitchen. Want me to make you a plate?"

"Perfect." I watched him weave away through the crowd.

"So, are you two going to get married already or what?"

I laughed. "Excuse me?"

Carlee rolled her eyes. "Please. You don't even look at other guys. And I have never seen a guy that crazy about a girl before. You're, like, his entire world."

I shrugged, smiling. "I can't imagine ever finding some-one better than Lend. He just—he knows me. Totally. Everything. And miraculously he still likes me."

"Likes? Girl, he head-over-heels-freaking-loves you."

"It's mutual!"

"Find me one like that, okay?"

"He's one of a kind." Way, way, way more than Carlee would ever know. She just laughed and we danced for a few minutes before I left the middle to watch from the edges and wait for Lend. The Vicious Redhead, my old soccer nemesis, was awkwardly grinding with a tall, skinny kid who was one of the stars of the basketball team, and Carlee was now surrounded by no less than four guys. I was surprised at how many of the kids I recognized under their masks, and how many of them I considered my friends. Maybe I wasn't on the fringes of normal society. Too bad I'd already volunteered for, like, ten clubs. Probably could have thrown an awesome party and called it good.

I scanned for Arianna but didn't see her anywhere. Turning to look out the window, I noticed a small point of light like fire, going in and out.

It took a minute, but I made it through everyone, nodding and grinning to birthday wishes, before bursting out the open front door. A bunch of kids lingered there, talking and laughing on the wraparound porch, but I walked straight off and into the trees that hugged the borders of the yard.

"You know you aren't supposed to be smoking those things," I said.

Arianna swore, surprised, and dropped her cigarette on the ground. "Great, that was my last one." She ground it out with her foot.

"Come in," I said, taking one of her hands, but she pulled back.

"Nah, not my thing."

"Arianna, seriously. This dress? The masks? It's incredible, and you did it, and you should be in there with me."

I could barely see her in the dark, but I think she smiled. "Vicariously living through you is enough for tonight. Tell me it's the best party you've ever seen."

"This party kicks the masquerade episode's trash."

"Got that right."

I took her hand again. "You're telling me you spent all that time on masks and didn't make one for yourself?"

Her voice was soft. "You know I already wear one."

I scrambled for words, but she squeezed my hand and let it go.

"Get back in there or I'm never doing anything nice for you again. And if you don't have the best night of your life after I spent all that time on this stupid party, I'm gonna turn you and make you spend eternity playing MMORPGs with me."

I hugged her tight, feeling her tiny body through my dress. "Thank you."

"Go be a teenager."

"That's my specialty," I said, grinning at her and going back to the house.

The rest of the night passed in a blur of color and noise and laughter. There were no fistfights, no furniture thrown through windows, nary an overdose or tragic revelation, so it wasn't quite the same as the *Easton Heights* episode, which I was grateful for.

Around 1 a.m. people were mostly filtering out, stopping to wish me happy birthday and to congratulate Lend on a party well thrown. David had been around on the periphery all night and looked exhausted as he pushed furniture back in. Lend was beat, too, beneath his always flawless dark-haired dark-eyed hottie glamour, but I was still buzzing.

When the last guest left, Lend leaned his head on my shoulder heavily. "Meet me on the porch in five minutes," he whispered.

"If you're surprising me with another party, I don't think it can top this one. Or that you'll make it without passing out."

He laughed softly. "No more parties. Pretty sure that'd kill me, immortal or not. Just a little present." He kissed my neck then went upstairs. I grabbed an afghan off the back of the couch and walked out, wrapping it around myself. The house was too brightly lit to see many stars, but it was a gorgeous night.

I wondered what more Lend could possibly have in store when I saw the light, bobbing and twinkling on the trail that led to his mom's pond. It winked on and off a few times, then slowly started moving away.

I bit my lip and smiled. He must have gone around the

back way. I couldn't imagine what surprise he had for me at the pond, but I couldn't wait to find out. I stepped off the porch and followed the light as it stayed always the same distance ahead of me, barely visible.

I could just make out where the edge of the pond would be through the trees; dozens of pale lights shimmered around its edges. He must have set up out here, too. I shivered, anticipating spending time with him, alone, on such a magical night.

Then I came through the trees and saw that Lend wasn't there and the lights weren't lights at all.

They were people.

Well, no. *People* was definitely the wrong word.

WINTER SOULSTICE

My eyes flicked around the group gathered at the edge of the frozen pond. I saw the three black-haired and mournful beauties from the diner—now definitely floating above the ground, their filmy dresses fluttering in a nonexistent wind. Banshees? Then there were Nona and Grnlllll, who had that same glowy salamander thing on her arm I'd seen them talking to once. The dragon, because this situation couldn't suck as much without a dragon. A little furry thing that looked sort of like Grnlllll but with massive, luminous orbs for eyes. It was holding up a small lantern—the source of the winking light. Of course. A will-o'-the-wisp, how fabulous that I'd meet one now. At least it hadn't led me to my death in a bog. So far. Kari and Donna, the traitorous seals. And there, floating over the pond, bleep! It was the stupid sylph who had flown off with me. I still had a part of its soul crackling around in me, and neither of us was happy about that.

The lights I'd seen around the pond were obvious now— the glow they each had centered around their hearts, their bright, immortal souls like dim lanterns behind fabric.

No faeries, though. That was something, I suppose. I didn't like my odds against most of these things, but at least I didn't have to worry about being whisked into the Faerie Paths.

"Child," Nona said.

"Stop right there. Enough with this 'child' nonsense. In case you hadn't noticed, I had a birthday. Which makes me seventeen. You are welcome to use my *name*, but if you're going to ambush me like this, the least you can do is treat me like an adult."

"Happy birthday, Evie!" Donna said, grinning.

I couldn't help but smile, exasperated by her enthusiasm. "Thank you. But somehow I doubt this is another party."

Someone in all black melted out of the woods next to me and I tensed, shocked to see Arianna. I frowned. "You're part of this? Did you set all this up?"

She rolled her eyes. "Please, so not my crowd. I saw you wander off into the woods alone and followed."

A huge crack echoed through the air, and water and ice shot up in a fountain from the middle of the pond, slamming back down and breaking more of the frozen surface. The fissure pushed straight through to the bank in front of me, water spraying up as the ice creaked and groaned and moved to the sides. The pulsing cold in my veins left over from the fossegrim I'd partially drained swirled as if in recognition. It had *better* not be him in there.

I stepped back, waiting to see what would come out of the water. It bubbled up into the form of a woman, and I let out a surprised breath. Cresseda—Lend's mom. Lend's mom whom no one had seen in months.

"Evelyn," she said in her rushing-water voice. As usual she glowed from the inside, far brighter in the night. Her features were perfect and strange and beautiful, and I could see points of starlight through her.

"Did you want to see Lend?" I asked. He'd be relieved to see her, even if I wasn't.

"I am not here for my son. It is time to take your path."

"You do mean the path back to the house, right? Because that's the only path I'm considering right now." I bit my lip. Maybe I shouldn't mouth off to the elemental I kinda hoped was my future mother-in-law.

"Eyes like streams of melting snow," she said, and it was all I could do not to roll my melting snow eyes. "Cold with—"

"I know the prophecy," I said, holding up a hand to stop

her. "I already did that. I let all those souls Vivian trapped go. Just like you told me to."

Cresseda shook her head, droplets of water flying everywhere and turning to ice before they hit the ground with musical plinks. "That was not the end of your journey. You have more to do."

I sighed, clenching my jaw. "What's that?"

Nona stepped forward. "You will send us all home." She smiled gratefully at me, reaching out to take my hand in hers. I folded my arms tightly in front of my chest again and stepped back.

"So you guys want me to open a gate now, too? Is that why you're working with Reth? Did he make you do this?" I scanned the tree line but didn't see him anywhere. Didn't mean he wasn't around, though.

"It is because of the faeries we are all here." Nona's voice was sad.

The three floating banshees drifted closer. They opened their mouths and spoke as one, their voices full of grief and the promise of death, mournful and tired and beautiful. They made me want to cry myself to sleep as they harmonized in chant.

"Greed and desire
Not peace, but fire
Coveting creation
Created damnation
Pulled alongside

A gate thrown too wide
Now our home calls
And darkness falls."

I rubbed my temples, feeling a headache coming on. "A for effort, ladies, but F for clarity. You do realize that your weird poem things *never explain anything.*"

Donna bounced forward. "I can explain! I can explain!"

"Be my guest."

"The faeries didn't like where we were. They wanted more, so they opened a gate! Using all our energy! But it was too big and they couldn't control it, and we all got sucked through, straight here! It was scary, and cold. The faeries wanted to be able to create, because they couldn't before, but here they could. But being here is wrong, and it's killing all of us, slowly, changing us from what we should be. And pretty soon we won't be able to leave, ever! So now you can open up the gate and let everyone go back to where they should be!" She paused, then leaned forward conspiratorially and whispered, "But I like it here. It's more fun."

"So, wait. You're all here because of the faeries?"

Kari and Donna nodded enthusiastically; everyone else nodded somberly.

"All the paranormals in the world, all the elementals, everything supernatural—you were never here to begin with?" That meant Lend wouldn't even exist if it weren't for the faeries. Then again, I wouldn't either. Dangit, maybe I did owe them, after all.

"No, child," Nona said. "We were victims of the faeries' pride and greed."

"Victims? Sorry, but most of you don't seem very victimish to me. What about hags, and fossegrims, and redcaps, and all the other sharp-toothed nasties"—I looked pointedly at the dragon—"in your group? I don't feel very bad for anything that's spent all those centuries preying on innocent people."

"It makes sense," Arianna said, her voice soft but thoughtful.

"What?"

"When you introduce an alien species into a new environment, it has to adapt or die out. And usually the way it adapts is by preying on the native species. Look at the dodo birds. They were fine until people came to their island with cats and dogs and pigs, then they became prey."

"You do realize you just compared our entire race to dodo birds."

She shrugged. "If they were never meant to be here in the first place, it's not their fault they had to become predators."

"Thank you, Animal Planet." I turned back to Nona. "But what about vampires? And werewolves? Even zombies. They started out normal; they didn't come here with you."

"Vampires were created by the Dark Queen in an effort to make an Empty One. You know this. The others I cannot explain, but even without our kind your world has mysteries of its own." She smiled.

"Okay. Fine. So, you were all brought here against your will and now you want to go back. You want me to just throw open a gate and let your little group skip on through?"

Cresseda shook her head. "No. All will have a choice this time. We have already started the Gathering." Paranormals had a way of talking with capitalized letters I still didn't understand. "It is nearly complete. And when we are together, we shall all leave this world."

Arianna drew in a sharp breath next to me.

"*All* all?" I asked. "Like, every paranormal in the world? Including the faeries? And just how big a gate do you think I can make? Because I don't think I can make another one, period. Last time it was mostly an accident, and it almost killed me." The night felt even colder against my skin as I remembered what it felt like to channel all those souls through a gate in the stars. The burning, the agony: I really thought I wouldn't survive.

It wasn't that I didn't get what they were saying or what they wanted, or even that I thought it was wrong. It wasn't their fault they were here, and I knew they deserved a way home, wherever that might be. But the idea of making another gate terrified me, and I wasn't willing to risk dying to try. They shouldn't expect that of me. They couldn't.

"I tire of this," the dragon said, and when it opened its

mouth I could see embers glowing from within. "The wee thing talks too much."

"Evelyn," Cresseda said, drawing my attention back to her. "Come with us now. We will help you do what you were made for, and make you whole."

I looked from glowing paranormal to glowing paranormal, finally settling on Cresseda. They'd been here for thousands of years already; surely they could tough it out a few more. "I wasn't *made* for anything. The faeries created this problem; they can solve it on their own. And I don't need anyone to fix me."

I turned my back on them and walked away.

OLD FLAMES

$\mathcal{I}$ was halfway to Lend's house when a huge spurt of fire shot up into the sky from the pond. I yelped and ran, the afghan trailing behind me like a dark shadow. It slipped and I looked back to grab for it, slamming right into Lend.

We both fell on the ground. "Are you okay?" he asked, searching my face. "What was that?"

"Probably the dragon. I think I pissed it off."

"The dragon's here? Why? What were you doing?"

"I got lured down to the pond by a bunch of paranormals. Including your mom."

"She's there?" He sat up and looked in that direction;

the fire was gone now, thank goodness, but I thought I heard voices arguing.

"Yeah. Listen, Lend. They want me to open the gate for them and all the other paranormals. Your mom asked me to." And suddenly it hit me—when she said all the paranormals on earth, she was including Lend in that. Ah, bleep. "They want to leave. All of them. Go back to wherever they came from. Probably with you," I whispered.

"What did you say?" I couldn't tell from the tone of his voice how he felt about it.

"I said no. I just—I'm done. I don't know how to do what they want me to, and the idea of trying terrifies me. I'm done with the supernatural drama, tired of being caught up in the middle of it, tired of being a pawn in their stupid prophecies and petty fights. After everything that happened with Vivian and Reth, even Jack—I don't want any of it. No gates, no other worlds, no being used. I just want here. With you."

He was quiet for a while . . . too long. Oh no, what if he wanted to go with them? What if he thought his mom was right and that I should try to open a gate for them? Would I try if he asked me to? Would he take me with him? Did I even want to go with him if he chose that? If I survived opening the gate, that was.

He reached out a hand and stood, helping me up. With one last look in the direction of the pond, he put his arm around me and turned us so we faced the house. "It's your choice, Evie. And for the record, I think you made the right one."

"Yeah?"

He squeezed me. "Yeah. Let's go home."

"I don't think we should go," Lend said, frowning at his dad the next morning.

"Nona asked very nicely. They only want to talk," David said.

"I've already heard what they had to say." I sat next to Lend on the couch with my arms crossed. His thumb pressed circles into the tight muscles along my neck. "I'm not interested."

"She implied there was more to it than you let them say last night. Something with what the Unseelie Court is doing."

"Again, not my problem. I didn't ask to be involved in any of this." It was easier to be annoyed with them than to feel compassionate. If I was annoyed, I could dismiss what they wanted instead of feeling guilty for not helping.

"But you are," Arianna said softly from the doorway. I hadn't heard her come in. She looked beyond tired, her shoulders stooped, hands shoved in the pockets of her black jeans. "At least get all the details before you decide to turn your back on them."

I threw my hands up in the air. "Fine. We'll go to the

diner, Nona can tell me everything, and *then* I can say no. Okay?"

David and Arianna nodded, and Lend stood. "Let's get it over with, then."

We piled into the car, Arianna in front with David. He looked at Lend in the rearview mirror. "Did you talk to your mother last night?"

"Nope. And I'm not going to if she's trying to take advantage of Evie and force her to do something she doesn't want to."

I put my head down on his shoulder. We were in this together, and Lend was right. We made our own choices, regardless of where we came from or what we were. He'd taught me that. I wasn't going to choose to be used. I put my hand over Tasey's reassuring bulk in my purse. I didn't belong to IPCA *or* to the paranormals.

The diner was empty when we got there except for Nona, Grnlllll, and the selkies. Scowling, I sat down next to Lend at a table. Arianna hesitated, then muttered something about picking up some of her stuff and walked straight back through the kitchen and upstairs. I guess she didn't belong at this conversation anyway since she wasn't one of the paranormals looking to go back home.

David pulled up a chair and Nona sat across from me. "Thank you for coming, Evelyn."

Well, at least she wasn't calling me child. "Yup. I'm here. So talk."

"It is not only for our sake that we ask this of you. I know how you have struggled to build a place for yourself in this world. But even that place is threatened by the faeries' continued presence here. We have indeed been working with the Seelie Court."

"I knew it!"

"But only because their desires align with ours. We have let go of our ancient enmity in order to move forward. I would ask you to do the same."

I sat back and shook my head. "It's not your place to ask, Nona. I've got nothing against you, really, but I don't like any of this. You'd make me sacrifice everything I have— quite possibly my life—for something I don't think I can even do. And I don't *want* to. If the faeries got you all here without an Empty One, they can figure out a way to get you back." There was no reason for me to be in the middle of this. I was sixteen—wait, seventeen now—and this shouldn't be my problem.

"It is not simply that. Being here has separated all of us from what we were and should be. We have dwelt here too long, and we can feel that the time is drawing quickly to a close where it will be possible for us to rejoin eternity. If we cannot get back soon, *very* soon, we will become permanent fixtures of your Earth. Some of us have been too far removed already. But it is more than concern for ourselves. The Dark Queen has been making—"

Light drew my eyes and I whipped my head to the far

end of the diner. A faerie door traced itself onto the wall and, in all his golden glory, out stepped Reth.

"I can't believe you brought him into this!" I said to Nona, standing in a rage.

"Time to go, time to go, time to go," Reth said, striding straight toward me and grabbing my arm. He looked strange, though, his usually pristine clothes slightly rumpled and an expression on his face I'd never seen there before and couldn't quite place.

"I'm not going anywhere with you!" I yanked my arm back, and then I realized what the look on his face was—panic. Reth didn't *do* panic.

David and Lend both stood, and Lend put himself in front of me. "Get out," he said.

Reth ignored him. "Nona, we're discovered. Gather everyone; I will do my best to keep Evelyn alive long enough to meet you."

"Excuse me?" I stretched my fingers out, eyes narrowing. I hadn't forgotten Reth's part in all this, what his court did to my mother—using her to make me and then discarding her, letting her die somewhere, broken and alone, while my alcoholic faerie father lost me. "The last time we were together I said I'd kill you if I ever saw you again. Do you really want to find out if I was serious?"

"I sincerely hope I have the chance to. But now we are leaving." He shoved Lend aside and wrapped an impossibly strong arm around my waist, pulling me backward.

I screamed as Lend and David jumped on him, but Reth flicked his free hand and tossed them both aside. "I am sorry about that."

"Stop!" I shouted, bucking my legs to try and throw him off balance long enough to get my hand around to his chest. He grabbed both my wrists with one of his long-fingered hands to immobilize my soul-sucking powers, but then froze.

"Wretched fates. Too late," he whispered, staring out the window. I matched his gaze and was nearly blinded as white light exploded in the middle of the street, followed by a window-shattering boom.

FOUND AND LOST

My mouth opened in a scream, but I couldn't hear anything as I ducked my head against Reth's chest. I blinked rapidly, trying to get my eyes to adjust, then looked back out. Where the street should have been was a wall of black nothingness. And stepping out of it was the most terrifying creature I had ever had the misfortune of seeing.

The Dark Queen.

She was just as I remembered: hair pooling down her back, iridescent like oil in the sun, skin pure white, lips violet and full and cruel. Perfection, terrifying and overwhelming. And in her whirlpool eyes I saw death.

Nona stood straight in front of the gaping window frame. My ears finally cleared and I caught the end as she said, "You have no claim." Her voice took on a deep echo, a cracking and groaning of growing things unnaturally accelerated. She raised both hands in the air and roots shot up, slamming through the asphalt and wrapping themselves around the Dark Queen's legs beneath her gossamer white dress.

The Dark Queen smiled, a knifing look, and her mouth moved in a whisper. Nona trembled, and the roots shook, faster and faster until they split into pieces. Nona shrieked and fell to the floor, her glamour falling away as small cracks spread along her oak-brown skin.

Grnlllll ran forward, jumping up onto a table and out the window. The roar that issued from her tiny gnome frame made the ground tremble and buck; I fell to my knees as the tiles beneath my feet rolled. The road, already broken up from the roots, crumbled into jagged pieces around the Dark Queen. She flicked a hand, sending Grnlllll flying into the side of the building.

The ground immediately stopped shaking, and her bottomless black eyes looked straight into the diner. "I want the Empty One." Her voice rippled out like a shock wave; I felt it go through me, felt it pierce my heart, overwhelm it, leave nothing in its wake but a vacuum that only she could fill. Yes. I would go.

I started to stand, but Reth pushed me to the floor and

put a hand over my heart. I gasped as the heat invaded, pushing out the vast emptiness the Dark Queen had put there.

"Give her to me, you golden fool, or I will unmake you."

I felt Reth's hand tremble on me; he'd turn me over. He had to. He wouldn't die for me. I was shocked to realize I didn't want him to die here, either.

Suddenly Arianna's voice rang out from above us. "Hey, witch! That's the fugliest dress I've ever seen!"

I looked up to see the Dark Queen pelted with the contents of our apartment fridge raining down from the second floor window. She raised a hand and I screamed. Not Arianna, I couldn't lose her, too. Then a plate smashed against the Dark Queen's perfect white arm from the side, distracting her.

Kari and Donna stood in the doorway of the diner, loaded with every dish they could hold, throwing them with remarkable aim. Cups and bowls crashed off the Dark Queen, not doing any real damage but sure as anything pissing her off.

"Dad! The pans, in the kitchen! Iron!" Lend said. David nodded and ran back.

"Behind the counter, now!" Lend hissed, grabbing Reth's arm and pulling us both back to the flimsy shelter where we all crouched. "We'll wait until my dad distracts her with the iron and then get away through a faerie door."

Reth nodded, and I let myself hope for one second that

we'd get out of this, that we'd escape her and somehow be okay. Then there was a horrible noise like an animal in pain that cut off far too sharply, and Donna screamed, sobbing Kari's name.

"Enough," the Dark Queen said, her voice pushing out and somehow making the very air feel different, thicker. Reth's golden eyes widened in horror; he put a hand out on the wall.

Nothing happened.

Lend watched, and I saw his face as it sank in. We weren't going to get out.

"It's okay," I said, my voice breaking. "It's okay. You guys stay back here. Try to help the others. I can't let her hurt anyone else. She won't leave until she gets me."

"You," Lend whispered, then looked at Reth. Something unspoken passed between them. "Keep her safe," Lend said fiercely.

Reth nodded. "Always."

Lend leaned forward and smashed his lips into mine, kissing me desperately, then pulled away. "I love you," he said, his glamour melting off so it was him, just him for a heartbeat, and I got ready to stand and be lost forever. Then he replaced his water self with:

Me.

"No!" I screamed, but Reth wrapped his arms around me and traced one finger down my throat, freezing my voice.

I screamed and screamed, ripping my throat to shreds but no sound came out. Lend-as-me stood up, lifting both hands in the air.

"I'm coming," my voice said. "Stop."

He walked out from behind the counter and I couldn't see him and she'd kill him and I'd lose him forever and I couldn't live in a world where he wasn't.

I kicked against the counter as hard as I could, trying to force Reth to let me go, but his arms weren't flesh, they were permanent, there was no give. I slammed my head back into his chest again and again, but then I felt more than heard her faerie door closing as the air thinned again and I knew it was over and my world had been destroyed.

Lend was gone, and it was my fault.

I slammed my head against Reth again in rage; he pulled me closer and said, in a voice tender and sad, "Sleep."

And then it was black.

SHOCKING
ENCOUNTERS

Shh, shh," Vivian said, cradling me and stroking my hair in our dark, star-filled dreamscape. "Where have you been? I've been feeling strange lately; I wanted to tell you. But what's wrong? What happened?"

"Lend. She took Lend. The Dark Queen took him, and I'll never get him back again. It's over. Everything."

Her hand stopped, even her breathing stopped. "She— she came out of the Faerie Realms?"

I nodded, sobbing so hard my stomach hurt.

"It's . . . she's never done that before, Evie. Ever.

Something must be happening, something big. Things must be changing."

"They want to leave. The elementals and everyone, they're working with the Seelie faeries. They asked me to make a gate. It doesn't matter now, nothing matters now. Maybe I should make them a gate so I can burn myself into oblivion."

"Don't say that! Don't you ever say that. Your soul is worth more than any of them can ever understand." She pushed back and took my face in her hands to glare into my eyes. "You hear me?"

I shook my head. "It doesn't matter."

"Don't be stupid, Evie. It always matters. Now, listen: Did she kill him?"

"I— No, I don't think so. She just took him. He . . . he changed into me. She thought she was taking me."

Vivian laughed, a short, mirthless sound. "Go, Lend. Bet she's not happy when she figures out she dirtied herself with the mortal realms to bring back the wrong person."

"You don't think he's dead?" I whispered, not daring to hope.

"No, he's too interesting a prize. The faeries who raised me talked about the Dark Queen all the time. She loves collecting pretty things, and if she's going up against the Seelies and all the elementals, she's not going to throw away the son of a water spirit. She's too smart for that, too cunning. She'll cut her losses and figure out how to use him to gain an advantage."

I let out another sob, thinking of Lend in her clutches, remembering what she had done to those poor people I saw when I was in the Faerie Realms with Jack. She'd done more than break their bodies—she'd stolen everything that made them human. The thought of what she could do to Lend . . .

"Deep breaths, Evie. This is good. I promise. She's not going to hurt him. Yet."

"Yet?" Gee, thanks, Viv. That was really reassuring.

"Exactly. Yet. Which means that you had better get your butt in gear and figure out a way to save him and take her down."

"How am I supposed to do that? She's the freaking Dark Queen. Have you ever seen her?"

"No."

"Well, I have! And both times it was all I could do not to throw myself at her feet! Around her I've never . . . I've never felt so *nothing*. I'm nothing compared to her. Not even a grain of sand in eternity. She's everything."

Vivian rolled her eyes. "She's totally overrated. And she has your Lend. You can do this. You have to."

I wiped my tears away, clenching my jaw. I could do this. I had to. Lend was the only choice I'd ever wanted to make, and as long as he was alive, I wasn't about to stop fighting.

"I love you, Viv," I said, needing her to know that it was

true, that someone could love her in spite of everything she'd done. I might never get a chance to see her again. Oh, who was I kidding—I was about to take on the Dark Queen. I was definitely never going to see Viv again.

Her face lit up in a smile that almost made her glow. "Ah, stupid, you know I love you, too." Vivian held up one hand, palm out, and I put mine flat against hers. Her smile shifted, a vicious slant to her eyes. "Magic hands, remember?"

I nodded. "Magic hands."

"Find the Dark Queen. Take it all."

I woke up to the skeletons of trees framing the sky. Someone was crying softly and I turned my head to see Donna, cradling a seal in her arms, stroking its fur and whispering to it. Next to her Grnlllll lowered Nona halfway into a hole in the ground, then motioned with her pawlike hands; the dirt filled in around the tree spirit and Grnlllll sat heavily, staring at Nona's body with half-lidded eyes.

I wanted to feel sad, wanted to find out if Kari would be okay and if Nona could somehow fix herself by being planted like that, but I couldn't. There was nothing I could do to help them right now, and if I let myself mourn, it would take time and energy. I didn't have room left to worry about anyone except Lend. I wouldn't lose anyone else to the Dark Queen. It's what Nona and Kari would want; they loved Lend, too.

"Where's David?" I sat up in Reth's arms, then pushed out of them and stood. We were on the banks of Cresseda's pond; he must have brought me here while I was asleep.

"I believe he's trying to secure help. Cresseda should be here shortly, along with most of the elementals. Including that rather distasteful dragon and those horrid, depressing banshees."

"Doesn't matter. Take me to the Dark Queen. Now."

"I may be wrong, but I don't believe your boy sacrificed himself so you could get killed."

"I'm not going to get killed. I'm going to kill her."

Reth laughed.

I punched him.

It hurt.

Me, not him, unfortunately. He just stared at me with those depthless golden eyes, and had the nerve to look sad. I waved my hand back and forth, trying to shake out the pain. "You think I can't do it?"

"I've no doubt you think you can. But, Evelyn, my love, I've fought to protect you for years now. And, unlike you, I won't so lightly disregard your Lend's last wish that I keep you safe."

"I'm not yours to keep safe! And if you had done something instead of just sitting there holding me back, Lend would be with us right now."

"Yes, but you would be lost."

"Are you going to help me or not?"

"Of course not."

"Fine. I'll get there myself, then."

I turned and stomped up the path toward the house, mushy dead leaves muffling my steps. Lend's car was still here; I could figure out this driving thing well enough to get myself back to the diner. I needed Tasey, and my cell phone, and Raquel.

I was out of faerie names now that Reth had a new one, Fehl would kill me at first sight, and my creepy alcoholic faerie father was banished to the Faerie Realms forever. Raquel, however, had a whole bunch of faerie names at her disposal. And if I had their names, I could control them. And if I could control them, I could get to the Faerie Realms. Too bad I'd given up my communicator. Raquel would help me—all I had to do was get in contact with her.

I broke out of the woods at the house and nearly ran into two tall, broad-shouldered men in suits. Frowning, I looked at their faces. Yellow wolf eyes beneath their blue and brown ones. Werewolves. Must be here to help Lend's dad.

"I think everyone's meeting at the pond with a bunch of elementals," I said, hoping that maybe together the werewolves and elementals would come up with some miraculous plan, but not counting on it. I didn't have time to wait for them to decide on a course of action; in fact, I seriously doubted anyone besides David would be willing to risk themselves to save Lend. It was up to me.

"Evelyn?" one asked.

"Yeah," I said, waving a hand dismissively and moving to walk past them. Lend always hung his keys on a ring near the door. I'd get those, and—

"You're under arrest for violating statute one point one of the International Paranormal Control Charter."

I stopped. "Wait, seriously? Seriously? You guys are here to *arrest* me?" I started laughing. "Wow, you so picked the wrong day. Come back next week, okay?"

Before I could move one of them shoved a shiny silver Taser at me; the last thought that went through my head before I collapsed, shaking on the ground, was that, bleep, being tased really sucked.

NEW JEWELRY

Oh. My. Galloping. Gremlins. My head hurt so bad that when I opened my eyes, everything was the same shade of blinding white. My tongue felt thick and dry and too big for my mouth, and my entire body ached. I squeezed my eyes shut and then opened them again, trying to blink away the whiteness.

Which was when it hit me. The white wasn't in my eyes. It was outside—and all around me. I sat up from my small cot and stared in horror at the seven feet by seven feet cube of a room I was in. My hand went immediately to my neck. My necklace, with the iron heart that Lend gave me, was gone.

My heart raced, panic setting in. No, this was wrong. They just brought me in to chew me out, or demand I work for them again, or—

I reached a hand down to my ankle and was immediately sick to my stomach over the small bulk beneath my jeans hem. No, no, no, no, no.

I'd been bagged and tagged. The ankle bracelet I was wearing was as familiar to me as Tasey; I knew exactly how it worked, and even then it was all I could do to keep my fingers from trying to rip it off.

I'd only get electrocuted again.

I stared at the open doorway, tormenting me with a free pass to freedom—or at least, freedom for anyone who hadn't been tagged. And if I had to guess, I'd say I wasn't in Containment or the normal cellblock. If they had any brains, they'd have put me in the Iron Wing.

Which wasn't to say I thought they had any brains at all, because the second one of them came in the room, he was going to get the surprise of a lifetime. I didn't think they knew what I could do besides seeing beneath glamours. They never knew that Viv and I were the same. Raquel wouldn't have told them; I had to believe that.

Which meant that I was armed, and they had absolutely no idea.

Normally I wouldn't even consider using my abilities on

a werewolf, much less a human. Their souls were already so fragile, everything about the idea felt wrong. Even Vivian never sucked a normal human dry. But there was no way I was going to sit around in lockup while my boyfriend was being held prisoner. I didn't care what it would take to get out of here.

"HEY," I shouted, walking barefoot right up to the doorway. "HEY. I wanna talk to Raquel."

No response. I went back to my cot and tried to pry it up to throw out in the hall, but it was bolted to the floor. Figured. I grabbed the scratchy gray blanket and tossed it out into the hall, followed by the thin mattress.

"HELLO! You better get whoever's in charge the bleep in here or you're going to regret it! People know I'm missing! And by people I mean paranormals the likes of which you can only imagine in your worst nightmares!"

Well, that was probably a lie. I'd walked out on them. And why would they think to look for me here? Still, I was going to play every card I could. "You think last April was bad? Wait and see how many of you are left standing if you keep me in here, you bunch of—"

"Evie," a gruff voice said and Bud, my old trainer, came into view. He looked older than the last time I'd seen him, and much sadder.

"Bud! Listen, you have to let me go. This is a huge mistake."

He shook his head, the heavy creases in his grizzled face deepening. "Sorry, kid. Things have changed around here." He looked both ways down the hall, then leaned in closer. "And not for the better."

"Bud. I just—I have to get out of here." Tears of desperation pooled in my eyes. "My boyfriend, he's been kidnapped by faeries and I'm the only one who can help him. Please, Bud, they're going to hurt him. Help me. Where's Raquel?" I wasn't trying to manipulate him by crying, really I wasn't, but the second I wasn't angry I was overwhelmed with fear and hopelessness.

He looked torn, then shook his head. "I'll tell them you're awake. I wish there was something more I could do for you, I really do." Frowning, he walked out of my vision.

I cried harder. Then I straightened and wiped my eyes. I was not going to cry in front of anyone else here. Ever. They were screwing with the wrong girl.

I paced my room—one-two-three-four-five-six-seven, turn two-three-four-five-six-seven, turn two-three-four-five-six-seven, turn two-three-four-five-six-seven.

One. Get out of the bleeping Center.

Two. Get to the Faerie Realms.

Three. Kill the Dark Queen.

Four. Save Lend.

Five. Make IPCA pay.

Six. Help the paranormals figure out another way home.

Seven. Finish plans for the Winter Formal.

Simple enough.

One. Get out of the bleeping Center, assuming anyone ever came to talk to me.

Two. Get to the Faerie Realms, assuming I could somehow get a faerie name and then control that faerie even though half the faeries wanted me dead and the other half wanted to use me.

Three. Kill the Dark Queen, assuming I could get within twenty feet of her without falling under her thrall and also somehow drain her before she snuffed me out of existence.

Four. Save Lend, assuming he was still . . .

"Get me out of this freaking white cell! Come on!" I screamed. "Get. Me. Out. Now. If my boyfriend gets hurt because of this, I swear I will come back here and BURN THIS PLACE TO THE GROUND!"

"Now, now," said Anne-Whatever Whatever, stepping in front of my doorway but just out of arm's reach. "Calm down, Evelyn."

"Let me go. You have no right to do this, and you have no idea what you're messing with."

"Actually, we have every right. You've violated enough sections of the charter to qualify for lifetime lockup."

"I'm not a member of IPCA anymore!"

"No, but you're not a person, either, not legally. You remain a Level Seven paranormal of unidentified origin.

Which means that I have final say in any and all containment policy."

My insides turned to ice, and I stood straighter, glaring at her. "What do *you* know about being a person?"

She sniffed primly. "We have a lot to discuss. This would all be much easier if you'd cooperate. Wouldn't you rather be useful, make a difference to humanity, than be locked up in this cell for the rest of your life?"

I laughed. "Don't talk to me about humanity. I know a pair of freaking seals that have more humanity in their flippers than you do in your whole organization. You want to talk about protecting humanity? If you don't let me out, the best person I have ever known will get hurt. If you have any shred of human decency in you, you'll let me go right now so I can save him."

She raised an eyebrow, and I continued, desperate.

"Let me go right now, and I swear I'll come back. I'll work for you however you want me to, whatever you want me to do. You want me to come back full-time to the Center, I'll do it. You have my word. But please, please, please, let me go. *Please.*"

She cocked her head. "What I think you fail to realize is that you're not in any position to bargain here. You'll do what I want you to because you have no other choice. Think about that, and we'll talk again tomorrow."

She started to walk off and I felt like I was going to

explode. "Stop! *Stop!* I want to talk to Raquel! She's a Supervisor—you have to let me talk to her."

Anne-Whatever Whatever stopped and looked back at me with a small smile on her face. *"Was* a Supervisor. Have a good night, Evelyn."

SPARKS FLY

You've got to be kidding me," I said, lying spread-eagled in the hall with only my ankle inside the room that kept me prisoner here. They really should have thought of that and tagged my neck or something. Judging by the looks the tall, annoyed werewolf guard was giving my ankle, he was thinking the same thing. And still staying out of reach, dang it all.

"Please confirm." His voice was low and terse. "Werewolf or not?"

He had a woman by the elbow. Her shoulders were hunched inward, her face terrified, eyes darting every which way avoiding mine. Her corkscrew-curly brown hair was wild and unbrushed, but her clothes seemed nice.

See, with werewolves, unless it's a full moon there's really no way to tell. Silver only affects them when they've wolfed out, and no one else can see their true nature like I can. And since the full moon had just passed, they had no way to confirm what she was until the next one. Somehow they thought I would do it for them.

I looked up into her yellow wolf eyes and felt nothing but compassion and pity. "Actually, you're way off."

"Oh?" the guard asked.

"Yup. She's not a werewolf, she's a chupacabra. Have you noticed a lot of missing goats lately?"

He growled his frustration. I bared my teeth back at him in a smile. "Tell Anne to come see me." It had been at least six hours. Or twelve. Or a hundred, for all I could tell, and I was ready to rip my hair out.

He turned, and the wolf woman finally made eye contact with me. "Hey," I said, "it's going to be okay. And if you see a faerie, any faerie, tell them IPCA has the Empty One."

"Ignore her," the guard said, pulling on the woman's elbow roughly.

"What's your deal? I mean, come on, why are you working with them?" I sat up, ankle still safely in the room. "Don't you get it? I can help you! Get me out of here and I'll take you with me."

His face turned a peculiar shade of red as he turned and loomed over me. "Help me? You've already helped me plenty. You know who bit me, who turned me into a monster? One of the werewolves that *you* set loose on the world, doing your little good deeds and 'rescuing' them from IPCA. I'm here because of you. Now get back in your room and rot, or so help me I will come back here with more than a Taser."

He stalked off down the hall and around the corner out of my sight, dragging the wolf woman in his wake.

"Well, that's just great," I muttered. "I make friends everywhere." While I had to admit that his situation did totally stink, and I could see why he would want someone to blame, I *wasn't* going to feel guilty about it. A) I didn't have time, and B) freeing all the Center's werewolves had freed Charlotte, my tutor, reuniting her with her family. I couldn't hold myself responsible for the actions of every paranormal I'd ever come into contact with one way or another.

Okay, maybe I could have done more to make sure they were all accounted for and had plans in place to control themselves at full moons. I banged my head back against my doorframe. Not my fault. Not my fault. Not my fault.

A voice from one of the other cells I couldn't see into drifted toward me. "*Leibchen*, are you still sad? I could help."

Yeah, because being trapped with no way to get out and save Lend and all IPCA against me wasn't bad enough, my block mate was the creeptastic uber-vamp stalker I partially drained on Halloween. He kept trying to start up a conversation, but even his voice set my teeth on edge. And then there was the matter of the part of his soul I was carting around inside myself.

But thinking about draining him made me wonder . . . if I could still feel nervous energy from him, and rushing chill from the fossegrim, and sparks from the sylph . . . I scooted back into my room, ignoring Uber-vamp. If I could concentrate the energy from souls enough to open gates between worlds, I should be able to do something else with it. Maybe.

It was worth a shot. I rolled up my pant leg, then closed my eyes, breathing deeply. Focusing inward, I tried to pick out the sense of the sylph's soul, the sparking, dry heat, the rush of wind. There! And there! Willing it to come together, I mentally directed it to my hand, and then to my pointer finger. It took a while, but eventually I could feel it building up, gathering there like a miniature storm. I opened my eyes and saw sparks dancing along the length of my finger beneath my skin. I squealed with happiness, and they scattered.

Bleep. After repeating the process, I finally had all the sylph energy more or less concentrated. "Here goes nothing," I muttered, then reached down, put my finger against the ankle tracker, and willed the sparks to leave.

And then screamed as currents of electricity shot back

and forth between my finger and the ankle tracker. I shook all over but couldn't control my muscles enough to move my finger. Finally it stopped and I collapsed on the ground, my nose assailed by the smell of burned plastic and skin.

I moaned softly, biting my tongue against the pain in my ankle and willing myself not to scream. After what felt like forever I was able to sit up and survey the damage. Angry red marks were already bubbling into blisters around the ankle tracker, which, as far as I could tell from the warped surface and faint smoke still drifting up, was out of commission.

I braced for an alarm, but none went off. Which meant I probably had a few minutes tops before the computer system registered that my ankle tracker was down. I stood up and gasped over the pain screaming through my ankle.

Okay, electricity burns? NOT. FUN.

But I could hurt later. Right now I had to get out and save Lend.

I limped over, then hesitated at the doorway. I didn't think I could handle another shock, but there was no avoiding it. Taking a deep breath, I pushed my foot across the threshold into the hall.

Nothing.

"Thank you, you crazy sylph," I whispered, then hobbled hurriedly down the hall away from Uber-vamp's voice. I had never known this wing existed when I lived here, but Jack had brought me here to visit Vivian. Just after my

entire life fell apart and just before he left me in the Faerie
Paths to die. So I hadn't been paying the best attention, but
I was pretty sure the door was at the end of this hall.

I paused. Vivian was still here, on the other end of the
hall. I had trusted Raquel with her care, but now that
Raquel was somehow out of power, I didn't want to leave
Viv alone and asleep. But I didn't have time to grab her,
and even if I did, I didn't think I could execute what was
probably already an impossible escape while carrying her
on my back.

I shook my head. I'd come back for her soon. She'd
wanted me to get to Lend as fast as I could; she'd understand. I needed to get out of this hall. After that, my only
hope was to run into a faerie. I hurried to the end of the
Iron Wing and opened the door.

Where I found myself face-to-face with Anne-Whatever
Whatever herself.

I pulled my hand back to punch her. "What are you—"
she started, when her eyes went wide and she collapsed on
the ground, revealing Tasey in the hands of a teen boy with
blond curls, blue eyes, dimples, and the most impish smile
I'd ever seen.

"Hey-oh, did you miss me?" Jack asked.

HAVOC

$Since$ my hand was already pulled back, I went ahead and punched Jack.

"Bloody— What was that for?" he asked, hand over his nose.

I stepped past the unconscious body of Anne-Whatever Whatever lying on the white tile floor and snatched Tasey from the blond nightmare. "Are you kidding me? The last time I saw you, you left me *for dead*."

"Well, yeah, there was that. But I thought rescuing you from IPCA might make up for it a bit."

"I'm in the middle of rescuing myself," I snapped.

"And how were you planning on getting past her?" He nudged the prone body with a none-too-gentle foot.

"Improvising."

"And once you were past her, you were going to get out of here . . . how?"

"Shut up!" I turned and tried to stomp down the hall, then cringed in pain from my ankle. Okay, no dramatic stomping. I opted for emphatic limping instead, which unfortunately allowed Jack to catch up quite quickly.

"Come on, Ev, listen. I'm sorry, okay? I came back for you that day on the Paths!"

"If you leave someone on the Paths, you can't ever find them again."

He scratched his head and looked down at the floor. "Yeah, I kind of figured that out. I really am sorry, though. And I'm glad you're not dead!"

"Go. Away." I didn't have time to deal with him the way I wanted to, which mostly revolved around tasing him into oblivion. Lend came first. If Jack showed up again later, fine, but for now I wasn't taking any detours.

"I was wrong! I know I was wrong. I was just so mad at you. And, you know, sometimes when I get mad, I do stupid things."

"You weren't 'just mad' at me!" I snapped. "You manip-ulated me! You created this whole path of destruction in my life to try and force me into doing what you wanted me to! You're as bad as IPCA and the paranormals and everyone else! I want nothing to do with you." I stopped and looked him straight in the eyes. "I mean it, Jack. I never want to see you again."

Hurt flitted across his cherubic features, then he grinned. "Well, it's not really up to you."

I rolled my eyes and kept walking. Transport was my best bet for finding a faerie. I'd have tried running, but I figured it was in my interest not to attract any attention. Plus I honestly didn't think I could run with the level of pain in my ankle.

Jack continued. "'Cause, umm, there's another reason I'm here."

"Shocking. Not simply the goodness of your heart. I can't believe it."

"Yeah, well, I couldn't have found you on my own. None of this was my idea." He paused, eyeing Tasey warily. "I mean, I'm all for it. Yay rescuing Evie! But I was . . . well, I guess you could say I was drafted."

"Drafted?"

"Forcibly."

"Well, consider yourself undrafted and bug off." I turned a corner and almost ran smack into . . . Bud. So not good.

I considered using Tasey, but couldn't bring myself to do it. I remembered all the hours he'd dedicated to training me, even though I was the worst student ever. I still held the Taser ready in my hand, but I had to at least try to talk him out of turning me in. "Bud . . . please."

He looked shocked to see me, then frowned. "Remember that knife I made for you? Stupid pink handle?"

"I— Yes. It got lost when I was escaping from here last time. Sorry." I blushed guiltily, then wondered why I was worried about a silly knife, and why Bud hadn't sounded an alarm yet.

He sighed in an annoyed way. "Well then, it's probably best that you'll never get the companion knife I made right before you left. Pity, too, because it was a particularly nice piece of work." He held out a small package wrapped in black cloth and I took it, wordless with surprise. "It's also a pity that I've got to get to bed right now and didn't even notice you in the hall as I hurried by."

A hint of a smile made his eyes light up and I beamed, tears filling my own. "Thank you."

"Don't know what you're talking about. In fact, I don't even know who you are. Or that I've seen you. So I suggest you book it."

He stomped past us and I tucked the wrapped knife into my jeans pocket, vowing to someday pay him back. Not everyone at IPCA was bad.

Where, oh where was Raquel? I needed her. And with this new and definitely not-improved IPCA, I was more than a little worried about her. What if she was in trouble? What if she needed me?

No time. Raquel could handle herself against IPCA.

Lend couldn't handle himself against the Dark Queen. He came first.

"Where are you going?" Jack asked.

"To Transport. I need a faerie."

"No, you don't."

"Yes, I do."

"I can take you out of here."

I laughed. "Yeah, sure, I'm gonna take a stroll through the Faerie Paths with you again. Because the last one was so pleasant." Then again, last time I *felt* myself straight to Lend . . . maybe I really could get to the Faerie Realms on my own. If I didn't find a faerie to take me there soon, I'd try it. I'd try anything.

"I swear, I'll never do anything like that again. I'm sorry. I don't know how I can convince you, but I mean it." He tried to take my hand, but I snatched it away.

He glared. "Okay, fine, you want a faerie?" He grabbed my elbow and tugged me down a side hall.

"Let go!" I said, pulling against him but trying to keep my voice down.

"Ta-da! Faerie!" Jack pointed at Reth, the very definition of beauty, leaning casually against the wall in a cream Victorian suit, the shirt open around his neck revealing perfectly sculpted collarbones, his golden hair just brushing along them.

"Evelyn, love, there you are."

"I— You—and you?" I looked incredulously from Jack

to Reth and back again. "This does not compute on so many levels."

Jack shrugged, shoving his hands sullenly in his pockets. "Reth found me, told me you were in trouble, so I agreed to help."

Reth cocked his head, giving Jack a curious look. "I seem to recall offering you the choice between having both your hands removed or pulling Evelyn out of that abominable iron-lined prison."

Jack didn't meet my eyes. "Like I said, I agreed to help."

I snorted. "Noble, as always."

Reth held out his elbow. "Are we quite ready to go? I, for one, would rather not spend much time here. Tasteless decor, and the lighting doesn't do your complexion any favors, Evelyn."

"Oh, for the love, you two are not in charge! And I don't trust either one of you for a stroll down the hall, much less through the Faerie Paths!"

Reth fixed his eyes on mine. "You have my word that you will come to no harm while in my care." He waved a hand at Jack. "And you have my word that if he does anything I find even so much as mildly annoying, he'll never walk again."

I bit my lip, torn. Reth was the easiest way to get out of here. But if I couldn't find Raquel, I could at least leave a token of my gratitude for a lovely stay. Both to show IPCA what I thought of their attempt to force me to work for them again and to maybe, just maybe, give myself an advantage in the upcoming confrontation with the Dark Queen.

"I need the IPCA faerie names," I said.

"Whatever for?"

"None of your business."

"Impossible," Jack said. "Trust me. If they were findable, I would have found them. They don't have records anywhere—computers or paper—that we can get to."

"Okay then, Reth. Can you get any of the IPCA-bound faeries here fast?"

He frowned. "I will do what I can." He walked through a faerie door that appeared on the wall, leaving me alone with Jack.

"So," Jack started.

"Talk again and I'll tase you," I answered.

He sighed, then slid down the wall to sit on the floor. He started whistling after a few minutes, but I tapped my finger against Tasey and he shut right up. As far as I could tell in the sealed, windowless, underground nightmare that was the Center, it was probably the middle of the night, since no one was bustling down the corridors. Not that I had issues with tasing anyone besides Bud, but I'd just as soon avoid any confrontations.

For now.

After what felt like an eternity but was probably only a couple more minutes, a faerie door traced its way back onto the wall and Reth walked out, followed by two faeries.

Each was as beautiful as the other, perfect, ethereal, obnoxiously serene. They eyed me with cool detachment; either they didn't know who I was or they didn't care.

"This is it?" I asked.

"All the faeries that aren't in use right now." He narrowed his eyes suspiciously at them. "And both Unseelie."

"Doesn't matter, I'll take what I can get." I turned to face them, ignoring the slight brain fog that being around that much faerie glamour always induced. I wasn't going to stare dazed and slack-jawed at them, tempting as it was. "I have a proposition for you. First, you tell me your true names."

Faeries were far too beautiful and otherworldly to roll their eyes, but the slight shift in expression they exhibited was probably the equivalent. It made me feel like the lowest creature on the planet, not even worthy of breathing the same air they did. Stupid faeries.

"You waste our time, child," the faerie on the left said. Her hair was the color and texture of snowy soft goose down and her long, white eyelashes popped against her nut-brown skin. Of course, her glamour dimmed all her real looks, but I could still see them.

"I don't. You tell me your true names, and I'll give you three commands. The last of which will be to choose a new name, which will free you from obeying any more commands. Ever."

That got their attention.

"Do you speak the truth?" asked the other faerie, his eyes so ice blue they actually made me shiver.

"Ask him." I jerked my thumb toward Reth.

He nodded, reluctant. "You remember my presence here. She freed me."

Well, when Reth had Lend at knifepoint, yeah. But this was a very different case. And this time I wouldn't precede the named command with a command to disregard everything IPCA had told them, which meant that they'd still have to abide by all those not-hurting-people rules. I hoped. I wasn't sure, but I really, really hoped.

"I will do it," said Goose Down Hair faerie. "Anything is preferable to walking these fools through the Paths for eternity. And to own my name again would be a wondrous thing."

"Good." I looked at the other faerie, and he nodded. "Reth," I said, "take Jack down the hall so he can't hear their names." The last time Jack had had a faerie name, he used it to command Fehl to hurt me as much as she could without killing me, hoping I'd drain her. I wasn't going to risk him overhearing one.

Goose Down Hair faerie stepped up to me and leaned down, her lips nearly brushing my ear as she whispered her name. "Theliantes."

I smiled. "Theliantes, before going home, cause as much havoc for IPCA as you can without hurting anyone. Theliantes, help me one time when I ask it of you. And,

Theliantes, choose a new name."

She straightened, her white dress spinning around her as she smiled, sharp teeth eager. She took a deep breath and closed her eyes, then her glamour melted away, revealing her in full faerie glory, positively glowing with power. Reaching out a single finger, she touched my cheek. "Until you need help, then."

Her laugh sounded like birds on the wing as she threw open a faerie door and disappeared into the wall.

"Your turn," I said to the Ice Eyed faerie. I had only just finished the three commands when the alarms blared.

RAINBOWS AND
BUTTERFLIES

Was that really necessary?" Reth frowned as the faerie disappeared. "You certainly don't need more Unseelie unbound and after you."

"Not like the odds aren't already impossibly stacked against me. And if IPCA can't function, well, that's one less thing I have to worry about."

Jack stood, hands over his ears, as he nodded up at the strobe lights. "That'd be our cue."

"Fine." Taking a deep breath, I tucked Tasey into my jeans and held out both my hands, Jack on one side and Reth on the other. "Take me to the Dark Queen."

A faerie door opened in front of us and I walked through, my hands warmed by the two creatures I swore I'd never go here with again. My ankle throbbed and stung, and by now I was limping so heavily Jack finally put my arm around his shoulder for support and I leaned almost all my weight on him.

"You know," he huffed, "for such a skinny girl you weigh a ton. It's like a miracle of physics or something. Are you perhaps made of lead?"

"Again, this would be an excellent time to shut up, since I now have a Taser *and* a knife." Not that I'd be able to reach either one with both hands occupied.

Fortunately, for once I wasn't nervous about the infinite empty black of the Paths. I was in too much pain and too worried about Lend to care. Well, care much. But I was about to face something much worse than my worst nightmares. Odds were, if I survived and was able to look back, I'd remember the nightmares I had about the Paths fondly in comparison to whatever would happen with the Dark Queen.

After a few minutes Reth spoke. "I hate to disappoint you, but you forget that you cannot force me to do anything, my love." Before I could protest we had stepped out of the Paths and . . . into the kitchen at Lend's house.

"Evie!" Arianna shrieked, almost knocking me over as she threw her arms around me. "I'm so glad you're okay!"

"What are you doing here? You should be with David, helping him!"

"I've been waiting for Reth and Jack to get back."

"You knew about their plan?" I asked, looking at the two cretins on either side of me.

"It was all the vampire's idea," Reth answered, sounding bored again as he wandered out the back door. "And rest assured we've now sealed this area from intrusion by any Unseelie faeries. I will not allow you to be taken again by anyone, regardless of faerie aid."

As the door closed behind Reth, Jack started to slink off in the direction of the front door. "I wouldn't," Reth said, his voice carrying forcefully even through the door.

Scowling, Jack sat down in a chair, put both feet on the table, tipped the chair onto two legs, and leaned his head back with his eyes closed. "I hate you again, Evie."

"Likewise. But, Ar, how did you know where I was?" I stepped forward to sit down and hissed from the pain. Arianna looked at my ankle and frowned, then led me over to sit at the table opposite Jack.

"Reth could tell you were back at the Center, but he couldn't feel where exactly you were or make a door there, so I figured we needed someone who knew the Center backward and forward. Once Reth found Jack"—she casually kicked out with her foot and knocked one of the chair legs, sending Jack clattering to the ground with a volley of swear words—"I knew they'd be able to get you out."

"Thanks." I smiled gratefully at her. "But I've got to get to the Faerie Realms, now." I looked at the clock and choked, panic rising even further. He'd been gone for twenty hours. I'd lost twenty freaking hours to IPCA.

"Not before we take care of your ankle."

I rolled my eyes, and she glared at me. "I'm serious, Evie. You're not going up against the Dark Queen already at a disadvantage. You can barely walk."

"And how do you propose to fix my ankle immediately? I'm not going to sit around and wait for it to heal."

She shrugged. "There's a unicorn out back."

Bleep. Of course there was. Arianna grabbed some kitchen shears and cut off the ruined ankle bracelet. I put my arm around her shoulders and hopped out the back door, where we hobbled past Reth and Grnlllll and, avoiding the path, went straight into the thick of the winter-barren trees.

I smelled it before I saw it, and the same unicorn I'd met on a field trip with Jack pranced up, pleased as anything to see me again. It wasn't mutual.

"It's so cute, isn't it?" Arianna said dreamily.

"Are we seeing the same creature? It's like a demented goat with a bone growth."

"You're going to hurt its feelings! Now shut up and sit on the ground."

I did as I was told, sticking my ankle out. "How is it going to heal me?" I asked, suddenly nervous. I pictured it licking my ankle and gagged. I could only imagine the diseases unicorn saliva had or what it carried around in its filthy, matted beard and hair.

Bleating reproachfully, it stared at me with its doleful, square-pupiled brown eyes.

"Oh, fine. Great, glorious unicorn, beloved of oblivious girls everywhere, please heal me. Now, if you don't mind."

With one last bat of its gunk-crusted eyelashes, it lowered its head and put its stubby horn against my ankle. I cringed, waiting for pain, but felt instead tingling warmth spread out, almost like having butterflies in my stomach. Only in my ankle. Butterflies . . . with *rainbows*.

The feeling of wholeness and well-being spread up my leg and into my entire body, and I couldn't stop grinning. The forest was beautiful! The tree branches, naked against the brightening sky, held unimaginable wonders. The hard-packed dirt beneath me was a treasure trove of unrealized potential, lovely for what it could eventually give life to. I could sit out here forever and just enjoy nature. I was so happy! And rainbows! Why did I keep thinking of rainbows? Who cared! Rainbows were totally awesome!

And the unicorn! I beamed at it, reaching out my hand to stroke it. There was never a creature more beautiful, more majestic. I'd spend the rest of my life out here, and we'd prance around the forest, worship the sunlight, bathe in the moonlight, and . . .

I shook my head, scattering the idiotic warm fuzzies that had invaded. "Whoa," I said, shoving the unicorn's head away. "That's enough of that." I looked down at my ankle, which was now completely healed, not even a scar left. I fixed a stern look on the unicorn. "I am not going to frolic in an eternal meadow of sunshine and moonlight with you, you rotten little fink. But thanks." I smiled, just enough to be nice without being too encouraging, and patted it quickly on the head.

I was going to soak that hand in bleach.

"Okay, let's get out of here." I stood, testing my ankle and relieved with the utter lack of pain. I still had an irrational desire to do an interpretive dance about rainbows, but it was a small price to pay for being healed.

"Don't you think you should—I don't know—wait? Have a plan? Get help?"

"I don't have time! Arianna, she's had him for almost a day! You don't understand what she is, what she does."

"I think you should talk to Cresseda."

"What— Why?" I narrowed my eyes. "And how did you know this unicorn was here?"

She shrugged, her normally perfect kohl eyeliner smudged. The sunlight was already getting strong enough to pierce her glamour; she probably needed to get inside soon. "I've been talking to them."

"You have." My voice was as flat as my stare and my chest.

"I think you should give them a chance. What they're talking about, what they've been through, it's not fair of you to shut them down. You don't know what it's like to want to kill things around you just because they're there.

You don't know what it's like to live somewhere you genuinely don't belong." I opened my mouth but she held up a hand, cutting me off. "No, Evie, you *don't*. Trust me. Because as much as you think you're torn between two worlds, as much as you think you've always missed out on this ridiculous idea of 'normal' that you have, the fact of the matter is you really can live normally. Because you're alive, and you're more or less human, and you belong here. You can make your life anything you want to. They aren't supposed to be here; they never were. I think you should let them help you with this, and then you should help them. They need you."

"No, *Lend* needs me. And I don't care about anyone or anything else." I fought the surge of guilt that threatened to overwhelm me as her face fell. "I'm sorry," I whispered, then turned and left her standing with the unicorn. There were no rainbows here.

HOLDING HANDS
WITH BOYS

Jack was balancing a spoon on his nose when I walked in.

"You," I said, knocking it off his face.

"Me!" he answered cheerfully.

"Take me to the Faerie Realms. Now."

"You always did have a great sense of humor, Evie."

I pulled the package Bud gave me out of my pocket, unwrapping a pure silver switchblade, the handle opalescent white. Classy, and it goes with everything. Who knew Bud had it in him. I flicked the blade in and out a few times, getting a feel for it.

"You know, I'd be a lot more comfortable if you'd put

that away," Jack said, eyeing it warily.

"Tell you what." I closed the blade with a satisfying snick. "Remember that time you tried to kill me because I wouldn't open a gate to hell?"

"The memory's a bit fuzzy . . ."

I opened the knife again.

"Yes, now that you mention it, I do recall something like that happening, although my motivation was certainly never to kill you. Can't you view it as me inspiring you to figure out how to use the Paths? I didn't actually want you to die."

"No, I really can't view it that way. And I still don't know how to use the Paths, which means that if you want all to be forgiven—and, trust me, you want all to be forgiven—you do me one final favor and then we agree to never see each other again."

He looked hurt, then his smile mask popped back into place. "But this has all made me realize how much I miss your sparkling personality and warmth."

I pulled Tasey from my jeans and flicked the setting to its highest level. "Do you mean 'sparking'? Because we can do sparking if you want."

Jack rolled his eyes and stood up. "Look. I know you still suspect I hate you, and, yeah, I did quite a bit, but I'm very mercurial. It's part of my charm." He gave me his broadest, most dimpled smile. "So while I hated you in that moment, I don't hate you anymore. No promises that I won't hate you again in the future, but what's life without a few surprises? And since I don't currently hate you, I'd feel awfully bad escorting you to a most certain and probably gruesome death."

"I'm not asking your opinion on my odds. All I'm asking you to do is get me to the Dark Queen. Then you are off the hook, completely and totally, forever."

"What about your mad faerie fellow?"

I grabbed a roll of duct tape out of one of the kitchen drawers. "Just give me your hand, you little monster. I'll deal with Reth."

"Fair enough." Jack held out his hand and I took it, steeling myself against the pit of terror in my stomach. Then I wrapped about twelve layers of duct tape around our joined wrists.

"Oy, I value those fingers. You've cut off my circulation!"

"I'll cut off more than that if you try to leave me in the Paths. This is insurance that you can't make a quick getaway."

He scowled at the floor and muttered, "I wouldn't do that again."

I walked him over to the nearest wall and he put his free hand against it, frowning in concentration as the light of a faerie door beamed and opened into the black.

"Are you sure about this?" he asked, giving me a surprisingly earnest look.

I pulled his hand, the edges of the tape digging into

my skin, and tugged him forward into the darkness as an answer. We walked together and I focused on the footsteps, on the feel of Tasey in my free hand, and on the reassuring bulk of the knife in my pocket.

"Do you have any sort of plan?" Jack asked.

"Not really."

"Eh, just as well. It'll be less of a disappointment when you fail."

"Thank you for your confidence."

We meandered, Jack struggling a little, as always, to find the door to the Faerie Realms. "In case you die, which I'm thinking is pretty likely, there's something I need to say. You don't even have to believe me, as long as you hear it. What I did . . . it was wrong. I know it was wrong. You are"—he paused, swallowing hard—"you *were* the closest I've ever had to a friend, and I used you, and I'm sorry. Trust me when I say it's not an emotion I'm very familiar with."

I shook my head, avoiding the sincerity pooling in his bright blue eyes. His manipulation of me had been both thorough and admirably well plotted. I wasn't going to let it happen again. I had no doubt he'd cut his losses and bail the second he thought he could do it without Reth hurting him.

"Ah," he said finally, breaking the silence that had stretched between us after his apology. "Here we are. Any particular place you want to come out?"

"Don't suppose you know where the Dark Queen holds court or keeps her captives?"

"I am a very smart boy, Evie, and extremely good at self-preservation. So, no."

I sighed. "I dunno. Anywhere in Unseelie territory, I guess."

He shrugged and opened the door; we walked out together into a forest of mirrors. Every tree was perfectly sculpted out of a brilliantly reflective material, each line of the bark a new facet, each leaf perfect, razor thin, and shining. A thousand fractured replications of the two of us stared back at me, distorted and strange and really, really bad for hiding. Even the ground was mirrored. Anyone anywhere near us would be able to tell immediately that we were somewhere we weren't supposed to be.

"This place gives me the creeps," Jack muttered.

"Not exactly ideal for sneaking around." I took a step forward and was rewarded with a crack that echoed through the entire forest, growing and doubling back on itself until the sound was overwhelming. Bits of mirror shattered and started falling off the trees, raining down all around us. A piece bounced off my hand, leaving a tiny line of blood in its wake.

I put both hands over my ears, accidentally tugging Jack's with mine, screaming, "Somewhere else! Anywhere else!" He yanked his hand back, and with a stomach-churning twist we were on the outskirts of a city. I squinted, totally disoriented. We were in New York. But no—those sky-scrapers weren't made of metal and concrete. Metal and concrete didn't move in subtle, writhing, slithering motions. Oh gosh. It was New York made out of millions of living snakes woven together, as far as I could tell from this distance. And the degree to which I did not want to get a closer look was pretty much infinite.

"Not very creative, are they?" Jack commented. "They couldn't make a *new* city out of snakes?"

"Seriously. I mean, New York is awesome and all, and who'd have thought snakes would be such a durable construction material, but couldn't they do better?"

"No, we really can't," Reth said, standing next to me and observing the city with a thoughtful expression.

I didn't even bother to be shocked that he'd found us so quickly. I looked at him from the corner of my eye, not wanting to turn my back on the snake city lest they decided to stop being buildings and start coming for me. "I'm doing this, and you can't stop me."

"I see. I cannot tell you how many times I've wished that, in place of a soul, I could fill you with an adequate amount of *fear*. You never seem to realize how hard it is to keep you alive, especially with you so constantly trying to achieve the opposite goal."

I certainly wasn't lacking in fear. If I thought about facing the Dark Queen too much, it was all I could do to breathe. I just didn't care anymore. The fear wasn't worth noticing because it didn't change anything about what I had to do. "It's not my life I'm worried about right now."

"You aren't going to find him here. And the longer you wander directionless around these cursed places, the sooner you will be found and incapable of helping the boy."

"You want me to survive so much, then help me! Take me to him and I swear I'll do everything I can to make it out alive."

"I can take you home in a heartbeat, you know."

I lifted my chin. "And I'll keep finding new ways to get back here if it kills me."

He stared at me, his heartbreakingly beautiful face devoid of any expression. Finally the corners of his perfect lips turned down ever so slightly. "I'll be very upset if you die."

I ignored the small, annoying, creeping warmth in my heart. He wasn't allowed to make me feel that way. "Does that mean you'll help?"

"Give me your hand."

I tucked Tasey into my jeans, pulled out my knife, and slid it through the duct tape, severing Jack's connection to me. Ripping the last of the sticky gray strands away, I laced my fingers through Reth's—then was surprised by Jack taking my other hand, his fingers circling mine.

"You're off the hook, Blondie. Go terrorize someone else." I gave him the best smile I could muster. He'd helped me when no one else would. He was still unbalanced and only helping me under duress, but it was something.

"Well, I don't know. It's bound to be exciting, if nothing else. I think I'll see this one through."

"Really?" He was free—completely and totally. And he was still here. He might have been sincerely sorry, after all.

He flashed an impish grin at me. "Really. Maybe we can light something on fire again."

"We can only hope." I smiled back at him, surprised and happier than I thought I could manage right now. With the two unlikeliest of allies, I was going to save Lend or die trying.

It wasn't a bad way to go, really.

"Off to it, then," Reth said, and the city snake-scape twirled away, replaced by . . . the most breathtakingly beautiful place I had ever seen in my life.

It was a riot of color, explosions of flowers carpeting every surface. Trees in the most brilliant shades of orange, red, and pink were clustered together, arching overhead and filtering the light so that everything was somehow softer and brighter at the same time, like your eyes were finally working how they were always supposed to. Jewel-toned butterflies the size of my face fluttered lazily on a breeze that smelled like sweet, sleepy contentment. The whole place was warm, and gorgeous, and very, very not scary. I turned to Reth, angry. "Where are we?" Of course he wouldn't have brought me where I asked him. I don't know why I expected anything different.

"Welcome to the Dark Court," Reth said.

Well, bleep. Not quite what I'd imagined.

DANCE, DANCE
REVOLUTIONS

I looked again at the obscenely serene and beautiful scene around us. There was nothing sinister, nothing threatening, nothing even remotely creepy about it. Unless you had really bad allergies, in which case the flowers might be considered evil.

"Are you sure?" I asked Reth, still dubious.

"Positive." His eyes darted around, scanning our surroundings as though he expected something horrid to come screaming out of the candy-colored trees.

"Well. Okay then." I was so confused. Why was this the Unseelie headquarters? Compared to that silver lake with black shores and red sky, this was somewhat lacking in the intimidation factor. I couldn't imagine the Dark Queen in all her soul-sucking black hole glory anywhere near this idyllic setting. "Any idea where they keep the prisoners?"

Reth waved a hand at the entire forest. "Anywhere around here."

"No jails? Or cages? Or, you know, chains?"

"You underestimate the power that comes with making humans happy and content. I seem to recall you overlooking several key problems with our relationship back when you allowed me to warm you."

I scowled. Oh, I so didn't like him. But he had a point. I hadn't cared that I was fifteen and he was ageless, or that we were entirely different species, or that he controlled every aspect of our time together. This was the same way, all happy and warm and nice smelling. Who would want to escape? "Let's find Lend and get out of here."

Maybe the Dark Queen wouldn't even be here. This didn't seem like her scene. It could be just a huge, elaborate, bizarrely butterfly-filled prison, after all. All we had to do was find the area Lend was in and hope he wasn't permanently screwed up by being in Happy Land for too long. Oh, please, please don't let him be permanently changed.

One of the huge butterflies alighted on my outstretched hand, fluttering its wings slowly. I looked closer, and realized that the brightly colored blue-and-purple scales all looked like miniature eyes. Interesting camouflage.

Then the eyes blinked.

"Bleep!" I shouted, shaking my hand until the creepy bug flew away. Jack gave me a weird look. "It had eyes! On its wings!"

"Of course it did," Reth answered, annoyed. "They already know we're here."

"Fabulous," Jack said, reaching down and plucking a crimson flower. A small scream sounded from it as he severed the stem. He smiled maliciously, then started stomping with abandon through the beds of blossoms, a chorus of tinny, shrill screams punctuating every step.

"Maybe you shouldn't aggravate the flowers," I hissed. "Let's find Lend and get out of here!"

"Lead the way," Reth said wearily.

I frowned and scanned the trees around us. There seemed to be a path through the flowers winding around the trees to our left. I figured it was as good a bet as anything. A path meant someone was using it, which would hopefully lead us . . . somewhere.

I walked over to it, followed by Reth and Jack. "I really need better plans."

"I wasn't going to say anything, but . . . wait, I already did." Jack shoved his hands in his jean pockets and whistled tunelessly. I scanned the trees constantly as we walked, but the only movement was those creepy butterflies, tranquilly drifting through the trees.

Wait—no, not drifting. Following us. "We have an audience," I said to Reth, nodding at the clusters of flying insects.

"I suppose we can't make the Dark Queen any angrier with us than she already is," he said, then his perfect mouth moved, silently forming words, and he gracefully waved his hands through the air in a semicircle. The warm breeze suddenly froze, and I saw frost eat across the nearest butterflies' wings. They stopped midair, then dropped to the ground with tiny clinking noises, frozen solid.

A serene smile spread across Reth's face. "I've always disliked insects."

"If the whole being-a-faerie thing doesn't work out for you, you definitely have a future in pest control."

We walked for a few more minutes, the air now devoid of fluttering spies, until the trees grew thinner, revealing a light-drenched clearing. Low, murmuring voices and sweet but strange notes of music drifted back to us on the wind.

"This is bad," Reth said, frowning.

"What? What's bad?" I pulled out Tasey and hurried forward, wondering if Lend was in the clearing, wondering what was happening. My feet seemed to dance ahead of their own accord in my eagerness to find him.

Jack, too, rushed with me, reaching out and taking my arm. Then he raised our hands above my head, twirling me in a rapid circle, which made perfect sense with the music. I spun around and around, my hair whipping out, then stopped, skipping forward again with Jack.

He laughed and I laughed with him, dropping Tasey on the path as we twirled together in flawless synchronization. I wanted to be wearing something as beautiful as I felt moving to this music. I wanted a dress made of spiderwebs and butterfly wings, with dewdrops for jewels. But it didn't matter, not anymore, not when we could dance together.

We kicked off our shoes in wordless agreement, then broke through the trees and fell into line with the other dancers. I didn't know the steps, I couldn't know the steps, but the music whispered them to me, told me what to do with my feet and my hands, but most of all what to do with my heart.

I laughed again, feeling lighter and freer than I ever had, my face flushed with exertion as I took someone else's hand, and then someone else's, and then someone else's, twisting and turning, exhilarated with the pure joy of movement. We were a circle, and then two, and then three, and then one again, writing patterns and creating tales with our movement.

I closed my eyes, felt the warm light on my cheeks, felt the wind in my hair as hands grabbed mine and twirled me around and around and around again. There was nothing but this, nothing but the dance and the music and the joy. My feet moved faster and faster, tracing their song of happiness on the ground, telling a story that would never end. I never wanted it to.

BUNDLES OF JOY

I was laughing breathlessly—doing pretty much everything breathlessly—because I couldn't seem to stop dancing
long enough to catch my breath, but I didn't want to stop,
couldn't even if I wanted to, everything was twirling and
laughter and motion and my feet, my feet wouldn't stop, and
they hurt, but they didn't hurt, they wanted to do nothing
but this forever, and the pain in my side wasn't pain, and I
wasn't gasping for breath, I was laughing, because I'd never
been this happy.

The faces in front of me blurred together in light and

movement and sound, one indistinguishable from the next, only their hands mattering as we moved in and out and around in patterns while our feet tripped along the inevitable choreography. One of the faces looked familiar, triggered something in my brain, but then it was gone again and so was the thought, the wonder; there was only the dance.

Forever, there would only ever be the dance.

My hands met others and I prepared to spin, but these hands were wrong—they spun me the wrong way, tripping my feet that knew which way they were supposed to go. My feet kept moving, kept trying to tap out the story the music told them to, but now the hands were lifting me, and my feet kicked and turned and twirled in the air, desperate for contact with anything so they could keep dancing, because the dance was everything, I had to dance, I had to, if I didn't dance I'd fly away into pieces, everything would stop, it would be dark forever, I'd—

"Neamh," a voice like the wind through golden sheaves of wheat said in my ear. "Come back to yourself."

The name coursed through me, lightning in my veins, pushing out the desperation of the dance. I blinked rapidly, shaking my head past the fog. "Reth?" His face was right in front of mine as he held me against his body, my feet several inches off the ground.

"There you are."

"I— What on earth just happened?"

"Well, nothing on *Earth*, obviously."

He set me down and I yelped, immediately collapsing to the ground. My muscles were trembling, my legs riddled with spasms of pain. I looked down at my feet and cried out in horror again—they were bleeding and raw, the bottoms one big mess of blister and ruined skin.

"I saw—there was someone there I knew. Is . . . oh, no, is Lend there? Is he in the dance?" I turned my face toward where I thought the dancers were, but Reth had brought me back into the trees and I could only see flashes of movement from the meadow. Now that I was out of it, the music was wrong, all wrong, all desperation and frenetic motion without any sense or beat or rhythm.

"Not Lend. Jack. Stay there," Reth said. "I'll see if I can recall him to his senses, although he never had many to begin with."

I cried softly, lying back on the ground, every muscle in pain. Gratitude to my crazy faerie ex competed with the overwhelming pain for my attention. Pain won.

A body thudded to the ground next to me, and I heard a whimper like a hurt puppy. I opened my eyes and turned my head to see Jack lying there, his face screwed up against the agony. He was in as bad shape as I was.

"Reth." My voice was hoarse and my throat raw from how hard I had been breathing. "How are we going to find Lend now? I don't think I can walk."

"Yes, that wouldn't be advisable at this point."

"I don't suppose there are any unicorns here?" I asked, hopeful. If I could get a magic patch job, we could get back to the business of finding Lend.

"No."

"Crap. How long were we dancing?"

"That's not really quantifiable in terms you'd understand. Long enough that you nearly lost what little soul you have to the dance. But not so long that you weren't retrievable. Honestly, mortals. You never understand too much of a good thing."

"Jack? You okay?"

He moaned, turning and smashing his face into the flowered ground. "Mmmph."

I took it as a yes. Or at least, that he hadn't lost his soul to the dance and that eventually we'd both be okay. But we didn't have time for eventually.

"Is there anything you can do?" I asked Reth. "This can't be it. I need to find him. Now."

"There is something. It will get you walking. But you won't like it, and it will do more long-term damage than good."

"Do it."

He nodded, still hesitant, then reached out his perfect, slender, long-fingered hands and wrapped them around my feet. I expected more of his heat, the creeping warmth and

later burning that he used to put in me, but gasped as a sear-
ing cold left his hands. For an instant there was blinding
pain, and then . . . nothing.

"That should hold for a while."

I looked down to see my feet shimmering with what
looked like a light dusting of snow. I stood, but the snow
stayed put, not getting brushed off or melting. All my muscles screamed at me, but I could stand, which meant I could
walk, which meant I could find Lend.

"Thank you. Do Jack."

"I think we should send him back," Reth said, glancing
at poor, broken Jack with something that looked shockingly like compassion in his golden eyes. "He hasn't your
resilience, and, admirable as it was of him to join us, this
isn't his fight."

I knelt down and brushed Jack's blond curls back off his
forehead. He opened his eyes. "You always did know how
to have fun," he whispered, trying to smile.

"I'm a laugh a minute. Can you get away from here?
Back to your room, where you'll be safe?"

"'M not going anywhere," he mumbled.

"Yes, you are. And when you're well enough to make it
through the Faerie Paths, go find Arianna. She has a unicorn who can fix your feet. And tell her that when"—my
voice cracked, but I hurried on—"when I get back with
Lend, we'll talk."

Jack looked up at me, guilt on his features. "I really am sorry, Evie."

"I know, you idiot. Now go."

He nodded, huge blue eyes sad, then held up a hand and rolled to the side, disappearing in a shimmer of light.

I stood again, groaning as muscles and joints I'd never even noticed let me know in the most painful way possible they existed, and took a few deep breaths to push past it.

"Onward?" I asked Reth. He nodded, holding out his elbow like a gentleman, and I put my hand through it.

My feet didn't hurt, but they couldn't feel anything, either, which led to a lot of stumbling on the uneven ground. Without Reth I would have been flat on my face, but even with him progress was slow.

And so we walked, the forest around us shifting from brilliant reds, oranges, and pinks, to rich blues, greens, and violets. Just when I was sure I couldn't go any farther on my trembling legs, we came to another clearing. This one had no music, and I stopped dead in my tracks.

It was filled with six women, girls really, all human, laughing and singing and lounging contentedly next to a babbling lavender brook. They glowed with health in clothes that looked like woven clouds.

And each and every one of them was pregnant.

"What—" I started, and then it hit me in a horrible rush of recognition.

"It would appear the Dark Queen has been busy

replacing Vivian," Reth said.

"Empty Ones," I whispered, unable to take my eyes away from the swollen bellies of the girls. They were making more of me.

HAPPY PILLS

I couldn't move, frozen as I stared at this meadow of girls stolen from their lives and brought here for the sole purpose of creating more Empty Ones, more homeless, placeless, half-mortal half-nothing girls like me.

"Why so many?" I finally asked.

Reth raised his eyebrows, considering the scene before us. "Safer, I suppose. This way if one doesn't work out, like Vivian, the Dark Queen has several others to fall back on. She is terribly efficient. Which is likely the reason why she has them here where she can keep an eye on them, unlike how you and Vivian were left in the mortal realms with minimal supervision. Though the whole thing is pointless."

"We have to save them."

"Do they look like they want to be saved?"

I had to admit they didn't. That was what was so horrible about it. They all looked so bleeping happy, so tranquil. One girl, a tiny blonde who was all belly, lay on the bank of the stream on a bed of flowers, smiling even in her sleep.

It was sick.

"We have to try, at least."

Reth shook his head. "If you pulled them away, like this, it might kill them. I am afraid we have no help to offer right now. And, need I remind you, helping these poor creatures is not why we're here."

I felt angry and impossibly sad watching those girls, but he was right. They weren't why we were here. That didn't mean I was going to forget about them, though. "Okay," I said, my voice hollow and quiet. "Let's go."

We skirted the edge of the meadow. I feared detection, but the pregnant girls were all so blissed out they didn't even notice us. Back under the cover of the trees, I stumbled along in silence for a while until I couldn't take it anymore. "Do you think she was like that?"

"I've found it is helpful when talking to use actual subjects and context so your listener can understand what, exactly, you are trying to convey."

I rolled my eyes. "Like you're so big on clear communication. I mean my mom. Do you think she was like them when she was pregnant with me?"

"In what way?"

"You know. Happy. Peaceful."

There was a long pause, and when Reth spoke again his voice had none of the sharp tones it often took on, only warmth. "Yes, I suppose she was."

"Until he left her."

"Yes."

"But while she was with me, while I was in her, she was happy. She wasn't scared, or lonely, or angry."

"No, I cannot imagine she was any of those things."

I nodded, unable to talk anymore. I didn't know if it made me feel better or worse that my mom would have been happy about me, for a while at least, until my stupid faerie father abandoned her. I guess it made me feel a little bit better, in a very sad sort of way.

Up ahead I heard voices through the trees and I stopped, worried about what we'd run into next. "What do you think it is?" I whispered to Reth.

"Those aren't faerie voices."

We walked forward and peered through the edge of the trees to see a small valley with homes, quaint and cheerful cottages in perfect rows. Outside, around those homes, were people.

Dozens of people.

People people, not faeries. I scanned the ranks, panicked, but none of them seemed to be pregnant. They were all colors, men and women, from children on up to middle age, going about what seemed to be a perfectly sedate farming life. Women in plain spun but beautiful dresses trekked back and forth from a stream, carrying buckets of water and baskets of brilliant yellow berries. Kids laughed and chased one another in the cobbled street.

It was like looking back in time at some medieval village. Except it was more like the Middle Ages on Prozac, where everything was clean and everyone was shining with good health instead of dirty and diseased.

"What are they all here for?" The only reason faeries kidnapped humans was to use them for their own purposes, as servants or slaves, or to torment them for fun. And they didn't do it very often, either, most faeries never bothering to come over to the mortal realms. This community free from faeries and filled with people doing relatively normal things made no sense whatsoever.

"Yes, what could they possibly be here for," Reth said, but his tone of voice was sarcastic, like he already knew. "Again, evidence of the Dark Queen's innovation and efficiency. And very bad for anyone who is unfortunate enough to be a part of it. She is—" He stopped, then pulled me behind the trunk of a tree. "Someone is coming."

We peered around the edge of the trunk to see a door open up in a flash of light, about fifty feet away. A faerie I'd never seen before, tall and thin as a reed with flowing emerald-green hair stepped through, and holding his hand was a young girl, and holding her hand was an older woman, and holding her hand was a teenage boy, and holding his hand . . . I watched, aghast, as a train of twenty people came through, each holding the hand of the person in front of them. When they were all out of the Paths, the faerie spoke to them; they all watched with rapt attention.

A few of the villagers, for lack of a better word, had gathered as well. The faerie nodded and gestured to them, and the villagers walked forward, smiling, their arms open in welcome. The new people filtered through into the crowd.

One little girl sat on the ground, crying as the faerie left, and a plump blond woman rushed over, taking her in her arms and patting her back soothingly.

"Reth, I can't— Please, we have to find Lend right now. I can't see anything else, I can't handle knowing this stuff and not knowing what it means or what's going to happen to them. Please, please, can't you find Lend faster?"

He stopped watching the people and turned to me. "I will do my best. The only way onward is forward."

I was so tired and numb I didn't even hurt anymore, my mind shutting down so I wouldn't have to think about what I'd seen or ponder its implications. Lend. Lend.

The trees shifted again, this time from cool colors to pure white. White trunks, white leaves, and white flakes drifting and sparkling in the light. I held out a hand to catch one, expecting snow, but it settled there like a little drop of sunshine.

I hated this place. I hated that it was beautiful and warm and welcoming, and that it hid so much evil inside. Well, duh. *Faeries.* Of course it was that way.

Reth stopped suddenly and I drew up short, almost losing my balance again on my sensationless feet.

"Can you feel her?" he asked, and his tone chilled me in spite of the flakes of warmth swirling around us.

"I—" I paused, and closed my eyes. And there, yes, I could. It was like a tug, a pull toward emptiness, toward blissful oblivion, pulsing out and with every beat telling me that I was nothing, nothing, nothing, hers, hers, hers.

I squeezed Reth's hand, hard. "I'm scared."

He laughed his silver laugh. "High time for that."

"Don't— Please, don't let me lose myself, okay? The first goal is to save Lend, but I'd rather die than lose myself to her or help her in any way."

He locked my eyes with his. "Evelyn, my love. I will not let that happen."

I nodded, biting my lip. He wouldn't, not if he could help it. I trusted him on that. "Okay. Okay. Any tips?"

"Remember who you are."

I laughed, part shrill panic and part bitterness. "And what if I have no idea who I am?"

He shook his head, exasperated. "Repeat your real name in your head. Don't say it aloud; whatever you do, don't give it to her. But hold on to it and it should help."

I took a deep breath. Neamh. Neamh. Neamh. I was

me, and she couldn't have that, just like she couldn't have my Lend. Another deep breath, and another, all the while holding the image of Lend's true face in my head. "Let's do this."

Reth put my hand in the crook of his elbow again and we walked forward, together, through the trees and into the heart of the Dark Queen's court.

WHAT'S IN A NAME?

We stepped out of the trees and into the middle of a throng of faeries. My heart beat like a wild bird in my chest, fluttering against my rib cage and desperate to get away.

The faeries were all standing, arrayed like satellites around the gravity of the Dark Queen. I had expected thrones of gold and gems, but she sat in the middle of everything on an enormous, deep purple calla lily. Her dress today shimmered with every color imaginable, a prism in fabric form, and her black-oil hair danced with life along her bare, alabaster arms. On either side of her stood a faerie, one with midnight-blue hair and eyes, her face dotted with tiny points of light like stars shining beneath her skin. The other was the Goose Down Hair faerie from the Center. The one I'd set free, straight back to help my greatest enemy.

And there he was . . . Lend. My hands flew to my lips to stop from crying out in joy, because he was here, my Lend was here, I'd found him! He was at the Dark Queen's feet, lying perfectly still, in his real form and thus nearly invisible under his clothes. He wasn't—oh no, no no no, he wasn't dead, he couldn't be dead. If I'd lost him forever, my world was over. A small, animal sound escaped my mouth, then there was the slightest shift, a twitch of his hand, and I let out a muffled sob. He was still alive. I could still save him.

"Ah," the Dark Queen said, snapping my attention back to her. Maybe I couldn't still save him. I tried to avoid looking into her pure black eyes, instead focusing just above them on her high, smooth forehead. "The Empty One comes to me."

Her voice shot through me like a hook, catching on my back and then drawing me forward. My feet moved against my will, again.

"Approach, child."

She was swallowing me whole, I knew it, I could feel it happening, but I couldn't care. I was silly to think I could ever do anything against her. I had no right to exist, no right to even be. She preceded existence. She superseded creation. To say she was more than me was laughable in its simplicity. She was more than anything. She was a god.

She would be my god. I would go to her feet and worship her, do anything and everything she asked of me, anything to be near her, to have my nothingness absorbed and absolved by her, to—

I stumbled on my icy feet, falling to my knees and scraping my palm. I turned it over and looked at the bright dots of blood.

My blood.

Me.

Neamh. Neamh. Neamh. *Me*.

I took a deep breath, then stood, shocked to see I'd already covered all the distance to her and was standing directly in front of Lend. Careful not to let any expression show, I set my face into a mask of need and adoration and lowered my head in pretend obedience.

Even though I couldn't see her face, I *felt* her smile triumphantly. "Did you bring me this toy as an offering?" she asked, and I tried not to react as Reth answered immediately behind me.

"Yes, my lady. Please accept it with my humblest gratitude for my continued existence." He was lying; I only hoped she didn't figure it out.

She tapped one long, ice-white finger against her knee. "You shall exist. For now. But only because I think your betrayal will plague my sister more than your death. Now, you," she said, leaning forward and gesturing with her finger. My head rose, pulled up on an invisible string.

She cocked her head, a gesture I'd seen on Reth so many times, so beautiful I could barely stand to look at her. "What have you brought me as an offering? What can you give me to convince me not to end you right now? I have no need of you, not anymore. A few years yet and we will be free."

My mind raced, desperate. I stuck my hands in my pocket, wrapping one around the knife as though it could somehow give me the answers. I could give it to her, but, no, it was pitiful as far as gifts went. She didn't crave things, she wanted power.

Power.

I looked into her eyes, suddenly hopeful.

"I can give you my name."

Her face froze, then her violet lips parted in a hint of a smile. "Your true name?"

I nodded eagerly, stepping forward over Lend. "My true name. But you have to do something for me."

Her smile faded and I felt it like you feel a cloud passing over the sun; even with a firm hold on my mind it made me desperate, anxious to regain her sunshine. "You would dare ask something of me?"

"Let him go," I said, my words rushing out. "Lend. Let him go, and I'll give you my true name, and I'll do anything you want, I'll open any gate anywhere, I'll be yours forever. Anything."

She didn't blink, hadn't blinked this whole time, never looked away from my eyes and I knew I was seconds away from losing myself. I couldn't lose myself, not if this was going to work.

"You have far too much spirit for an Empty One," she said, leaning forward. "You cannot command me in anything. I enjoy this boy, so pretty like glass. Do you suppose he is as fragile as glass? Would you like to find out?" She raised a hand toward him, and he whimpered softly in his sleep.

"No!" I shouted, and she smiled again.

"I shall keep him, and you will tell me your name to save yourself. And even then, perhaps I will end you anyway."

Blinking against the tears, I nodded and opened my mouth.

"Your name is for me alone," she warned. I leaned closer to her and she bent her graceful, long neck down, putting her ear next to my face. I closed my eyes, the fear and joy and pain washing through me this close to her. I didn't deserve to be this close to her. I'd never deserve it, and I'd never get it again, and I wanted to sink into her darkness and never come out.

I pulled the knife out of my pocket and jammed it into her neck.

She screamed, the meadow around us shifting and crackling with lightning at the sound, the light disappearing. I fell backward, tripping over Lend's body.

"YOU!" I shouted, pointing to the Goose Down Hair faerie, barely visible in the writhing darkness that surrounded us now. "You have to help me one time! Attack the Dark Queen until I'm gone!"

Her eyes lit up with rage and death and she took a step toward me, hands outstretched. Guess that answered whether or not the previous commands would bind her. I closed my eyes, waiting to be killed, but when the hands didn't come around my neck, I opened them again. On the throne, standing over the Dark Queen, the Goose Down Hair faerie sobbed as she jammed the knife deeper into the Dark Queen's neck.

"My lady," the faerie shrieked in grief and terror, "my queen, I love you." She said it again and again as she slammed her hand against the knife, driving it in farther.

I dropped down, wrapped my arms around Lend, and screamed, "Reth! Get us out of here, now!"

Strong arms grabbed me, and with a bright flash we were pulled out of the Faerie Realms and into the blessed darkness of the Paths.

POWER NAP

I sank to the ground, holding Lend and blinking against the cold, bright sunshine streaming down on us. The gravel of Lend's driveway dug into my knees, but I didn't care.

We were here. We did it.

I looked up at Reth, the sun behind him creating a blinding halo around his head. "Thank you," I said, tears streaming down my face. "Thank you."

He reached down and tucked a strand of hair behind my ear, then leaned over and put his fingers briefly on Lend's forehead. I reached for his hand, but without a word he turned and walked away.

"Evie? Evie! Oh my— Lend?" Arianna started toward us, then ran into the house and yelled something. She sprinted back, joined by David.

"Is he okay? What happened? Is he—"

I shook my head, then nodded, not knowing what to say. All I knew was that he was here, with us. I had no doubt I'd pay for what I'd done to the Dark Queen. She couldn't be killed by something as simple as a silver knife; all I'd done was borrow more time. Time that never should have been mine to begin with, so what was another threat of death hanging over my head? With Lend here I didn't care. I'd take her wrath, all of it, anything.

David reached down and took Lend out of my arms, straining but carrying him into the house. Arianna helped me up and I cried out with pain. My feet had finally thawed.

"What did you do?" she asked, horrified, but I just shook my head, taking her arm for support and hobbling after David. I needed to be where Lend was.

We made it to the house and I tracked smears of blood on the hardwood before I sat heavily on the floor next to the blue couch where Lend was lying. He was still breathing evenly, for all appearances deeply asleep.

"Do you think he's okay?" I whispered, looking up at David, whose worry and heartbreak mirrored my own.

"I'm sure he is." David's face turned into a mask of bravery as he smiled and knelt next to me. "Evie, what you did,

I can't even begin . . . thank you." He wrapped me up in a hug and I buried my face into his shoulder.

"I had to bring him back."

He nodded against my head, and even though I knew he was as terrified as I was, I let myself lean against him and pretend for a moment that he was my dad, that I had someone like that who could be strong for me when I didn't have any strength left. I wanted Raquel here. I wanted Lish here. I wanted the mother I'd never known. But I could pretend Lend's dad was enough.

"Evie, we need to fix your feet," Arianna said when I let go of David and sat back against the edge of the couch.

"Yeah, they kind of hurt. But there is no way we're letting a unicorn inside the house. You'd never get the smell out."

We both choked out a laugh. Arianna and David wanted to carry me out to the unicorn, but I waved them away. I wasn't leaving Lend's side until he woke up. I put my head down on the couch next to Lend's. He would wake up soon. He had to wake up soon.

"Do you think Cresseda would know something, be able to help?" I asked.

"She might. I'll go see." David nodded and hurried out the door.

"So, how did you pull this off?" Arianna asked, sitting next to me with her legs against mine.

"I have no idea. But Jack helped before he got hurt and

had to leave. And Reth did, too. I wouldn't have been able to do anything without Reth. He was kind of amazing, actually."

"Guess there's a first time for everything."

"Seriously."

I saw my purse across the room and asked Arianna to hand it to me. I pulled out my phone to see several missed calls and texts from Carlee. The most recent read: "where r u meg said u were supposd to email her dance plans shes pissed and wont stop bugging me. also my mom is making me watch white christmas please call save me must go shopping." I hesitated, then texted back. "Lend sick. Not fun. Will call when better."

Please, please let me be able to call her soon. She texted back immediately, as usual, offering soup. If only.

I looked up as Donna came in with David, her usual exuberantly bouncy step subdued. I was hit with a wave of guilt. I hadn't even thought of Kari or Nona or Grnlllll this whole time. Now that I had Lend back, everything I'd been avoiding came rushing in.

"Donna, is Kari—" I couldn't finish the sentence, but Donna gave me a brave, heartbroken smile, then shook her head.

"I'm so sorry. And Nona?"

"It's too early to tell," David said softly, but it didn't sound hopeful. "We're going to take Lend to the pond. There are a bunch of paranormals down there; they might be able to help or tell us something, and Cresseda wants to see him."

David put his arms under Lend's knees and arms, picking him up with a sharp exhalation, then cradling him and walking out the door.

"Help?" I asked Arianna and Donna. They stood on either side of me and I put my arms around their shoulders. Donna's were lean and sinewy, powerful. Arianna's were frail and felt like I would break her if I put too much weight there. It couldn't be helped though.

We'd barely made it to the trees and already my feet were in such agony I didn't know how I'd get down to the pond. "I'm sorry." I gasped. "I can't. Where's the unicorn?"

"Probably by the pond. Want me to run ahead and try to bring it here?" Arianna asked.

"Allow me," Reth said from behind, scooping me into his arms like I was nothing and striding down the path with his usual graceful gait. Arianna and Donna were quickly left behind.

"Reth, I . . ." I paused, then took a deep breath. "I'm sorry."

"Whatever are you sorry for?"

I shrugged. "How about threatening to kill you, for starters."

"That is an excellent place to start, although I must tell you those threats were rather more endearing and humorous than frightening."

I rolled my eyes. "Whatever. You really came through for me when no one else could, and I know Lend wouldn't be here without your help. So thank you." I leaned my head against his shoulder and it seemed like he almost missed a step, but then he continued on as graceful as before. I lifted my head back up, staring ahead and straining for my first glimpse of the pond. "Why did you do it? Help me, I mean. I know you don't love Lend."

His golden voice was as deliciously warm as it had always been, wrapping around me in a comforting blanket, insulating me from the bite of the December air. "No, but I do love you, silly creature that you are."

I nodded. I felt like I should say something back, but I honestly had no idea what that something was.

We came out of the trees to even more paranormals and elementals gathered around the banks. The water was still frozen solid, but a small hole near the banks boiled furiously, steam dancing into the air.

David saw me and shook his head. "I thought he was waking up for a minute on the walk here, but he didn't." He laid Lend gently on the ground in front of the ice hole and Cresseda appeared in a geyser of water.

Reth kept me in his arms, angling me so I could see everything. The unicorn, bless its dirty, filthy heart, trotted up and set to work on my feet as they dangled in the air. I focused as hard as I could on Cresseda to try and avoid being overwhelmed by the rainbow-sunshine-butterfly-moonlight happy cloud the unicorn was creating. It mostly worked, although I had to shake my head and wipe off several goofy, sloppy smiles.

Cresseda's voice had an undercurrent of storm water, angry floods, and tsunamis breaking the surface of her normal tranquillity. "What of the traitor queen?"

I raised a hand. "I kind of stabbed her. In the neck. She's probably not happy."

Cresseda nodded, her clear features reflecting the sunlight in a fierce way, almost painful to look right at. "You have my gratitude, Evelyn."

"Will he be okay?" I asked, my voice catching.

Cresseda reached out a water hand toward Lend and was quiet and still for almost a full minute. Finally, she nodded, and her voice rang with the melancholy of the tides. "He is still ours."

I let out the breath I was holding. He'd be okay. He'd be okay. It was all worth it.

I motioned and Reth set me down, my feet still tender and raw, which surprised me. They weren't as bad as they had been but last time the unicorn had healed me completely. In answer to my unasked question, Reth said, "I am afraid that, as I said, my patch did more harm than good. A unicorn's magic cannot combat my own."

I shrugged. "It doesn't matter. We did what we had to. They'll get better eventually."

Cresseda nodded at Reth. "Son of the Light Court, all

is not forgiven, but I thank you for your service to my son. And I trust you to never reveal or use my Lend's true name again."

"That's how you could find him?" I asked, looking up at Reth, but for some reason he avoided my eyes. Of course it made sense that Cresseda would have given him Lend's true name (although I'd had no idea he had any besides his normal one). Reth knowing my true name meant he could find me anywhere, anytime. . . .

Instantly.

"Wait a second," I said, everything clicking into place. "You—you could have found him immediately. You knew *exactly* where he was the second she gave you his name. So our little detour through the horrors of faerie land—" I closed my eyes and shook my head. Of course. Of course Reth wasn't being selfless by helping me. He just wanted me to see what the Dark Court was doing, how they were hurting people so I'd be more sympathetic to what the Light Court and the paranormals wanted me to do. The entire thing—always, like always—was just another way to manipulate me.

EAU DE FAERIE

Evelyn," Cresseda said, but I stopped her.

"Were you all in on it?" I glanced around the shore at the gathered paranormals: selkies and banshees and a gnome and a sylph and a few other things that were new that I didn't care enough to study. "Did you really risk Lend's life just so I'd see what the Unseelies were like? I already know what they're like! I already know they're terrible! I can't believe you"—I pointed right at Cresseda's watery chest where the light of her soul shimmered—"his own *mother* would do that. Every minute he was with the Dark Queen was dangerous. Who knows what she did to him!"

Cresseda shook her head, droplets spinning off like liquid light. "I simply gave Reth Lend's name and asked him to help you in whatever way he could."

I rolled my eyes. "Yeah, because Reth's opinion on how to help me has always been spot-on." I raised my scarred wrist from where he had tried to force more soul energy into me. "Brilliant move. For someone who's been around for eternity, you don't learn very fast. You. Don't. Trust. Faeries! Ever! Especially not him!"

Okay, forget that I had been guilty of trusting him. I couldn't believe how grateful I was, how willing to forgive him for past offences.

"I took the path that was necessary." Reth's voice was firm and unapologetic.

"By whose standards? No, whatever, don't answer that. David, can we take Lend back to the house now? It's freezing and I don't like the company here."

Arianna put a hand gently on my shoulder; I hadn't realized she was behind me. "Lend's home. That's all that matters."

I shook her hand off, tired and devastated and needing Lend to wake up, just wake up.

"Please stay and hear us out, Empty One," a beautiful dryad asked, her skin a soft mossy green beneath her glamour, large brown eyes pleading.

"My *name* is Evelyn." My voice caught. I couldn't handle the mixture of hope and sadness in her eyes, couldn't shoulder the burden of the entire paranormal world. I'd worked so hard for my life. They'd find another way. I wasn't an Empty One, not anymore. I was an Evie.

David sighed. "Will you go put his pillow and blankets on the couch? We can watch him easier down there. I'll bring Lend back to the house in a minute."

"Yeah."

I turned on my heel and hobbled toward the house. My feet were still tender, sore, and freezing but I didn't care.

"Hey," Arianna said behind me; I walked faster. She ran to catch up, keeping pace with me. "Seriously, why won't you listen to them? You saw how bad things are in the Faerie Realms. You could stop it."

"Yeah, I saw it. My feet? That was because of the field trip Reth took me on—a field trip specifically designed to make me sympathetic toward his group of faeries. To convince me to do what they want me to. That's all any of them are trying to do: force me to be what they want me to be. I don't belong to them!"

"Just because he tricked you into seeing it all, does that change how bad the things you saw were?"

I shook my head angrily, trying not to think of the girls blissfully unaware that they were carrying around Empty Ones inside them, nothing more than tools for the Dark Queen. Then there were those locked forever in the dance. And the village. All those lives, stolen, destroyed on a whim by creatures that shouldn't be here at all.

Creatures I could send back forever.

This shouldn't be my responsibility!

Arianna put her hand out on my arm and forced me to stop. "Listen," she said, her voice soft and intent. "Just because someone else—even someone you don't like— wants you to do something, doesn't mean it's not your choice. Doing the right thing is still doing the right thing. And if you make the right choice, whatever that is, it's still your choice, no matter who wants you to do it. They can never force you to. But you can choose to."

I put my hands up over my eyes and breathed into them. "I need some time. I'm . . . I'm scared. Of all of it. I need Lend to wake up and be okay before I can think about any of this."

"Okay." She put her arms around me and leaned her forehead against mine. "But promise me you'll *think* about it. Really think about it. I spent way too many years doing things just because my parents didn't want me to, and I ended up dead. I know what I'm talking about. Promise me."

"Yeah," I said, my voice exhausted.

She hugged me close, then shoved me away. "Let's go fix up the couch for Lend, then you need to take a shower. You stink like a faerie, all flowers and sunshine and evil manipulation."

"I thought he was going to wake up again on the way here; he was stirring and starting to put on glamours. It shouldn't be long." David smiled tiredly at me after tucking Lend in, and I nodded.

I crawled on the couch and scooted in to Lend, spooning against the whole length of his body and tucking my head into his neck under the curve of his chin. I put his arm over my waist, taking comfort in its familiar weight.

Sleep was coming on heavy and desperately needed when I heard Arianna swear. "Where did you come from?"

Jack's voice answered, whispering. "Is she okay?"

"Yeah, she's okay."

"She bloody did it." His voice was filled with wonder and admiration.

"Stabbed the Dark Queen herself."

He snorted. "Oh, she's in for it now."

"As usual, but— Crap, your feet, too, huh? Come on, out back. She needs to sleep."

They padded away softly, and I slipped into slumber.

"Did you do it?" Vivian whispered, everything dark and hazy, her voice sounding far away. Usually she was right next to me, as real as life.

"I got Lend back." I turned in a circle, but didn't see her anywhere.

"Good girl." She sounded happy, but her voice was getting farther away.

"Where are you?"

"I don't know."

"Can't you be here? I miss you. I wish—I wish I could bring you back with me like I brought Lend."

I could barely hear her now, like she was speaking from a great distance. "Why do you wish that? You shouldn't."

"But I do. Where are you going, Viv?"

"I don't know, stupid. Just sleep."

When I woke up my mouth was dry, my throat irritated, and my stomach grumbling angrily from neglect. I squeezed Lend's hand where it was still draped over my stomach, but there was no response and it stayed as clear as water.

I rolled off the couch, turning to make sure he was still sleeping, still breathing.

"Wake up," I whispered, leaning in and leaving a lingering kiss on his forehead. "Please, soon."

With a sigh I took wincing steps out of the room and around the corner into the kitchen. David's fridge wasn't as well stocked as it had been when Lend and his enormous appetite lived here. I grabbed a loaf of French bread and sat heavily at the counter.

How long would it take Lend to wake up? And what if he never did?

No.

I couldn't let myself think that, because if I thought it, it could become true. He would wake up. Soon. I looked up at the ceiling. I'd never had much religion in my life, but I knew for a fact there were things out there besides us. You couldn't carry the soul of your mermaid best friend in your own body without knowing that.

"Hey, Universe?" My voice was soft, tentative. "If you're listening, I need my boyfriend to wake up. If he wakes up, I swear I'll do anything. I'll open gates, I'll help all the paranormals, I'll never judge people wearing Crocs again. Just let him wake up. Please."

"Well, good morning, bright eyes!" Jack's voice came from the other room.

I sat up straight in shock, hearing Lend let off a string of swearwords. "Where is Evie? What did you do with her?" he croaked out, voice cracked and heavy with sleep.

Thank you, Universe! I shrieked with joy, falling off the stool and hitting my hip against the table. Careening off it, I ran back into the family room just to see Lend's head disappear again behind the back of the couch.

"Lend, you're awake! You're—" I stopped dead in my tracks having come around the edge of the couch to find Lend, once again, crystal clear and unconscious. "Lend? Lend!" Kneeling next to him I shook his shoulder, soft at first, then harder. He didn't respond.

Standing, I turned and saw Jack staring at both of us, confused.

"What did you do to him?" I screamed.

"I didn't do anything! He woke up and looked ready to kill me, business as usual, perfectly healthy. Then you turned the corner and it was lights out."

"If you did anything . . ."

Jack raised both hands in the air. "Evie, I swear."

I sat on the edge of the couch, Lend rolling slightly with my weight so his stomach was against my back.

Very funny, Universe.

I NEED A LITTLE SPACE

I sighed, knocking my head against my knees in time to my heartbeat. He had to wake up again. He had to. I'd been sitting here next to him for the last fifteen hours straight, eating on the floor, not even daring to go to sleep myself in case he woke again and I missed it.

A light hand came down on my shoulder. "Evie, you need some rest."

I looked blearily at Arianna. "What if he wakes up?"

"I'll sit here with him. If he so much as flutters an eyelid, I'll come get you, okay?"

"I can sleep down here next to him."

"You know you won't be able to; besides, it's too noisy."

She had a point. Paranormals had been drifting in and out of the house. Vampires, werewolves, pretty much everyone that David knew through his underground organization had stopped by to offer help. The fact that it was night now actually increased traffic, due to the need for no sunlight and lots of secrecy. Besides David's friends, there were all the weird ones, like the dryad who I kept catching watching us through the window.

Then there was the dragon, whose strange high voice could be heard drifting through the trees, answered by the banshees singing phrases that made me want to throw myself off the nearest cliff, or dig a hole six feet under the ground and go to sleep not only for a few desperately needed hours but for forever.

Yeah. No rest to be had down here.

"Promise you'll come get me?"

She nodded and gave me a hand to stand up. I searched Lend's face for any hints that he was going to wake up soon, but still, always, there was nothing. Brushing my lips against his, I sighed and left the room, tromping up the stairs.

I'd barely gotten to the top when Arianna shouted. "Evie! Evie!"

I turned so fast I tripped, falling down the stairs and landing at the bottom in a bruised but happy heap. "Lend?"

"Evie?" he called, his voice still hoarse.

Laughing, I got up from the floor and ran around the

corner into the family room.

Just in time to see his glamour drop back off as he collapsed *again* onto the couch.

"No!" I screamed, darting forward and grabbing his head in my hands. "Not again! Don't go back to sleep!"

I buried my face in his chest and curled his shirt in my fist. "Wake up, wake up, wake up."

I heard Arianna's soft steps shuffling away, but then she paused. "Evie, leave the room."

"What? Why? What if he wakes up again?"

"Just walk out of the room. Go to the kitchen or the stairs or somewhere."

"Ari, I—"

"Do it!" she snapped. Glaring at her, I wiped my eyes and stood up, walking into the kitchen and wondering why she'd lost her mind.

"Arianna, what on earth is going on?" Lend asked.

I turned and ran back into the room and Lend immediately dropped.

And so did my stomach and my heart. Oh, no. No, no, no. I looked at Arianna and she nodded. I turned and marched mechanically back into the kitchen.

Lend woke up again.

"Okay, this time we both keep our eyes closed," I shouted from the stairs. Squeezing mine shut, I put a hand on the wall and felt my way into the family room.

"No good," Arianna said. "He's asleep again."

"Bleep!" I screamed, opening my eyes and kicking the wall.

David put a sympathetic hand on my shoulder. "At least he's waking up at all," he said softly.

I tried to nod, but I couldn't. What good was a world in which Lend and I couldn't be in the same freaking room? If there was a wall between us he'd wake up, but as soon as there was physical proximity, bam, unconscious Lend.

Shoulders slumped, I walked back out of the room and sat heavily on the bottom stair in the foyer.

"Evie?" Lend called.

"Yup."

"Apparently that one didn't work."

"Nope."

At least we could talk to each other. I'd already explained what happened in the Faerie Realms, telling him the whole tale of how I got him back. He hadn't said much about what happened to him there, his voice catching every time he referred to the Dark Queen. I wished I could hold him and tell him it was okay now.

Problem was, if I was holding him, he couldn't hear me.

Other problem was, it really wasn't okay now.

"Did you eat or drink anything in Faerie?" I asked, rubbing my eyes in exhaustion.

"Again, no. Nothing. I knew the rules. I didn't touch a thing. I wasn't even conscious for long before . . . she . . .

made me fall asleep. I guess I have a knack for annoying authority figures."

I snorted, remembering how crazy he made Raquel when he was locked up at the Center. Raquel, Raquel, where *are* you? She should have called me by now. I was really starting to worry. Why didn't I try to find her when I was in the Center?

Shaking my head, I wrapped my arms around myself. "Yeah, true. You excel at obnoxious. It's always been one of your most attractive qualities."

I wished I could see him smiling. I was sure he would be. My cell phone beeped with a new message. From Carlee, of course. "Found perfect winter formal dress 4 u. is $$$ mite have to sell ur kidney will b worth it. call me bratt we need to tlk colors & decorations." My finger hovered over the callback button, but I set the phone down sadly instead. No Winter Formal until I figured out how my boyfriend and I could actually be there together. Conscious.

I stood up with a sigh. "I'm going to go find Reth."

"What? Why?"

"He might know something about this. I think . . . I think she cursed you, Lend. Reth might know how she did it or how to fix it." Please, please let him know how to fix it. Talking to Lend through walls was not nearly good enough for me, and the idea that I'd never be able to see him awake face-to-face again made me . . .

I couldn't even think about it.

"Don't go alone," Lend said, his voice tight with concern.

"I'll take Jack."

"Oh, wonderful, take the other psychotic guy in your life to go find the first one."

I laughed and rolled my eyes, wishing I could run my fingers through his hair to mess it up. "Relax. They're both behaving. Sort of."

"Take Arianna."

"That means Jack stays with you."

There was a pause. "Fine. But don't forget what I'm sacrificing for you."

"You both realize I'm standing right here, don't you?" Jack asked, raising an eyebrow at me from where he leaned in the open doorway between the entry and the family room.

"We realize. We just don't care. I'll be back soon with answers, hopefully."

Arianna left the room and handed me a coat. I zipped it up and, avoiding the doorway to the family room, walked out the front door into the cloudy night.

"Any idea where to find the pretty creep?" Arianna asked.

"I was hoping he'd be down by the pond with the rest of the menagerie."

"Fair enough." We stepped off the porch and a deliciously warm hand took my own. I glared up at Reth.

"You needed me?"

"How did you know?" I narrowed my eyes suspiciously. Was he eavesdropping?

"You radiate need, my love. I can always feel it."

I sighed. "Can you fix my boyfriend?"

His smile lit up the dark night. "You really ought to know better than to ask a faerie for a favor by now."

DECK THE STERILE
WHITE HALLS

*R*eth watched as Lend passed out the moment I walked into the room.

"Interesting," was his only comment.

"It's faerie magic, right? Can you reverse it?"

His eyes caught the warm light of the family room so it looked like they glowed on their own. "I think we should see my queen."

"Can you fix him or not?"

He paused, then pursed his lips, shaking his head.

I sank down against the wall, staring despondently at Lend. His arm had flopped over the side of the couch and his face was smashed into the cushion, pushing his lips out. I wanted to go over to him, but touching him wouldn't help. I needed *him* to touch *me*. I'd never noticed how often he did, and missing his touch was a physical, palpable pain. Every inch of my skin ached, looking at him.

I needed to think. I wasn't going to go back into the Faerie Realms to visit Reth's queen. I didn't care if she was the queen of the "good" court—they were all bad, and hers was the court that had let my evil, alcoholic (well, carbonationaholic, I suppose) father destroy my birth mother to make me and then forget about me. I wasn't going to go to them for help.

If Reth couldn't fix this magic . . . what was different? I clapped my hands together and jumped up. "Reth can't fix this because he isn't the same type of faerie! We need an Unseelie faerie!"

"I think—" Reth started, but I cut him off.

"No, if the Dark Queen cursed him, we need a dark faerie."

Jack looked up at me from where he was doing a handstand in the middle of the room. "Brilliant! Want to hop on back to the Dark Court, then? Maybe if you ask really nicely, they'll decide they don't want to kill you."

"You, shut it." I glared and started pacing. I needed an Unseelie, but one that I could control. I couldn't get the Goose Down Hair faerie to help me again, plus she was probably dead or worse, considering what I'd made her do to her queen. And I didn't know her name anymore, nor did I know the name of the other faerie I'd freed or where to find him. I had no names.

"Raquel! I need Raquel!" I'd find Raquel and help her if she needed it, convince her to leave IPCA once and for all, and get all the faerie names she knew to help Lend. I ran into the kitchen, where David was at the table on the phone. He'd been desperately calling contacts all day, trying to figure out where Raquel was and how we could get ahold of her. I was touched at his concern. He obviously understood how much Raquel meant to me.

"David!"

He held up a finger for me to wait, listening intently. The color drained from his face and I felt sick. Whatever he was hearing, it wasn't good.

I heard Lend wake up in the next room. "This is getting really old," he muttered.

I put my hands on the back of the chair, bouncing nervously on my toes.

"Okay, thanks," David said, putting down his cell and staring like he didn't quite know what to do with it.

"Did you find her? Is she on some terrible, faraway assignment?" I hoped. Maybe Anne-Whatever Whatever had put her in an incredibly remote part of the world, doing grunt work like herding pixies. We could get her here, though, with Reth.

David's voice was soft, devastated, not carrying to the other room. "She's in lockup."

"She— What?"

"She's going on trial for treason. Tonight at seven." He put his head in his hands.

"No," I whispered. I didn't think my stomach could twist any more, but it kept finding new ways. Raquel *was* in trouble. And it was because of me. At least now I knew where she was. My tired brain sluggishly sorted through plans to get her out as I half listened to Lend, Jack, and Arianna, who were still unaware of Raquel's plight.

David grabbed his phone, then abruptly stood and left the room; I heard the familiar creak of his feet on the stairs.

"Can we switch rooms?" Lend called. "I'm kind of starving."

"I'll make you something!" Jack said, cheerfully skipping into the kitchen.

"Can you even cook?" I asked, a valid question considering he didn't eat normal food. He could only eat food in the Faerie Realms. Jack could help; he could get me to wherever Raquel was. And he knew the Center better than I did, even.

"Never underestimate what I can do."

"Oh, believe me I don't." I sighed. "Lend, do you want me to go around the back so you can come in here?"

"Yeah. Man, this brings whole new levels of suck into my life."

I tried to smile but couldn't quite manage it. I walked out the back door; the sky was just beginning to soften, heralding the coming of a new day. Then it hit me, what day today was. I'd lost track in the crazy shuffle of day-less nights and nightless days in the Center and the Faerie Realms, but I was pretty sure I knew when we were now.

Merry Christmas, Evie.

I ran around the wraparound porch, cringing from both my feet and the freezing air before bursting through the front door. I was not a fan of this whole winter thing. At least in the Center all seasons felt the same.

I jumped onto the couch, curling up in the corner in what remained of Lend's body heat. A lingering hint of Lend's particular smell remained, crisp and cool like a stream buried in the deep green of a forest.

Arianna was still in the armchair, staring at nothing in this creepy way she had where she didn't move and didn't breathe and didn't appear to be alive—or, well, undead—at all. I was glad she didn't want to talk, because I didn't either. I had to figure out how to rescue Raquel.

". . . why you are here in the first place," Lend finished saying. His voice had a distinctly menacing tone.

"Why, to make you the best omelet you've ever had, of course." There was a pause that I could only fill with my imagination. It involved Lend making *I'm going to kill you* motions with his hands. "Hey-oh," Jack continued, "I rescued our girl Evie from the Center and helped her get to the Faerie Realms to save you."

"*Our* girl is *my* girl. And that makes everything okay how?"

"It doesn't," I yelled. Would we never be able to have a quiet conversation again? "But it's a start."

"A start I intend to finish with this omelet," Jack said, "because after you've eaten it, all will be forgiven."

"I'm not eating anything you make," Lend answered. I closed my eyes, listening to the sounds of the fridge opening and drawers shutting slightly harder than they needed to. I was big on second chances for people who nearly tried to kill me, apparently. First I forgave Vivian, now Jack.

But not Reth. Never Reth.

Of course, of the three he was the only one who had never tried to kill me. Whatever, though. At least Vivian and Jack had being crazy and raised by the faeries as an excuse for borderline-homicidal tendencies. Well, Vivian's definitely went past the border and straight into hundreds-of-paranormal-deaths-quite-literally-on-her-hands land.

It was a very complicated land.

"So, we've got a problem," I said.

"What?" Lend yelled.

"We've got a problem!" I shouted.

"No, I heard that. I mean, what's the problem now?"

"I have the solution!" Jack interrupted.

"What?" I sat up, all ears.

"Bells!"

"What?" Lend and I asked at the same time.

"Get her a kitty collar with bells on it. That way you can hear her coming and get someplace where you won't be hurt by collapsing immediately into sleep."

There was a thumping noise, followed by an indignant "Ow!" from Jack.

"The problem," I said, "is that Raquel is going on trial with IPCA and I am not about to let them lock her up forever." She was *my* Raquel. How dare they. My fear was quickly shifting to anger. Tasing me was one thing. But if they thought they could get away with persecuting the very best person they'd ever had working for them, they had another think coming.

"Where?" Jack asked.

"At the Center," David answered, coming down the stairs, but he was cut off by Lend snapping, "You aren't involved in this, Jack."

"Oh, I think you want me involved. I believe I'm the only one here who has ever been to a disciplinary hearing. Five, actually. I was shooting for my lucky number seven, but alas, IPCA and I parted ways too soon."

That settled it. A cheery band we'd make, no doubt. I'd been looking forward to starting some new Christmas traditions this year. Simple things. Reading the *Grinch*. Decorating a tree. Making cookies. Storming the Center to rescue the closest person I'd ever had to a mom. The usual holiday fare.

Merry freaking Christmas.

IN THE ABSENCE OF
RUBY SLIPPERS

This is the worst idea ever," Lend shouted from behind the closed door as Arianna finished pinning my hair under a brunette wig.

"I've been having a lot of those lately, but one of us wouldn't be here if it weren't for my most recent one."

"Well, you look the part, at least," Arianna said, standing back to admire her handiwork. I was in a fitted, sleek black pantsuit with a blouse underneath. The blouse was white. I hated it already. That, combined with the too-dark hair and colored eyebrows making my tragically pale skin even whiter, and I was not loving life. Still, sacrifices had to be made.

Jack was lying on the bed with his head hanging over the side, his face slowly turning more and more red as the blood rushed to it. He looked phenomenally bored for someone about to break into a secret international high security facility.

I slipped into my favorite stilettos, took one step, and fell over. "Ouch." Shaking off the shoes, I rubbed at my still-tender feet. The stilettos were so not happening. That did it. If I didn't already want to destroy the Dark Queen, the fact that she had ruined my ability to wear high heels put her at the very top of my hit list. She was so going down.

But not right now. With a longing look at my pile of heels brought over from the apartment by Jack, I instead turned to the other pile and put on plain black ballet flats.

I heard a thunk that sounded like Lend's head against the door. "This is stupid. Let my dad take care of it. He's been contacting everyone he knows who is still with IPCA, and—"

I walked over and put my own head against the door, pretending there wasn't anything between us. "And it doesn't matter. IPCA isn't the same. There are new people in charge, and they aren't messing around. I can help her. Raquel would do the same for me. She *has* done the same for me."

"I don't see what good it's going to do for you to waltz back in there and—"

"Can I tango back in there, instead? So much sexier than the waltz."

"Evie, I'm serious! You just broke out of IPCA! You're going to get tased and tagged again."

"I really doubt it. Faerie backup, remember?" I went to the window and looked down into the yard, where Reth stood in the midst of the dead brown grass, looking like a god of spring and sunshine who had seriously lost his way. He was staring straight up at me, although how he knew I'd look down right that instant I had no idea. Creeper.

I shivered a little, still not breaking eye contact with Reth. I was in over my head, I knew that, and I knew I'd owe him even more after this. I had no doubt I'd pay in a way I really didn't want to, and soon.

The door shook as Lend kicked it. "Pretty much the only idea I like less than you walking back into IPCA is you walking back into IPCA with only Jack and Reth for protection."

"They owe me."

"True," Jack said, standing up and swaying slightly as he shook his head to clear it. "Plus, I'm pretty sure Reth's threat to remove my hands if I don't help Evie is still under effect. And I'm always up for making hell at IPCA. It's a favorite pastime of mine."

Lend kicked the door again, harder. "Along with abandoning people in the Faerie Paths?"

"One time! I do that one time and no one's going to let me live it down? Just off the top of my head I can name five worse things I've done in the last year."

I put my hand on his shoulder. "Probably not the best way to get back in our good graces."

My phone buzzed on the dresser and I ran to it, hoping against hope it was from Raquel and none of this would be necessary. Maybe they'd let her out! Maybe . . . No such luck. Carlee had written: "omg met a guy soooooo hawt older 2 im dying merry xmas to me CALL." I twisted half my face into a smile, wishing I *could* call her for details. Alas, more people I loved needed rescuing. "Txt me details, cant talk now, xoxo." One of these days my life would be normal and I could be a good friend again.

The doorknob twisted. "I'm coming with you."

I ran over and held it shut. "No, you are so not. We can't carry your unconscious body around the Center. Besides, I need you here. If something goes wrong, I can't handle you getting hurt."

"Wait, so it's okay if I get hurt?" Jack asked.

"Yes," I snapped at the same time as Lend and Arianna.

"As long as you're sure, then," Jack muttered.

Lend jiggled the doorknob. "What about you getting hurt?"

"I've already broken into the Faerie Realms and stabbed

the Dark Queen. After that, a bunch of government suits? Not so intimidating."

"Please tell me stabbing does not factor into your strategy."

I laughed. "Of course it doesn't. I left my knife in her neck, anyway. I think I'm just going to run around and punch people, see if I can't find a teenage girl to tase me." I knocked teasingly on the door.

"If you really want to get Raquel out, then you need me. You can't turn into anyone and everyone you see. I can. So if you really want this covert mission to be a success, why on earth are you leaving your best asset at home?"

"I— Because you—"

I looked at Arianna for help, but she shrugged. "He's right."

"GAH!" I shouted, throwing my hands up in the air. "Fine!" He *was* right, of course. I couldn't risk Raquel's freedom on anything less than our best effort, and Lend should be part of it. Much as I hated to admit it.

"None of this would be a problem if you'd followed my plan to send all the faeries to hell," Jack said, his voice laced with annoyance.

"Do you *really* want to bring that day up again?" Lend asked, the door doing nothing to muffle the threat.

"So!" Jack said, clapping his hands and grinning at me. "We ready to go? What's the transportation plan?"

"I guess I'll go with Reth, and—"

Lend shouted, "No, you're not going anywhere alone with Reth."

"Fine, I'll go with Jack, and—"

"That doesn't work for me either."

I laughed drily. "Okay then, I'll click my heels together three times and say, 'There's no place like the Center, there's no place like the Center,' and then magically appear there!"

He was quiet for a few seconds. "You'll probably be safer with Reth." It sounded like he was speaking through clenched teeth. "And I can keep a better eye on Jack."

"Well, I for one am thrilled to spend more time with Lend. That's the top of my Fun Things to Do list. We should come up with a secret handshake!" Jack said, pushing me to the side and throwing the door open, which resulted in Lend falling to the floor immediately unconscious. "Oh, whoops." Jack smiled, his eyes gleaming. "Too bad. I like him so much when he's talking."

"Very funny. Keep him safe, okay? I don't think Raquel's in the Iron Wing—she would have heard me shouting. Look anywhere you can think of. They might have her in a random room somewhere. We'll meet in Raquel's old office in two hours, whether we've found anything or not."

He nodded, not looking at me as he poked Lend repeatedly with his foot.

"And, Jack? That threat Reth made about your hands? I'm going to apply it to Lend, too. Keep him safe. Or else."

I took one last long look at Lend, wanting to touch

him but knowing it'd only make me feel worse because he couldn't touch me back. Then Arianna wished us luck, and I went downstairs and out the door, where Reth was waiting, hand outstretched. He was holding Tasey, the rhinestones sparkling in the early morning light. "You dropped this in the Faerie Realms. It seemed a pity to part you two."

I wrapped my fingers around my trusty friend, maliciously hoping I'd get the chance to use her on someone.

PLAN T

You have no idea where Anne's office is?" I asked, grouchy and beyond footsore, seriously envying Jack's completely healed feet. We'd already been here for an hour and had nothing to show for it other than a few close calls with security patrols. I'd figured since I couldn't check every room for Raquel, searching Anne-Whatever Whatever's office for records was my next best bet.

"Surprisingly enough, I do not make a habit of concerning myself with the locations of offices of people I neither know nor care anything for."

"I thought you had some big vendetta against IPCA for controlling you."

"Have you seen anyone who ever once used my name against me? Present company excepted."

I frowned, checking around a corner to a hall that was, as usual, empty. This was so much less exciting than I had been afraid it would be. Reth walked calmly forward, never pausing, never frantically checking over his shoulder.

I wondered what he did to those poor suckers who had trapped him with his true name. I almost asked, but honestly, I didn't really want to know. "Wait—you didn't do anything to Raquel." I inwardly cringed. Raquel had used his name against him, and there I went reminding him.

"Hmm. An uncharacteristic oversight."

I snorted. "Yeah, mister always has a plan, you're constantly missing details." I shouldn't push the issue lest I convince him that he still had some vengeance waiting, but I couldn't help it. It was so unlike him.

He waved an elegant hand through the air as though brushing off my observation. "Some things are beneath my attention."

"Liar."

He stopped short, and I walked a few paces before realizing he wasn't beside me anymore. I turned and found myself sucked into his golden gaze.

"You are quite blind sometimes, my love."

"What do you mean by that?" I snapped. Then my

jaw dropped as he actually rolled his perfect, gigantic-bordering-on-anime golden eyes. That was *so* not a faerie gesture. "You just rolled your eyes!"

"It would appear you are a negative influence after all." He walked past me and I scurried to catch up.

But it had me thinking. I knew for a fact that on at least one occasion Raquel had directly screwed up his turn-Evie-into-a-fiery-immortal plans. If that didn't get her on his hit list, I didn't know what would. I looked at Reth, wondering if he'd left Raquel alone just because of what she meant to me. That line of thought made me feel strange and squirmy inside. It was easier for me to dismiss him when he was unquestionably a jerk. But he'd helped me so much, even if some of it was underhanded and calculating. I didn't know how to sort it all out in my head and my heart.

We hit a hallway that I knew contained a records storage room. Maybe it listed where they kept employees waiting for disciplinary hearings. I couldn't palm it open. "Any way you can open this door?"

Looking utterly and completely bored, he put a hand up to the door and pulled it back as though burned. "Iron."

"Brilliant. I can't unlock them, you can't get in them. We're useless."

"I do recall saying exactly that same thing before we embarked on this pointless excursion."

I rubbed my eyes. Being able to find Raquel, or even Anne's office, had always been a long shot, but I'd secretly hoped we'd run into someone that we could pump for information or something. I had no doubt that Reth with all his glamoured glory could get some poor sap to spill all sorts of beans. But we hadn't seen a single soul the whole time we'd been stalking the halls.

Wait. The whole time I'd been following Reth through the halls.

I looked at him, my eyes narrowed. "You'd really like it if this whole effort was a failure, wouldn't you?" Much as I doubted he cared one way or the other about Raquel's future, one thing he was invested in was me. And no Raquel meant no more faerie names, which meant no more touching Lend. Maybe forever.

He tilted his head to the side, face inscrutable.

"I can't believe this." I turned on my heel and stalked back down the hall. "Of course you wouldn't really be helping me." I knew where we should go, and without Reth to lead me in paths to deliberately avoid any and everyone, I was going to find something out.

I walked as fast as I could without looking crazy in case we did run into someone, quickly navigating the labyrinthine halls to my old training room. I pulled my hand up just short of trying to palm the lock. Odds were, nothing would happen, but what if they'd coded the place to recognize my hand and set off an alarm?

"Bleep," I muttered.

"Problem?" Reth said, leaning in way too close to my

ear. Faeries and personal bubbles, honestly. I tried not to shiver at the way his breath trailed warm and sweet down my neck.

"No." Screw technology, I would do this old school. I pulled my hand back, made a fist, and then knocked. Loudly. Repeatedly. Maybe a bit desperately, because I was fast running out of time and if he didn't open the door . . .

The door slid open, revealing the shocked and angry face of Bud. "What the—"

I pushed him back into the room and let the door close behind us, shutting Reth out in the hall.

"What are you doing back here?" His face was an unhealthy shade of red. "Are you daft? You were lucky to get out of here once. If they catch you again, you can bet that—"

"I need help. They're going to try Raquel."

He let out a heavy breath and rubbed his eyes, staring at the floor. "I'd thought as much."

"Do you know where they're keeping her? I need to break her out before the trial, because after that I might not ever be able to find her again." It was too terrible to think about. I wouldn't lose Raquel, not like I'd lost Lish.

He put his calloused, heavy hands on my shoulders and fixed his muddy brown eyes on mine. "Listen, kid. I always liked you. And I liked Raquel, too. But, trust me, you don't want any part of this. Best to leave IPCA to itself and get free and clear again, forever. Disappear."

I opened my mouth to argue when it hit me—that look in Bud's eyes? It was fear. Bud was like a grizzly bear. He was stronger and tougher than even a werewolf, and he didn't have any supernatural abilities other than his infinite capacity to yell at me for not practicing my self-defense techniques.

"What's going on?" I asked.

He dropped his hands and sat wearily on a beat-up folding chair surrounded by free weights against the wall. "This place, well, it's never been perfect but I always believed in the core of it. That we were doing good. But ever since Anne-Laurie LeFevre swooped in, it's all gone to pot faster than a gremlin can chew through the hull of a supertanker."

"With the arrests?"

"More than that. There are rumors—and I stay out of all this, mind you—but rumors of dealings with creatures we're meant to protect the world from. Things that sure as all heck go against our charter. Things it's safer for both of us not to know about. I'm asking you to leave it be. I'll keep an eye out for Raquel, but she made her bed with IPCA and she'll have to sleep in it. She wouldn't want you here any more than I do."

I scowled, my stomach crawling inside my abdomen like a living thing. Something serious was going down here to have Bud scared. I was in over my head.

Eh, what else was new. I shrugged. "Raquel wouldn't leave me. I'm not going to give up on getting her out."

He sighed heavily. "You always were too stubborn. I've half a mind to set off the alarm just to get you to run away."

"Aww, come on. You wouldn't do that. We both know I was your favorite student."

He snorted.

"No idea where they're keeping Raquel?"

"None. And if I knew, I wouldn't tell you. Get out. Have a life. And stay out of mine. You're more dangerous than anything else here."

"Psh. I'm the epitome of cuteness. See? Perky! That's me. Not dangerous."

He shook his head and opened the door. "Out. And please, kid, I never want to see you again."

"Thanks, Bud. Again. For everything. I'm pretty sure that knife of yours saved my life." He looked at my hands expectantly like I'd have it there. "Oh, uh, yeah. Kind of lost it." Before he could glare I hugged him, then walked out and heard the door slide shut behind me. I'd expected Reth to be waiting, but he was nowhere to be seen. What was the evil creature up to now?

No matter. That was probably as much information, worthless as it had been, as I was going to get. I turned and hurried alone toward Raquel's old office, letting myself hope that they'd found Raquel and she'd be there with them, sitting behind her desk and practicing her arsenal of sighs. As I passed a cross hall I caught sight of someone. My werewolf guard buddy from before. Bleep, bleep, bleepity bleep. Stopping short of putting a hand up to shield the side of my face, I walked as fast as I could without looking like I was panicking.

He didn't see me. He couldn't have seen me. Oh, please, please let him not have seen me.

"Hey! You!"

Could nothing go my way today? I broke into a run, skidding around the corner with Wolfie right behind me. I had just enough time to register Bud at the end of the hall and wonder what he was doing out there, when Bud melted away to reveal the water form of my boyfriend, collapsing to the floor in an unconscious heap.

Time for plan B. Or plan T, really. Time to see how much Wolfie liked Tasey.

PICTURE IMPERFECT

Wolfie growled, narrowing his eyes. "You know, the best way to get a predator to chase you is to run."

I snorted. "Oh my gosh, did you practice that line in front of a mirror or something?"

He lunged and I dodged to the side, but the hallway was too narrow to maneuver much. I had to keep him away from Lend. I turned to sprint in the opposite direction but was jerked back, my feet nearly slipping out from under me. Wolfie had my collar in his huge hand. I undid the buttons, reached into my suit jacket, and pulled out Tasey. He tried to yank me backward, pulling off my jacket with the effort.

Tasey on, I twirled to jab it into his stomach, but he was too fast.

Bleep, I hadn't fought a werewolf ever, and had never had to tase one who was actually expecting it. He grinned maliciously as we circled each other, each looking for an opening.

"I can smell your fear."

"Again with the lines! What do you think this is, a B movie? News flash: you are not a tortured hero and we're *not* going to have a hot make out scene after we fight." I feinted forward, but he twirled to the left and slammed his fist into the side of my head. My vision exploded into stars, everything narrowing and closing off as my brain tried to process the pain.

Taser, Taser, Taser, I thought, desperately trying to claw my instincts out of the blow-to-the-head stupor, but before I managed to, he had grabbed my hand and smashed it down onto his knee. Tasey clattered uselessly to the floor as he twisted my arm behind my back, forcing me to bend over in pain.

"Whose movie is it now?" he hissed in my ear, pushing me to my knees.

"That's quite enough of that," Reth said, and I'd never been so glad in my entire life to hear his smooth, golden voice. Wolfie abruptly let go of my arm. I jumped to my feet and backed up.

Reth had a finger underneath Wolfie's chin—the

werewolf security guard's face was blank bordering on slap-happy as he stared at Reth. Judging by the look on Reth's face, though, Wolfie was going to meet a very bad end. Immediately.

"Wait!"

"Hmmm?" Reth didn't look up at me.

"Don't kill him."

"May I remind you that you can no longer control me? This *thing* was going to hurt you."

"It's not his fault. I mean, he's a jerk, sure, but he didn't ask to be here." And it was a little bit because of me. Dang guilt. I picked up my jacket and Tasey. "Can you just make him go to sleep or something so he can't sound an alarm?"

Reth finally looked at me, his eyes narrowing. "You are far too attached to the transient lives of this realm, Evelyn. If you opened up your vision like you should, you'd realize that none of this matters."

"Matters to me. So please. Put him to sleep. *Temporary* sleep, not euphemistic sleep."

Finally, Reth's eyes relaxed and he turned back to Wolfie, tracing his fingers across the guard's forehead. Wolfie's eyes rolled back in his head and he dropped, none too softly.

I didn't feel bad about that. "Thanks. Where were you?"

"I had some business to attend to."

"What, like, forgot to fill out your last IPCA time card? Pick up your personal effects? Clean out your old cubby?"

He actually smiled, the corners of his perfect, straight

lips pulling up. "Something like that."

Positive he wasn't going to give me a real answer, I turned and walked the length of the hall to where Lend was still lying, peacefully asleep and, ah bleep, totally naked. Hadn't expected that one. I mean, it made sense that he'd come without real clothes so he could imitate anyone regardless of what they were wearing, but still. Not really the time or place for boyfriend nudity.

But I couldn't very well leave him here to wake up alone. Where was Jack? If he'd ditched out on Lend, he was so going to pay.

Raquel's old office door slid open, and the little demon himself poked his head out. "There you are. Had to use the Faerie Paths to get in and open it from the inside. Took a couple of wrong turns to get there." He looked down and saw Lend. "He's a terrible sentry. I would never fall asleep on the job."

"Shut up and help me get him inside." We each grabbed an arm and pulled Lend into the room. Reth sauntered in behind us, carrying Wolfie. "Can't you dump him some-where else?"

"Would you rather I leave him unconscious in the hall for anyone to stumble upon?" Reth walked to the corner and dropped him on the floor.

I set Lend's head down gently, then sat in the white chair at Raquel's desk. The whole place was as pristine as it always had been when she was here, but it felt wrong to be behind the desk in her place.

Jack sat in one of the extra chairs, draping a leg over the side. "We got nothing. Any luck?"

"None. An old friend says that IPCA's into some bad stuff, but he couldn't or wouldn't say what. It doesn't give us anything to go on." I opened the nearest drawer and my heart jumped painfully in my chest. At the top of the pile of papers was a photo of me. I was probably thirteen, on one of our field trips to the Museum of Natural History in New York City, posing like the huge T. rex. I reached out and trailed my fingers along the edge of the photo, touched that Raquel had printed and kept it.

Also, wow, braces and bangs were so not my friends.

Pulling out the photo and setting it gently on the desk, I rifled through the rest of the papers, but they were the usual government bureaucracy nonsense—forms and forms and more forms.

"I doubt you're going to find anything useful there," Jack said. "If you knew you were in trouble with IPCA, would you leave incriminating evidence in the unlocked drawers of your desk? It's probably between her mattresses or something."

"Yeah! That's where I keep my secret stuff."

Jack rolled his eyes. "I know. It's not very creative."

Resisting the urge to punch him again, I nodded. "Okay. Reth, how soon is Wolfie going to wake up?"

Reth didn't bother responding, simply glaring at me

like he couldn't believe I would question his efficiency in rendering werewolves harmless. He looked uncomfortable standing in the room. It wasn't that he was too big for it, because he was very lean and narrow although quite tall, but somehow it felt like he took up more space than the room could afford. Like it couldn't contain him. No wonder faeries never hung around inside if they didn't have to.

"Jack, have you ever been to Raquel's room? Could you open a door there?"

"Raquel and I didn't see each other socially much. I kept waiting for a dinner invitation, but alas."

I looked at Reth hopefully. "You?"

"Must we really waste more time? Not all of us here are immortal, and I'd think you and Jack would more carefully guard what little you have. We should go immediately to my queen."

"Can you get us in or not?"

He looked at the ceiling, his features dripping with disdain for the entire operation. "I suppose if you were to stand immediately outside her door I could use my sense of where you are to navigate into her room and open the door from inside."

"That's my pretty faerie boy!"

"If you ever address me like that again, I will make that abomination on your head permanent."

I put my fingers up to the brunette wig, horrified. "You wouldn't."

"I suggest you do not attempt to find out."

Swallowing hard, I pointed to Lend. "Can you take him with you so Jack and I don't have to carry him?"

Not taking his eyes off me, Reth picked up Lend, letting his head loll uncomfortably to the side, then walked through a faerie door and out of the room.

"That guy is scary," Jack said.

"Tell me about it." We left Raquel's office, checking both ways, then walking as calmly and quickly as we could. We were halfway to Raquel's room when I froze in terror at the sound of Anne-Whatever Whatever's voice.

EAVESDROPPING AND
READING NOTES

Looking frantically up and down the hall, I let out my breath, relieved. Anne-Whatever Whatever was nowhere to be seen. But I could still hear her, which meant she was way too close for comfort. I put my finger to my lips to shush Jack. He put a finger to his lips, too, but used the middle one instead of the pointer.

"Wait here," I hissed.

I tiptoed down the hall with my back to one of the walls until I got to the corner, where I could make out words.

". . . know about the deal. I assure you I haven't for-gotten." Anne-Whatever Whatever sounded equal parts annoyed and nervous. "We've been tracking their progress, and I'm confident they are no closer to making a gate."

How did she know about gates? IPCA didn't usually pay attention to faerie lore. I startled, nearly screaming as a hand came down on my shoulder. Jack gave me an exasperated look, leaning in to listen, too.

"And the Empty One?" This voice was definitely not Anne's. It was like birdsong formed into words, and something about it made a spot behind my eyes start hurting. I needed to see who that voice belonged to. I was sure it was a faerie voice, but which one? That wasn't how IPCA officials talked to named faeries.

"I've told you, she's a silly, stupid girl. We'll get her away from her protections and next time she won't escape the Center."

"Our displeasure is not to be taken lightly. Do not think you can try to gain an advantage over my queen by keeping the Empty One for yourself."

"You keep up your end of the bargain and get me more names, and I guarantee that Evelyn will never make a gate. Yours will be the only exodus from this world."

What the crap? If this was what it sounded like—and it sounded like the government agency charged with protecting the world from paranormals was conspiring with the very worst of the lot—it was big. Scary big. No wonder Bud had been nervous. I had to look, had to see if I could tell which court the faerie belonged to. If the Seelie Court was playing all the sides, I was so done with them. I started to lean forward; Jack's hand tightened around my arm like a vise. I shot him a glare. "I need to see," I mouthed. He didn't let go, so I ducked down and peeked my head around the corner.

Anne's back was to me, but I had a full view of the faerie. A faerie with midnight blue hair and eyes, her cold white skin dotted with pricks of light like stars. A faerie straight from the Dark Court. A faerie I knew for sure that IPCA didn't have named.

Which meant Anne-Whatever Whatever was making deals with uncontrollable faeries. Unseelie uncontrollable faeries.

Oh, bleep.

I pulled back, heart racing as I waited for the faerie to yell or sound an alarm. Nothing. Jack and I slipped off down a side hall, taking the long way to Raquel's unit. We made it without incident, then stood there. I shuffled my weight from foot to foot, trying to relieve some of the soreness and wondering how long it would take Reth to figure out where I was and get into Raquel's room.

The door slid open in reply.

Jack and I darted in, letting out twin sighs of relief. Lend, of course, immediately dropped to the floor. Naked, still. I doubted Raquel had anything in his size.

"He was rather upset waking up in the Faerie Paths with me," Reth said.

"I can't imagine." I quickly scanned Raquel's austere living room area. "There, help me get him into that closet."

Jack grabbed an arm and we dragged my poor boyfriend across the floor and shoved him into the tiny coat closet next to Raquel's vacuum. I added watching Lend walk to the things I missed most about him.

We closed the door and after a few moments a loud thunk sounded. "What the— Where am I? Evie?"

"Right here," I said, tapping on the door. "You're in a closet in Raquel's unit."

"Why?"

"Because I'm going to search the rest of her place and I didn't want you to risk brain damage by any more unconscious falls."

He muttered something unintelligible but distinctly grouchy and I turned, quickly scanning the room. Nothing here but a glass coffee table and a bland gray couch. I'd spent a couple of nights there after I'd gotten trapped in the Center, cleaning up a poltergeist this fall. The couch was both ugly and uncomfortable. Someone seriously needed to teach Raquel a thing or two about interior decorating.

I hoped I'd have the chance.

"You two look around here and the kitchen. I'm going to look through her room."

I walked in and my breath caught. I'd never been in Raquel's bedroom before; now there was no question in my mind why I hadn't been invited. Prominently displayed on her wall was a framed series of photos from when Raquel was a young woman. They looked suspiciously like engagement pictures, her black hair loose and flowing and her smile brighter and happier than I remembered ever seeing.

And the guy with her was Lend's dad.

Didn't see that one coming. And, oh bleep, what would Lend think knowing that his dad had been very serious with one of Lend's least favorite people in the world? Or at least I assumed they were very serious, given the number of photos that they were sucking face in.

"Well, that's interesting," I said.

"What's interesting?" Jack called from the other room.

"Something is interesting?" Lend shouted.

"No! Nothing! I mean, nothing important. Keep looking."

"I found a vacuum," Lend said.

"Brilliant!" Jack answered. "Just what we needed!"

Sighing, I went for the bed, surprised and pleased to see a deep green bedspread instead of white or gray. Shoving the top mattress to the side, I felt around and . . . my fingers closed around a file folder.

"Bingo!" I shouted, pulling it out and praying it wasn't filled with love letters or some other equally horrifying thing. "Between the mattresses!"

"See?" Jack said, leaning against the doorframe. "Told you I was useful."

"We'll see." I walked out into the living room and sat on the floor against the closet door. "Oh, Lend, in the hall we saw Anne talking to an unnamed Unseelie faerie about me. Apparently she's helping them keep me from making a gate."

Reth's attention snapped to me. "Are you sure it was an Unseelie?"

"Yup. The faerie was in the Dark Court, standing beside the queen. And I know I never saw her at IPCA, not even when they called all their named faeries in."

"Perhaps this trip was not a waste after all, then," Reth said. "We should go and inform my queen immediately."

"Not yet. Please."

He nodded sharply, but his eyes promised I'd have to pay him back soon.

"What do you think that means?" Lend asked.

"I dunno, but it's big. It goes against everything IPCA does to work with paranormals like that."

Lend's voice sounded tired, even muffled by the closet door. "Okay, that's something, I guess. What did you find in the folder? I'd really, really like to save Raquel and then nab a dark faerie who can break this curse."

I opened the folder, pulling out several sheets filled with Raquel's precise cursive penmanship. Oh, bleep, they were love letters, they were totally going to be . . . I could feel my cheeks burning by the time I realized that these papers were not anything close to love letters.

I passed the first page under the closet door as I pored over the second. It looked like a detailed accounting of werewolf and human IPCA employees: dates of when they started, specific duties, and for each . . . a date of disappearance. I flipped through sheet after sheet of names and information and dates, passing them on to Lend. Reth was standing in the middle of the room, again filling it more than his size made possible, while Jack juggled coffee mugs.

"Anne" was written at the top of the last page, followed by hastily scrawled notes about things Raquel had noticed, changes she'd seen, conversations she'd overheard. People whose names even I recognized—mostly politicians, and, bleep, the vice president of the United States?

And then, the final line: "Must convince Evie to help Light Queen or all will be lost."

Well, that was fabulous. Way to be cryptic *and* a traitor, Raquel. "Looks like Raquel joined Team Force Evie to Do Supernatural Crap." I passed the final sheet under the door and folded my arms as I waited for him to finish reading.

I closed my eyes, stewing over everything. What could make IPCA violate their own charter and work with unnamed faeries? What did they have to gain by conspiring with the Dark Court and keeping me from opening a gate? "I don't get it. Why does IPCA care what goes on with gates?"

Lend shouted, his voice excited. "They don't want you to open a gate because they'd lose their power! What would IPCA be without faeries? Nothing. It wouldn't even be IPCA anymore, it'd probably dissolve into all the various factions again. And there's no way transportation is all they're using the faeries they control for. What if they're using the magic to mess with the whole world? Influence people, control politics?"

I nodded my head, eyes wide as what he was saying sunk in. "They could do *anything* with what they have now. If I open a gate and the faeries they control leave the world, all that influence and magic is gone. Done. No more power, no more money, no more nothing."

"So why work *with* the Dark Court?" Jack asked, catching one of the mugs with his foot. "Shouldn't they be working against all the faeries to keep everyone here?"

I snapped my fingers. "Because! IPCA helps the Dark Court, and the Dark Court makes sure all the Light Court and other paranormals stay here forever! IPCA never has to lose control. Reth himself said the Light Queen would never attempt to make another Empty One."

"But even if the Dark Court manages to leave, the Light Court still has you," Lend said.

"It was pretty clear from the conversation we overheard that one way or another I'd be dead."

Something smashed to the ground. Jack looked at me, all the mugs forgotten. "I'm not going to let anyone kill you." He grinned. "If I don't get to, no one should."

"I'm touched." But I couldn't help smiling back at him.

After a few seconds Lend said, "But what about all these disappearances she has listed? What do they have to do with anything?"

"I wish I knew." Actually, I kind of wished I didn't know any of this. Lend and I were cursed to the ultimate long-distance relationship, we weren't any closer to Raquel, IPCA had gone crazy, powerful immortal creatures *and* a covert international government agency were gunning for my death, it looked like I would have to help Reth's side no matter what as the lesser of two evils, *and* I was pretty sure there was no way I would be getting those car-financing back-pay checks from IPCA now. The rate my luck was holding, Reth'd probably make me a permanent brunette by tomorrow.

ICE, ICE, BABY

What time is it?" I asked Jack.

He leaned into the kitchen. "We've got about twenty minutes before David's friend said Raquel's trial starts."

"Do you know where she's being tried?" Lend asked.

"Central Processing." I tried to keep the sadness out of my voice. At least I wouldn't have a hard time finding it. "I'm going to go to the hearing."

"What?" Lend, Reth, and Jack all said at the same time.

I shrugged. "Either all IPCA is in on this and we're completely screwed no matter what, or Anne is acting on her own, in which case we might have an advantage with our new information. Regardless, that's the only place we know for sure Raquel will be before she potentially disappears forever. I'm going to go, and I'm going to get her back."

I expected Lend to freak out, to yell that I couldn't do it and it was too stupid to even consider. Which was why his soft voice saying "Okay" caught me off guard.

"Wait, okay? Seriously?"

"Seriously," he answered. "I want this stupid curse broken more than anything. And I know you need to help Raquel. If anyone can do this, you can."

I beamed, suddenly flush with warmth that he believed in me that much.

"What can I do?" he asked.

"For this to work, we need to find a computer system to break into." I looked up at Jack. "I don't suppose either one of you have previously undisclosed hacker abilities?"

Jack shook his head. "Not one of my many talents, sadly. But if you have a cherry stem I can show you a really cool one."

"I'm not great," Lend said. "You need Arianna."

"I think you're right. Jack, can you take Lend back and bring Arianna here?"

"But—" Lend started.

"No, there's not anything you can do here. Go back home and figure out what, exactly, your mom and the others want me to do. If I'm going to make a decision about them, I need all the information I can get. Also please put some clothes on because sleeping, nude Lend is a huge distraction I can't deal with right now."

He laughed. "Okay, fine. Be careful. And come back soon."

"I will." I stood and walked into Raquel's bedroom, then into her walk-in closet just to be safe. This wasn't a good time for Lend to pass out.

"I'll be back!" Jack yelled out. I was about to go tell Reth my newest Save Raquel plan when I noticed half her closet was filled with the clothes I'd left behind. It was touching that she'd kept them, and just what I needed to cheer me up. Bleep if I was going to stage a rescue in a freaking pantsuit.

". . . for the unauthorized release of a Level Seven paranormal, for the aiding and abetting of known IPCA fugitives, and for—" Anne's voice grated to a complete stop as I walked into the room.

I smiled cheerily at the shocked faces looking down at us from a raised platform that curved along the far end of the huge, circular room. Eleven people, all from different countries, sat along the polished, dark wood table. They were each dressed impeccably in suits, the women with no-nonsense buns. I wasn't sure, but it looked to me like most of them were exhausted under their severe exteriors.

As for me, I was in my best hot-pink shirtdress with a big black belt, matching black boots (worth the pain), and sparkly silver tights. I wasn't going for subtlety.

"What are you doing here?" Anne-Whatever Whatever asked from her spot in the center of the table, her jaw nearly unhinged in shock as the door slid closed behind Reth and me. I kept my hand tucked in Reth's elbow; in this lion's den, Reth was a bit like a security blanket. A crazy, magical security blanket who would probably hurt me again soon but for now would definitely hurt these people if they tried to hurt me.

There was a lot of hurt potential, really.

"I'm here to represent the defendant," I said.

Anne recovered quickly. She pulled out her communicator and typed something into it, smiling smugly at me. But then she looked down at her communicator and her smile turned into a frown. She pushed the buttons again; nothing.

"The communications system is down," she snapped, glaring at a vampire standing in the corner. He had a typically handsome glamour, dark hair and nearly black eyes, but both his faces—the glamoured one and the corpse one underneath—looked confused.

"I don't know—" he started, but she cut him off with another glare.

"Fix it."

He pulled out his own communicator and started tapping furiously. I so owed Arianna, that undead little genius.

"Shouldn't we get down to business?" I asked. For the

first time I let myself look over to the side, where Raquel was sitting on a simple, hard chair. She didn't have a massive desk to hide her, and seemed shockingly small there all by herself. Her suit was rumpled and some hair had escaped her perpetual bun. She met my eyes and looked impossibly sad. I wanted to hug her, but I had to wait.

"Evie, please," she said. "Leave."

"By all means, stay," Anne said. "Have a seat. We'll take care of you next."

"Yeah, see, I think someone else is going to be on trial next." Baring my teeth at her in a grin I pulled out my file folder. "I've got some interesting reading here. And I even brought copies for everyone so you don't have to share."

A distinguished-looking South African man on the end shook his head. "What is this? Another farce?"

"No, but bonus points for using a funny word. You really want to read what I have here. Anne, you'll be especially interested, since you have a starring role."

"Enough. Rhia—"

Reth quickly flicked his wrist at her; her mouth kept moving, but no sound came out. It was one of the most satisfying things I'd ever seen. Sure, that trick had sucked when he used it on me, but I wholly approved of it now.

"Whoops. I forgot to mention these are now closed proceedings. There will be no summoning of faeries, or my faerie friend will make sure it's the last thing you ever say." I walked forward, setting one of the photocopied sheets in front of each Supervisor. Several of them glared at me, but a few actually looked interested. One, a Chinese woman named Hong Li who had a bad habit of patting my head whenever we met at holiday parties even after I grew taller than her, actually looked amused.

Maybe not everyone here hated me, after all.

"Now, as you'll see, the top sheet is a detailed record of everything that Raquel has discovered about Anne's extra-curricular activities." I stepped back and watched, holding my breath. This was the critical part. Either this was going to blow the top off Anne's operations, or the rest of them were already in on it and I was going to have to figure out a new tactic, stat.

Hong Li skimmed the paper, then sat up straighter, putting on reading glasses and scanning it again. She looked up at me. "What proof do you have?"

"The evidence Raquel has gathered, which includes names—dozens of names—of missing people that have been filtered through IPCA, and my personal eyewitness account of Anne talking and making deals with an unnamed faerie of the Unseelie Court."

Anne slammed her fist down onto the table, still mouthing words furiously.

Hong Li looked back at me. "Evie, you have a history of lying and misleading this organization. How can we trust you now?"

I stared at her, willing her to see my earnestness. "Because

I have no interest in any of this. If I wanted to disappear, I could have. If I wanted to burst in here and break Raquel out, I could have done that, too. But I thought it was more important that you all understand exactly what Anne is doing, and just what it means for the rest of the world if she's successful. She's using you—everyone, the entirety of IPCA—for her own ends. And surely things haven't changed so much since I left that you've all forgotten why IPCA is here in the first place: to make the world safer. Not to help evil faeries, not to conspire with governments, and not to imprison and punish a woman who's done nothing but try to fulfill the Charter to the best of her ability."

Hong Li turned to look at the other Supervisors. Several looked outraged, still reading the sheets. One, a woman with a shock of curly red hair, looked terrified, all the blood draining from her face. And a couple of them looked entirely impassive.

"Let Anne-Laurie speak," Hong Li said to Reth.

I turned to him, noting the slightly murderous expression on his face that flitted there after she gave him a command, and squeezed his arm. "Go ahead."

He flicked his wrist, and Anne cleared her throat, standing. "Surely you aren't going to believe the words of a paranormal girl known to have betrayed everything we stand for. Do I really need to go over her crimes yet again? She's a stupid teenager with an inflated sense of self-importance and a dangerous level of arrogance."

The handsome black man raised an eyebrow. "Be that as it may, these are serious charges, and I think it merits discussion. There have been many breaches of protocol since you were made Lead Supervisor, and I for one vote for immediate review."

"I agree, Baruti." Hong Li turned to Raquel. "Do you have more evidence to back up the claims here?"

Raquel sat up straighter in her chair. "I do."

"Very well, we'll—"

"That's enough," Anne snapped. "We're done here."

"Excuse me?" Hong Li asked, indignant.

"I said we're finished. I deny the motion for review, and rule that Raquel is to be immediately and permanently locked up. As for the Level Seven, since she has proven she is no longer useful to IPCA in any capacity, she will be bagged and tagged and put into seclusion at a secret location."

Hong Li slapped her hand against the table and stood, too. "Since when can you—"

"Since I am the only person here with any vision or sense of the direction IPCA needs to go to continue to protect the world. If you want to cow to the ramblings of an aberration of nature, please feel free to join her. I am not about to let her destroy what we've built here."

"How can she destroy anything?" a blond man with impossibly square shoulders and a thick German accent asked.

"She's currently working with a rebel group to subvert our work. And aside from that, she's actively trying to open a gateway to another realm, which, in and of itself, could be disastrous for our world, but aside from that would allow all faeries to leave. Which would leave us entirely without their particular skills, and I think you all understand what that would mean. IPCA would dissolve. We would no longer be able to function at any capacity, leaving the world unprotected and at the mercy of the various paranormal elements we work so hard to contain."

To my horror, the blond man looked like he was actually weighing her words. The redhead trembled—where had they even gotten her?—and a couple of other Supervisors were nodding.

But Hong Li, bless her head-patting heart, was having none of it. "You admit to it, then? Conspiring with unnamed faeries?"

Anne rolled her eyes. "I don't have to answer to you."

"I beg to differ," Baruti said.

"Very well." Anne nodded to the terrified redhead and they both started spouting off faerie names as fast as they could.

The Supervisors all started shouting at one another as lines of white light snaked along the walls.

"Raquel!" I yelled. "Time to go!" She ran to us. Reth was already holding the door open. I smashed the emergency alarm button every room in the Center had, briefly flashing back to the last time I'd done it to warn everyone that Vivian had gotten in, just after I'd found Lish's body.

I would *not* lose anyone I loved tonight.

The alarm blared, so loud it made my teeth hurt, and all the lights dimmed as strobes went off. Reth said a word and raised his hand, making the air behind us shimmer and thicken like water as we ran out of the room and down the hall, Raquel and I on either side of Reth ready to take his hands.

"Too much iron in these walls," Reth said, not even his perfect hair disturbed by his running. "Back to where we came in, if you please."

I nodded, hoping that Jack and Arianna would take the alarm as my cue for them to leave. Jack was good at running, at least. Then I had a thought that made me feel sick. "We can't leave Vivian here; they won't take care of her. Do we have time—"

Reth jerked to a stop and threw me into the wall.

I didn't even have time to register the faerie before whatever she had done slammed into where I had been standing—and straight into Reth. He stumbled back, falling to the ground as I watched in horror. Reth was *Reth*. He was perfect, and flawless, and supernaturally tough.

"All mine," the faerie said, the same midnight-haired faerie I'd seen before. She walked up to me but I couldn't tear my eyes away from Reth on the ground. He let out a low sound, his golden voice tarnished, and tried to push himself up. He'd be too late. If she could do that to him . . .

Then I could do this to her. I lunged forward and slapped my palm against her chest, throwing open the connection there and pulling out as much as I could as fast as I could. It flowed into me, but instead of the living flame that Reth had, this soul was so cold it burned, like crystals of ice ripping through my veins, filling me and changing me and I had to stop it I didn't want this inside me but I wanted more no, no, I didn't want this, but—

"Evie!" Raquel pulled me away, breaking the connection, and I gasped, struggling to claw my way up from the ice crystals in my brain, this dark-blue, freezing haze of power cracking through my body. "Evie!"

I blinked, then finally managed to focus on Raquel's eyes.

"Okay," she said, her accent thicker when she was upset. "Okay, you're okay."

The midnight faerie staggered backward, slumping against the wall, and the sight filled me with shame and self-loathing. But I didn't have time for that, either. I stumbled forward and knelt next to Reth.

"Reth? Reth! Are you okay? We need to get out of here."

He pushed himself up from the ground, his arms trembling in a way that was so human and vulnerable it made my breath catch. I held out my hand and he took it to finish standing and, for the first time ever, my hand was warmer than his.

"Are you okay?" I whispered.

He looked at me and something—something was off. Something was not quite right underneath his glamour. Silently, he held out his other hand to Raquel as a door appeared on the wall in front of us and we walked out of the Center for what I very, very much hoped would be the last time.

DOUBLE DATING
DISAPPOINTMENTS

We came through at the edge of the trees by Lend's house. Reth stumbled forward, leaning against a tree for support, his golden glow dampened. Was it really just yesterday I'd come through with Lend, stumbling, while Reth was strong?

"What did she do?" I asked. I'd been too worried to talk in the Faerie Paths, terrified that Reth would collapse before we made it through and we'd be stuck there again. "Are you going to be okay?"

"I am better than you would be if she had hit her intended target."

I shuddered, taking his hand in mine. Either I was way warmer or he was way colder; I found both options equally disturbing. I already felt weird, with a disconnected buzzing like I'd taken too much cold medicine or something. "I have to go in with Raquel and fix this curse. Why don't you come in and . . . umm, lie down on the couch or something."

Reth gave me a humorless smile. "In all our time with each other, have I ever struck you as the type to nap on a couch?"

I snickered. "Not really. But it would be entertaining for me, at least. I'll bet you snore, even."

He looked indignant. "What makes you think I even sleep?"

"Do you?"

"Not in the same way you do. Go and waste your time trying to 'fix' Lend. I will try my best not to die waiting."

I took a step away, then turned back. "Wait, seriously? Are you going to die?"

He smiled, this time a genuine one. "I knew you cared. Not at the moment, but I will need you for something very soon."

It felt horrible, abandoning Reth when he was so hurt and messed up. And I knew that I'd do whatever he needed me to if it meant helping him. Lend had to be my priority right now, though. We were heading directly into the middle of a massive paranormal storm, and everything would change. I had to be able to really be with Lend *right now*, because right now was the only guarantee.

I nodded. "I won't be long." I turned toward Raquel, who was still standing in the same spot she had been when we came out of the Paths, a dazed expression on her face. "Raquel? You coming?"

"I honestly never thought I would see the light of day again."

"Aww, come on. With me on your side? Of course things worked out."

She tried to smile, but her eyes filled with tears. "Thank you, Evie."

I threw my arms around her in a hug. "You don't have to thank me."

"I really do. You wonderful girl. I've missed you so much."

"Well, now that we're both unemployed fugitives, think of how much time we'll have to hang out!"

She laughed drily, and we walked with our arms around each other to the house. I opened the door and yelled, "Evie alert! Coming into the family room!"

"You made it!" Lend shouted back. "Just a sec, I'll go to the kitchen. Raquel's with you?"

"Yup!"

"Good job! Jack and Arianna got back a couple of minutes ago."

I walked into the family room to find Arianna and Jack

sitting on the couch, arguing. "But there would have been no point to you being there if it hadn't been for my computer prowess."

"But your computer prowess wouldn't have mattered if you couldn't have gotten into the Center in the first place."

"Being a glorified taxi does not make you the bigger hero."

"Being a nerd who can tap on a keyboard or being able to navigate the dark eternities of the Faerie Paths . . . hmmm . . . which is a rarer and more valuable skill . . ."

I put my hands on my hips. "Okay, kids, take it elsewhere. Raquel and I have work to do."

"Evie," Raquel said. She was staring at Jack in horror.

"Oh, that." I waved a hand dismissively. "It's all good. Jack's been helping us."

"Don't you remember how he tried to kill you?"

Jack rolled his eyes. "Boring. We've all moved on."

"Really?"

"Not really," I said. "But he's behaving. And everyone needs a glorified taxi now and then."

"Admit it: you all adore me." Jack bowed dramatically as he left the room. Arianna smiled tightly at Raquel and left after him.

Raquel collapsed onto the couch and closed her eyes. "You're working with Reth and Jack? Have you lost your mind?"

"Oh, that happened ages ago. But I've had to do a lot of rescuing lately, and those two come in handy."

"Do you trust them?"

"No, we don't," Lend called from the kitchen.

I smiled. "But, I don't know, I think I've forgiven them. They're both complete idiots, and sometimes they're evil, but they always have a reason, you know? I don't approve of them or trust them, but I understand them. I've done some things I'm not proud of, but at the time they felt utterly necessary. And I'd do them again." I shuddered at the memory of the midnight faerie's soul, tried not to feel the frosty spread of it through my veins, the distance it seemed to put between my body and me, even the room around me. "Anyway. Right now they're on my side, and I'll take whatever help I can get."

"As long as you—"

"Raquel!" David said, running into the room. Raquel stood up to greet him and he swept her into his arms and— oh good heavens I never wanted to see anything like this in my life—he smashed his lips against hers.

"Dad?" Lend called from the kitchen. "What's going on?"

"You don't want to know!" I said, my voice high and strained.

They broke apart, gasping, and David held her at arm's length, looking at her like he'd devour her. I didn't know whether to laugh or throw up.

I dug my toes into the carpet, staring at it. "So, uh, I saved Raquel."

Raquel laughed, and David joined her. They sounded slightly manic. "You're free now," he said.

"Of all of it," she answered, and I looked up to see them locked in a gaze I'd previously only observed between actors on *Easton Heights*—one filled with all the things unspoken over the years, all the betrayals and fears and pain left behind in favor of overwhelming love. It was beautiful.

Oh, who am I kidding, it was awkward as all heck and I didn't have time for it. "Okay! So, you may have noticed Lend is in the kitchen."

"Mmm hmm," Raquel answered, reaching up to smooth down a stray piece of David's hair.

"Yeah, that'd be the big faerie curse."

"Faerie curse?" She actually turned toward me; David took both her hands in his.

"Yup. Really funny one, too. See, any time Lend and I are in the same room or can see each other or could actually, you know, touch, he falls fast asleep."

"Oh." Raquel frowned.

"So I need your help. You know all the names of the IPCA controlled faeries, right?"

She nodded, her frown deepening.

"Well, it was a dark faerie curse, so I figure we need

a dark faerie to undo it. So you call an Unseelie faerie, we give him or her a named command to break the curse, ta-da, we can double-date!"

"Wait, who can double-date?" Lend asked.

"I'll let your dad tell you. So. Faerie?"

Raquel heaved a sigh, along the lines of her famous *things never get easier, do they?* sigh, and, boy, I agreed with her.

"To be honest, I don't know which court most of the faeries belong to."

"You don't? How can you not know? It seems like pretty vital information to me. You know, 'Are you a member of the evil court kidnapping humans and plotting world domination, or a member of the moderately less evil court who just wants to get the crap off the planet?' sort of a survey when you get them."

She raised her eyebrows. "Do you have any idea how hard it is to get information of any type at all from a faerie? Figuring out which court they belonged to was never a very high priority as long as we could control them."

"Gah! IPCA keeps coming up with new ways to massively fail me. But you said you didn't know which court *most* of the faeries belonged to. Do you know any?"

She nodded, reluctant. "Yes, there's one I know for certain is from the Dark Court."

"Great! Let's call him."

"Her. You know her, too. Fehl."

Ah, bleep. Of course. The one faerie Vivian had mostly

drained, who was now running around the Faerie Realms, feral and twisted. Also the one faerie I'd commanded never to come near me again.

"There has to be someone else." I didn't even know if Fehl had enough strength to make it to Earth anymore.

Raquel paused, deep in thought, then nodded. "There's another I'm fairly certain is Unseelie. I'm not positive, though."

"I'll take it!"

"We'll have to manage this very carefully, Evie. From what I saw, it would appear that entire court wants you dead."

"Yeah, well, you know. Stopping their custom-made Empty One, stabbing their queen in the neck, breaking their mirror forest, I'm not really Miss Popularity there."

"Stabbing— You what?"

"Long story. Faerie? I'd really like to hang out with my boyfriend while he's, you know, conscious."

"Seconded," Lend shouted.

"Are you sure it's a good idea to invite an Unseelie faerie here?"

"We're very well protected," David said. "There's pretty much every elemental you can think of hanging out around the house, and Cresseda has put up numerous safety measures."

"Very well," Raquel said. She didn't even blanche at Cresseda's name. David's fingers laced through hers probably had something to do with her newfound grace regarding the elemental who stole David from her. "Althenam."

We all waited, barely daring to breathe, until a line of white light traced itself along the wall. A faerie, long and tall and beautiful with hair as orange as fire, stepped through, her eyes widening as she saw me.

Raquel said her name again, and she snapped her attention (and vicious glare) toward my former boss. "In the kitchen is a boy under a faerie curse. Undo it without harming him, then wait for further orders."

I had to hand it to Raquel—she had the whole named command thing down. I tended to suck hard-core at it.

I bounced nervously on my toes as Raquel and the faerie went into the kitchen. I'd be able to hug Lend soon! And hold hands! And make out like crazy! And then figure out how to help Reth with whatever that faerie did to him. And then figure out how to deal with whether or not to open the gates, and how. But still!

After what felt like an eternity I heard the faerie speak again. "I cannot undo it."

"Are you Unseelie?" Raquel asked.

"Yes," the faerie hissed. "But this curse is not a pattern I can weave or unweave."

"Very well," Raquel said, and then she sighed, a sigh of defeat. I slumped onto the couch. "Althenam, leave this place, never return, and reveal its location and occupants to no one." She paused. "And never return to IPCA or answer their calls again."

I couldn't hear the faerie door, but there seemed to be a certain shift of energy, like that vaguely disturbing silence that settles in when the power shuts off, signaling the faerie was gone.

As were all my hopes.

MORE MONSTERS IN
THE DARK

We'll figure something else out." Lend's voice was soft and barely loud enough for me to hear from around the corner. Raquel had run outside with David, already shouting the names of every faerie under IPCA control. I had to hand it to her—I hadn't even thought to use her to free them from IPCA. It didn't mean Anne-Whatever Whatever wouldn't have faerie help from the Unseelies, but it would sure make her life harder. I didn't have the energy to follow them, instead slumping against the wall to the kitchen.

"What if—" I stopped, swallowing hard. Nope. I couldn't even say it aloud. We'd figure something else out because we had to. Time for a subject change before I lost it. "What did your mom say?"

"Mostly that she thinks my hair is getting too long and I should cut it."

"That's not helpful."

"That's my mom for you." He was trying for humor but his voice caught, and I wondered if he was thinking about how if she left and he didn't, he'd never ever see her again.

"So," I said, sitting on the floor against the wall as close to the kitchen doorway as I could get without Lend dropping like a rock, "do you want your Christmas present?"

"You got me something?" He sounded surprised.

"I've been working on it for a while."

"I, uh, didn't find you anything yet. I was actually setting up for your party, not Christmas shopping like I said."

"Being kidnapped by the Dark Queen and then cursed gets you off the hook for a lot. Besides, my birthday party totally counted."

"This isn't how I wanted our first Christmas to go. We were going to go all out, pick out a Christmas tree on Christmas Eve, decorate it, watch cheesy holiday movies, drink hot chocolate, let my dad make his eggnog and then complain about how disgusting it was, then I was going to deck out my entire room in mistletoe . . ."

"Wait, you mean you didn't plan for us to be stuck in different rooms for the holidays?"

"Well, that part's kind of nice." I heard his head bang

against the wall where he was sitting right on the other side of it from me. "I mean, who wants to actually be able to touch their super hot girlfriend? Overrated."

"I know, right?" I tried to laugh, but it came out choked. I swallowed, forcing my tone to come out light. "And I totally dig watching people sleep. It's so sexy."

We were both quiet for a bit. With my last brilliant idea a failure, the reality that maybe we could never fix this hung like a chain around my neck, cutting off the air. I'd fought so hard to get—really get—Lend. From escaping the Center to stopping Vivian to overcoming my own stupid issues, I'd been fighting for this relationship since the day I first saw his water eyes. I couldn't have come this far just to lose him physically forever. It wasn't fair. And I was sick and tired of things not being fair.

"So, where's my present?"

I wiped under my eyes. "Oh, right. You have your laptop in there?"

"Yeah."

Smiling, I grabbed my laptop off the coffee table and emailed him the link, then waited.

"Ooh, I've got mail." After a few seconds I heard the video playing, and Lend laughed. "How long did this take you?"

"I had a lot of time on my hands while you were in finals." I leaned my head against the wall as I heard the soundtrack to the clips. I'd gone through all four seasons of *Easton Heights* and found every single time any of the characters said "I love you," then (with copious amounts of help from Arianna) pieced them all together back to back to back, with one of Lend's favorite songs as the soundtrack.

"I love you!" "I *love* you." "I LOVE YOU, idiot!" "You are so— I hate you! I love you!" "Shut up and tell me you love me." *"Te amo!"* Ah, yes, the guest arc of the Spanish hottie. That was a good season.

Given the number of relationships that show cycled through, the video lasted several minutes. When it ended, I heard Lend's laptop closing.

"Well?" I asked.

"I love you," he answered.

"I love you, too." I put my palm against the wall, fingers splayed out. I would fix this. I didn't care if IPCA was taking over the world, or dark forces were conspiring to keep us apart, or if in opening the gate to another world I'd maybe die or Lend would leave this world forever. He was mine, no matter what I had to do to make it work.

"Umm, so, what was that you were saying when my dad and Raquel were in here? About double-dating?"

I rubbed my eyes. "You should really ask your dad about it."

"I don't want to ask my dad about it, I'm asking you."

"Your dad and Raquel are—were—well, they were *really* happy to be back together. Like, together together. I found some pictures in Raquel's room and I think we've solved the mystery of what the deal was between them. I think they were engaged or something before your dad met your mom. And, uh, they've rekindled the spark."

Lend was quiet for a long time. Too long.

"Are you okay?"

"He's still married."

"What?"

"My dad. Is still. Married. To *my mom*."

I hadn't even thought of that, although I guess it would be difficult to sign a divorce agreement if your hands were made of water. "Yeah, but they haven't really been with each other in eighteen years."

"She's my mom, Evie. And what, now that she's going to leave the planet he's suddenly jumping all over a woman who stands for everything he and I have fought against?"

"Whoa now. You heard. Raquel's not IPCA anymore. And she's never been as bad as you make her out to be."

"Sure, because stealing my dad is really cool."

"Who is she stealing him from? Your mom left him forever ago, and I'm pretty sure she stole David from Raquel in the first place!"

"What is *that* supposed to mean? I wouldn't exist if my parents hadn't loved each other!"

I looked up at the ceiling, breathing deeply. "That came out really, really wrong. Of course I'm glad your parents fell in love. They made the best thing in the entire world. And it is really weird that your dad and Raquel might be dating now. You have every right to be freaked out. Just, please, give her a chance, okay?"

He didn't answer. I could feel knots forming in my shoulders and neck. It was like my whole body was ganging up on me because it hated not being touched by Lend. Subject change time. "Did you find anything else out while I was gone?"

His voice was still terse. "Not much new, although it's getting crowded out there. They're gathering paranormals from all over. Everyone who wants to leave."

"So they're taking it for granted that they'll actually have a gate?"

There was a pause. "I thought—I thought you were going to try to open the gate. Not that I want to push you, but . . . I don't know, I think it's the right thing to do."

I scowled up at the ceiling, picking at the rug under my fingers. "Well, yeah, it probably is, but it pisses me off that they're just assuming I will."

Lend laughed, the sound making some of the tension in my shoulders relax. "Yeah, that's paranormals for you. Always bossing people around. Prophecies this, prophecies that."

"And do any of their prophecies say please? No, not a single one." I rolled over onto my side, my nose practically touching the wall, and put my hand against the wallpaper. Amid the dry, static wind of the sylph's soul; the manic, buzzing energy of the vampire's; the fluid motion of the fossegrim's; and the horrible, cracking, burning frost of the faerie's, I tried to sense my own soul, tried to find that part of my core that was me and only me. But how could I find it when I didn't know what it felt like unless I was touching Lend?

I sighed. "I'm scared. Of it all. Of what will happen if I don't try to open the gate, yeah, but even more of what might happen if I do. Not only do I have no idea how to do it, but the last one I opened . . . I really thought I was going to die. Everything went rushing out of me so quickly and if it hadn't been for Lish's soul signaling me to stop, I don't think I would have been able to close the gate, or to stop my own soul from flying out, too. I might want to help the paranormals, but I'm not willing to give up my soul for it."

"Of course not! No one can ask you to do that. No one should. If you decide to do this—and I mean you decide, not anyone else—then we'll figure out how to make it work so you come out safe and sound. Besides, I wouldn't let you sacrifice your own soul. It's mine."

"Uh, I think you mean my *heart* is yours. That's a little more romantic and less stalker creepy."

"Well, regardless, you know mine is yours, right? Heart, soul, whatever. It's all yours."

I smiled and buried my face in the carpet so my cheek was resting against the cool wall. "I know."

After a few quiet minutes during which I nearly fell asleep, Lend spoke again, his words soft but shaking me to my core. "What if we can never fix this?"

"What?"

"This stupid thing keeping us apart. What if we can't break it? Because I'm not going to accept a life where I can't touch you."

"I don't know what else to do, besides hitting up the Light Queen for help. And I really don't want to."

"It just doesn't make any sense! I've been thinking about it—I haven't been thinking about anything else—and why would the Dark Queen do this? I mean, why curse me so that I can't physically be near you? It seems so . . . childish, you know? Like, if she didn't want me to escape or she wanted to punish me if I managed to, why not curse me to die? Or to never wake up at all?"

I frowned, sitting up. "I hadn't thought about it that way. I kind of thought it was a genius evil curse, but with what we know about her, it does seem sort of silly."

"She didn't strike me as much of a prankster in the short but overwhelmingly terrifying time we spent together. Epically cruel, sure. Cleverly mean, not so much."

"Not being able to talk to you face-to-face and touch you is pretty epically cruel, Lend."

His voice came out tortured. "I know. But still."

"Yeah. Maybe she couldn't just kill you? Because of, I don't know, your mom?"

"Maybe."

"I should ask Reth about . . . oh, crap!" I was the worst

person ever. I stood up. "I totally forgot about Reth."

"What about him?"

"He got hurt. A faerie tried to attack me, but he pushed me out of the way and it hit him instead. He seemed pretty bad off."

"How did you get away, then?"

I rolled my eyes in aggravation and glared at the ceiling, hating what I had to confess. Lend knew how much it affected me, taking souls, and I always felt guilty and dirty, like he was judging me even though he tried not to. "The faerie came after me when Reth was down and I sucked out some of her soul."

"Good."

"I— Good?"

"Yes. Good."

I shuddered. "You don't have the creepy, icy thing in you. It's not good."

"You here, safe and alive? Good."

I smiled sadly and knocked on the wall three times. "I"—knock—"love"—knock—"you"—knock.

He knocked three times back.

I wavered, then blurted out, "Will you go through if I open the gate?"

"No," he said, but there were a few seconds of hesitation before it slipped out, and those few seconds filled me with dread and loneliness so deep it was colder even than the midnight faerie's soul. He didn't know.

He knocked on the wall again. "Go check on Reth. But be careful. I haven't slept on purpose in way too long, so I'm going to bed. And since I'll be asleep anyway, come sleep next to me when you get back in, okay?"

I forced my voice to come out light and teasing. "Only if you're wearing footie pajamas."

He laughed. "I'll see if I can find a pair. See you soon."

"No, you won't," I whispered too softly for him to hear, then walked out the front door toward the trees. It was dark now, and bitterly cold. I had no idea how many hours I'd been awake at this point—the last time I remembered sleeping was on the couch just after saving Lend. I was so tired I wished I were the one who'd drop instantly to sleep, because then I'd "accidentally" walk into the room with Lend and have a perfect excuse for not doing things I knew I should.

Alas. Miles to go before I sleep.

"Reth?" I called, wrapping my arms around myself and squinting into the darkness. The hairs on the back of my neck rose as I remembered being tased out here. In spite of what David said about protections, maybe I shouldn't be here alone. "Reth?"

"He's not here," Arianna said, and I jumped and shrieked in fright. She was standing just past the tree line. I swallowed hard, disturbed. I could see her soul, glowing in the black night. I couldn't usually see hers so brightly; I hadn't been able to see any this clearly since the night I took all the souls from Vivian. Just how much had I taken from the midnight faerie, anyway?

"Chill, Evie. You look like you've seen a ghost. Which, for the record, are way less cool than vampires. Reth's with everyone, hanging out at the pond, being immortal and whatnot. It's pretty rocking."

Great. Exactly where I wanted to go right now. To the pond, with dragons and sylphs and selkies, oh my.

"Of course that's where he'd be, because my night keeps getting awesomer. What are you doing out here?"

"You know. Hanging out. Being all immortal and what-not."

"Where's Jack?"

"He went to the Faerie Realms to eat and sleep. Said he'd be back later."

"I have to find Reth and make sure he's okay. Come with me?"

"Now, now, you aren't afraid of monsters in the dark, are you?" I caught a flash of her eyes, winking wickedly at me.

"No," I said, shivering. After all, I was one of them.

I walked slower and slower as we got closer to the pond. I could see them already, bobbing and dancing and swirling through the night, all the lights of the souls there. The souls waiting for me to save them, to send them home.

Oh, bleep, I didn't want any of this. I didn't want this pressure, this weight on my shoulders. This whole mess had nothing to do with me. But it seemed like no matter how hard I fought against being involved in paranormal drama, I kept getting sucked back in. I guess it was my birthright, the only thing left to me by my broken and gone mother and my broken and gone faerie father.

I stopped, staring through the trees at the pond, at this world and this life that I was integral to but completely not a part of.

And then . . . I thought of all the paranormals who meant something to me. Nona and Kari, who had sacrificed themselves to keep me safe. Lend's mom, and everything she'd done for him. Even Reth, who put himself in harm's way to protect me. Lish. My Lish. All these paranormals needed me, and as much as it terrified me, could I really turn my back on that? Could I really refuse to at least try to help them, no matter what it might cost me?

Could I really value my own soul over all the beautiful, brilliant souls in the darkness in front of me?

"Evie?" Arianna asked, noticing I wasn't keeping up with her.

I wiped my eyes, overwhelmed. "Go ahead. I'll be there in a minute."

She nodded and walked through the edge of the trees to the pond. I heard a low murmur of voices greeting her and wondered how much time she'd been spending out here. Under other circumstances I could imagine hanging out down there, gawking at all the strange paranormals, maybe even getting to know the cranky dragon. But in that day-dream Lend was with me, holding my hand. And there wasn't terror and pressure and doom hanging over everything.

I sighed and leaned against a tree.

"I assume you are looking for me." Reth's voice sounded more like copper rather than his usual gold.

"Yup, I suppose I was. How are you feeling?" I stood straight and turned around, then gasped. His soul. I'd for-gotten what it looked like. But . . . it was different, too. Whereas before it had been unmoving and crystalline, now it seemed to shiver around the edges.

He smiled at my reaction, the stupid smile of his that was like he knew something you didn't. And he knew some-thing I didn't pretty much all the time, so it was pretty much every smile on his face.

"I need to go to the Faerie Realms," he said.

"Okay. Good. You should go." I looked to the side, both-ered by the intimacy of the moment. It wasn't like I knew anything more about him by being able to see the shiny, shivering gold of his soul, but it still felt weird. I wanted to make him put on another shirt, or a coat. Or a tent.

"Are you ready?"

"For what?"

"To come with me."

"I— No, I'm staying here."

"Judging by the fact that you are here alone, your latest plan did not work."

"Brilliant, Sherlock." He raised his eyebrows quizzically and I shook my head. Faeries weren't exactly big on understanding the cultural lexicon.

"So you have only two options left. Appeal to the Dark Queen, or appeal to my queen. Might I, as someone infinitely concerned with your continued survival, recommend the latter?"

I pulled on my ponytail, nervously wrapping my fingers in it. "I don't know. Can't she come here?"

"No, she cannot. And if I recall, you owe me several debts. I am collecting."

I opened my mouth to argue, then realized there was no point. He was right. I owed him, big-time. And I was out of options for how to fix things here by myself. If throwing myself on the mercy of the Light Queen meant I got to feel Lend's fingers on my skin again, well, so be it. And maybe she could help me figure out how to save the paranormals without losing myself in the process.

I took a deep breath. "Okay. What do I have to do?"

"Unless you plan on creating a door and walking the Paths alone, you really ought to take my hand."

"I mean when we get there, you jerk."

"It will be as simple as falling asleep." There was a teasing note to his voice that made me nervous.

I looked toward the house, imagined running away from all this and spending the night curled up next to Lend. But then I imagined waking up in the morning and knowing he couldn't wake up until I left. And no amount of running away would change the sheer number of souls around the pond, waiting for me, needing me. So I took Reth's hand, an action that was becoming all too familiar now. It felt a bit cooler than it had even an hour ago.

"I knew you'd choose this." The least he could have done is sound smug about it, but his tone was simple and matter-of-fact, like there was never any doubt that he would win. I stuck my tongue out at him and we walked together through the Paths toward what I absolutely would not ever consider my destiny. His steps were not quite as fluid as normal, and for once I didn't have to hurry mine to keep up. He opened another door and we stepped out into the Faerie Realms.

Which were as empty and pitch-black as the Paths we'd just come from.

DREAM DATE

"Umm, Reth?" I blinked, trying to find anything for my eyes to focus on, but there was nothing there. Unlike the Faerie Paths, I couldn't see Reth—not even the glow of his soul. I clutched his hand tighter, his skin against mine the only evidence I had that he was still here. "I think you made a mistake. This isn't the Faerie Realms."

"Wrong, as usual," he said, and I could hear the smile in his voice. "It's simply not finished yet."

"What are we doing here, then?"

Another voice, a voice like the light of the full moon, pure and white, enveloped me. "You are here to dream."

The voice seemed to wrap me up; I could almost feel it on my skin, and I could definitely feel it in my soul. It tugged at me, much like the black hole gravity of the Dark Queen's voice, but rather than making me want to lose myself in it forever, it made me want to find myself through it.

I knew I couldn't see anything but I couldn't help twisting my head around, my eyes straining. I wanted to— needed to—see who was talking. "Who's there?"

"Close your eyes, child of impermanence and eternity. Sleep."

I snorted, fighting the soporific glamour of the voice. "Yeah, that's not going to happen. This isn't exactly my ideal sleeping situation. I usually like a bed, and a blanket, and the comfort of knowing where the bleep I am and that I won't be attacked or killed or lost forever at any given moment."

"You are as safe as ever you have been. Sleep, and dream, and understand."

I startled as lips brushed against my forehead, but my eyes closed against my will, sweet and sudden sleep slipping over me like a sheet of water.

I opened them to see the Dark Queen, in all her porcelain-skinned beauty, and next to her, hands clasped, was a faerie of equal power and grace, her skin black and warm as ebony, her hair a white cascade of rainbow light to contrast the Dark Queen's oil-slick black. Even though the Dark Queen looked different from when I'd seen her—her features even less human, the borders of her body almost blurring with light—I knew it was her just the same. They stood on an empty and brilliant plane, bright and beautiful and serene. In the distance I could see what looked like trees, but the two women were alone here.

The voice that had spoken to me in the darkness whispered in my ear. "Too wicked for heaven, too good for hell. We wanted more. We had eternity, and each other, and the faeries under us, and the multitudes that dwelt with us in the unchanging space between heaven and hell. But we saw what the other plane had, though they, too, were stuck between heaven and hell."

"They move," the Dark Queen said, ignoring my existence, her eyes seeing something impossibly far away. "They move forward. They *create*."

"I want to create," the other faerie answered, and I recognized the moonbeam voice from the darkness, aching with desire and longing. The Light Queen.

"What is the joy in eternity if we cannot change?"

"Dear sister," the Light Queen said, "if I cannot create, I want to perish instead."

"But we were not given dominion there. We were gifted our land; who can tell what will happen if we leave it?"

"I no longer care."

The Dark Queen narrowed her eyes. "Then I shall make a way for you to go there."

"It is too wicked." The Light Queen raised her head, crystal tears frozen on her cheeks. "We cannot."

The Dark Queen smiled her razor smile. "If I am too wicked for heaven, I am certainly wicked enough to do this."

The scene broke apart in scattered beams of light, re-forming over a shining pink body of water. The Dark Queen and the Light Queen stood together, one hand raised on either side, their contrasting hands clasped in between them. An entire congregation of faeries waited behind them, all standing tall but some with more confidence than others. I gasped as I recognized Reth, looking older and younger at the same time.

"You cannot do this thing," a voice like a waterfall said, and I saw Cresseda rise out of the water, far more solid and corporeal than she ever was on Earth. "You will destroy yourselves."

"We will not destroy," the Dark Queen said, and every faerie leaned almost imperceptibly toward the gravity of her voice. "We will create. We will be *more*."

"Leave then, and be done with it." Cresseda's voice poured down like a wave of judgment on them. "But we will have no part of this."

I saw then that the water was swirling with life, with souls, and my perspective shifted to encompass all of it—it was an ocean, a home to every water spirit. Behind the faeries was a forest of trees, each with leaves of flame. The trees nodded their agreement, bending away from the Dark Queen. Even the ground itself pushed back, forming a crater around the faeries.

"We have all spoken," voices said in unison, voices that sounded like the rumbling of stones, the rustling of leaves, the crackle of flame, the rushing of water. "We accept what we have been given and reject you."

The Dark Queen raised her chin in defiance, a smile twisting her violet lips. "Not *all* have spoken."

A breeze started, and part of the souls in me recognized it. The sylph, in its true form as shapeless air. It spun, faster and faster, until it was howling, surrounding everything. "We want to fly," it said in a voice almost unhearable through the violence of wind. "We want to be free. We want to see new places, taste new things, fly unbound and boundless."

Cresseda shouted something but the noise was swallowed by the wind, now a hurricane force with the faerie-filled crater at the very center. I watched in fascination and horror as the glowing souls of the trees, fire, water, and earth were torn from their places and caught up in the screaming wind until the faeries were surrounded by a swirling vortex of light.

"We will be reborn," the Light Queen said, her voice reverent.

"We will give birth," the Dark Queen said, and together

they raised their arms, hands out, all the faeries around them doing the same thing. The lights of the souls spun faster and faster until they were a solid wall and then a soundless, horrible rip shuddered through the land, like the very air was being sucked from my lungs, so wrong and so unnatural I wanted to scream, but I couldn't do anything except see.

The Light Queen's face fell. "What have we done?" she whispered.

"What we must."

"We cannot do this."

The Dark Queen's eyes flashed in anger. "I do this for you. And there is only one way for you to stop me. Will you break our bond? Will you utter my true name and betray me, the other half of your heart?"

"I will never," the Light Queen whispered. The Dark Queen took her hand, and as one the faeries ran forward, breaking through the wall of light and disappearing.

I thought it was over, that it was the end, but the lights didn't stop, the souls of the other paranormals weren't flung free of the sylph's wind. The faeries had left a gaping wound in their wake, a tremendous black void that the lights were pulled toward; and now under the howl of the hurricane I could hear the voices of all the other creatures, screaming as one in terror and agony as they were dragged away—the water, the earth, everything that had made up this world. When the last light, that of the wind itself, was sucked through and disappeared, the darkness collapsed inward and left the landscape so empty and devoid of spark and *wrong* I wanted to scream, I wanted to die, I couldn't be there anymore, I had to—

"Wake up, child."

I opened my eyes, my heart pounding, and sat up. "Where are we?" I couldn't get my heart to stop racing, my body still in panic mode, as I looked around. Reth stood next to me; we were no longer in the pitch-black. Now we were in a cave, brilliant light reflected and refracted by the thousands of stalagmites and stalactites that looked like they were made of pale pink spun sugar. The entire thing seemed impossibly fragile, like a shout would bring it shattering down around us, but that only made it more beautiful.

I looked to my right, and there was the Light Queen, exactly as I'd seen her in my dream. Only . . . somehow less. I couldn't quite put my finger on it, because she was just as beautiful and perfect, but it felt like she was shorter, or thinner—diminished in a way I couldn't describe. The lines of her body, instead of blurring to take part in everything around her, trapped her, contained her soul, cut her off.

"The sylph," I said, understanding. "It harnessed all the souls, and then you two used their power to rip a gate through to our world. But you didn't close it, and everyone else got pulled through, too." Just how Donna and Kari had explained it; now I'd seen it for myself. I shook my head in disbelief, then asked, "Where did you take me?"

"We have not moved," the Light Queen answered.

"Where did this all come from, then?"

"You."

"Last time I checked, my powers don't extend to making shiny pink rock formations." And, in the catalog of powers to have, that one was frankly useless. Although it would make a good party trick.

"This was the great tragedy, the great failure of our grand plans. Because unlike humans, who create with every thought, with every dream, with your very bodies, even here we were powerless on our own to create so much as a new thought. We assumed that by coming to your world we would be given the gift of creation, but it was never ours to have."

"Sucks to be you?"

She smiled. "It does indeed. But we found ways around that, as you have demonstrated. It is not creation to take what humans make and form it how we want, but it is as close as we get. And my sister will leave me forever before she will give up the power that human dreams give her."

I frowned. "Wait, so all this—everything in the Faerie Realms—you make from dreams? Any dreams, or the dreams of the humans you steal?"

"Those are most powerful, dwelling already in the land of dreams, but we can pull from your realm. Thoughts, hopes, desires, dreams. Here we take the material you give us and make it into imitations and repetitions of reality."

So faeries used human dreams to make the Faerie Realms and everything in them. Maybe that's why being here for a long time changed you, like it did Jack, made you less able to live in the human world.

Thinking of Jack in the Faerie Realms made me think of all the other people I'd seen there, which, when connected with the Dark Queen's determination to get back to where they came from without losing their ability to create . . .

"She wants to open a gate and take humans back with her, doesn't she?" I asked.

The Light Queen nodded solemnly. "Even this mockery of creation is more than we had there. She would have it all—eternity and the ability to shape it. My Seelie faeries refuse to once again bring unwilling creatures somewhere they do not belong. Thus the great chasm that has grown between us. She would sooner trap us all here than go back to our home without human dreams to feed off."

So pretty much all those poor saps I'd seen were nothing more than cattle to feed the Dark Queen's need to "create." "Why didn't you go back? After you got here, I mean. And why are the rest of the paranormals on Earth and not in this realm, with you?"

"We were scattered coming through the gate. Without the energy of all the souls together and a way to focus it, we could not open a gate again. Coming to Earth changed our forms—gave bodies to things that had been mere spirit, trapping them and shifting them and changing many beyond recognition. Some adapted better than others. For the faeries, our threads to eternity were shortened, thinned, until we feared they would snap entirely. It took us many generations to carve out this space between, where we were able to form a buffer between ourselves and time, living outside it. We would have protected our spirit cousins here as well, but since it was our folly that ripped them through the gate with us, they have never forgiven us."

"So that's how—" I paused, not wanting to refer to Melinthros as my father. "That's how faeries can make Empty Ones? You force them to live on Earth for long enough and it breaks down what makes them a faerie?"

"Yes," she said sadly. "I have never returned to the mortal realms. Those who make frequent trips do so at great personal sacrifice." I looked at Reth, who still stood next to me, had been standing next to me this entire time, silent and watching. Reth who never needed to come back to Earth after I freed him from IPCA. Reth who was looking dimmer by the hour after taking the midnight faerie's attack in my place.

The Light Queen followed my gaze. "My golden son has given much because of his love for you and his devotion to me. He may yet give up all."

Well, bleep. It was so much simpler to hate him.

"I know you hold depths of anger and bitterness toward the fey, child, but please understand our desperation. And please know my deep respect for humans and human life. Such beautiful, fragile animals, so fleeting and easily broken and yet powerful beyond anything faeries can ever hope to be. We cannot create but live forever, unchanging. You change with every breath, dying even as you live, but your thread to eternity and immortality is reborn with every new generation."

I was busy avoiding Reth's eyes, not wanting to think of him like that, as someone who was nobly sacrificing to be around me and protect me. Not wanting to accept that he really loved me the way he was always saying he did. My head was already the oddest combination of fuzzy and buzzy from being around the Light Queen.

I sighed, knowing what I had to do and hating that it was what these scheming faeries had been trying to make me do all along. But at least this way it was *my* choice, just like Lend and Arianna had said. And I wasn't doing it for the idiot faeries, anyway. I was doing it for the others, the ones that had no choice in all this, the ones that had never asked to come here in the first place. I could understand that.

And I found, to my surprise, that once I made the decision, *really* made it, I wanted to do it. I needed to do it.

I wouldn't leave those paranormal souls to whatever fate they'd face here, not the way I'd been abandoned. I flexed my fingers, trying to calm down my wildly beating heart. There was no going back now.

"Okay," I said. "I'll do it."

YOU CAN'T CHANGE ME

I stood straighter and looked her in the eyes, a luminous brown like life itself, containing all the other colors at the same time. "I'll try to open this gate for you, on a few conditions."

She smiled. "We faeries do love a good condition."

I rolled my eyes. Didn't I know it. "First, I will not kill myself to open the gate. If I can't do it, I can't do it, and I'm not going to drain any more innocent paranormals to get more energy. What I've already got is all you're getting. Second, you absolutely must take all the faeries—every last one, including the Dark Queen and all her minions—with you. I don't want any of you staying behind where you can keep messing around with my world. Third, we have to save all those humans the Dark Queen has kidnapped and figure out a way for them to be able to go back to their lives. None of them are going through with you. And fourth, you break this bleeping curse the Dark Queen put on my boyfriend."

"The first three I accept; no innocent paranormals will be harmed, I will ensure that every faerie forever leaves these realms, and no humans will be taken with us. But I am afraid I do not understand the fourth."

I narrowed my eyes, trying not to be lulled into the calm that radiated from her stupid, moonlight voice. "Your evil sister took my boyfriend, Lend, Cresseda's son. I got him back, but she cursed him or something because whenever we're in the same room he immediately falls asleep."

She blinked slowly. "My sister did that?"

"Yeah, and I can't figure out how to break it. We had an Unseelie faerie come, but she said she couldn't."

"I cannot fathom it. My sister's arrogance would not allow her to even consider the possibility you could get the boy away from her once she had him. She has always underestimated mortals. Why she would see the need to glamour him is beyond me. What do you think?"

She turned to Reth, who avoided her eyes, staring determinedly into the sparkling pink distance. "You are the queen. Why are you asking me?"

"Because I value your opinion."

"Excuse me," I said, since obviously she wasn't used to Reth's sneaky circular way of talking. "You do realize he didn't answer your question, right?"

Reth glared at me, then looked back at the Light Queen. "I could not say what I think."

The Light Queen narrowed her eyes. "Could not say, or will not say?"

"Slim difference between the two."

"My golden son, the mortal realms have changed you. Would you deceive even me?"

I snorted. "You don't know Reth very well if you think he's ever straightforward about anything."

His full lips twitched toward a smile. "Will not say."

"I command you to."

The smile bloomed, full and sly. "Ah, but not even you know my name now."

Her huge cat-shaped eyes went round with shock. "Have you no loyalty?"

"I do. I am loyal to myself and I am loyal to what Evelyn should become. Everything I do is to those ends, to securing the eternity we should have together. You can trust that I will do whatever it takes to help her make that gate and transport us home. But how I get there is up to me entirely, and I am done following any sort of command from you. None of the direction you have given me from the beginning has accomplished anything or moved us forward to where we are now. Evelyn should be full, should be as we are by now. Your excessive caution and then refusal to allow me to act have held everything back, forced me to stay on Earth while you remain here, disconnected and free from the taint of the mortal realm. I do as I see fit. Fortunately for you, my desires coincide with your own."

I'd never been quite sure what the term "gobsmacked" meant, but I was pretty sure that was the only way to describe the look on the Light Queen's face.

"Now, if that's everything, I will be taking Evelyn back so those of us who are actually involved can finish the preparations."

I expected her to strike him down with some crazy finger lightning like these all-powerful beings always seem to have in movies, but to my surprise her face shifted into a gentle smile. "You surprise me. How remarkable to see so much change in one of my own."

Reth frowned sharply like she'd said something incredibly offensive. "Evelyn, time to go." He held out his hand, but I took a step back and folded my arms.

"She might be okay with your remarkable change, but you didn't answer her questions and I didn't get what I came for. I'm not doing anything—*anything*—until one of you figures out how to fix Lend."

The Light Queen gave Reth an amused smile. "Time to do as you see fit?"

He stalked over and tried to grab my hand, but I snatched

it out of the way. He stood straight in front of me, golden eyes burning. "We can't very well do anything for him from here, now, can we?"

"Wait, you can fix it? You could have fixed it all along?" My voice was getting higher and louder, echoing off the pink rock formations with a gentle tinkling bell sound. "What is—"

He grabbed my hand and the landscape shimmered around us, and with a stomach-twisting blur we were back in what I recognized as his room from when he brought me here before. It felt like an eternity ago, back when I was still with IPCA and he was trying to slowly fill me with more soul on his own. I closed my eyes and steadied myself against the lush red velvet chaise longue. Although I kind of wanted to puke all over his room, because really, it'd serve him right.

"Okay." I opened my eyes, pleased to see that the room had stopped tipping to one side. Reth was reclining on the couch, arms folded petulantly across his chest, his face flushed. I'd never seen it that way. "What is your problem? You could have fixed Lend all along?"

"No, I couldn't have."

"Yes, you could have! What would have changed between now and when we first rescued him?"

"You've come to your senses, that's what. Although stubbornness may be a quality some admire, I find your overabundance of it quite distasteful. You take an enormous amount of leading to reach the correct conclusions."

"You know what I love? I love being manipulated! It makes me *so happy* and *so willing* to do whatever I'm being manipulated into!"

His mouth curved into a puzzled frown.

"It's called sarcasm, you stupid faerie nitwit." I picked up the nearest object, a froofy pillow with gold thread in intricate swirling patterns, and chucked it at his head. He stared at me, aghast, and I was pleased to see I'd managed to muss his perfect golden hair. "And I'm sick of being manipulated! Jack screwed with my life to try and make me do things, too, and remember what happened? I didn't do it! So don't think that you're making me do anything. You're not. I only do what I decide to."

Reth stood, fury radiating off him as he walked around the couch to stand right in front of me. "Yes, you decide what to do, you silly little girl. It is your decision, it always has been. All I did was give you the information you didn't trust others to merely tell you. You always have to see things for yourself, so I made sure you saw what needed to be seen."

"Yeah, your detours in the Dark Court, brilliant. Fine. Whatever. But why haven't you fixed Lend yet?"

"Because when you are happy, you don't do anything! If you are content, the rest of the world and those who need you fall away into the background. And I for one knew that things needed to move. When you can't have what you want, you become focused. I know you well."

"You don't know anything about me!"

"I know more about you than you understand about yourself! You'll see when you're made whole. That's what this is all about. You cannot see how things will be when you're changed, when you're whole."

"I don't want to change!"

His slender hands curled into fists. "You don't want to change? Do you have any idea what I've been through for you? Why do you think I keep coming back to that horrid, dirty, decaying world of yours? Because you changed me! It makes me sick to think of how I have shifted away from what I should be!"

I leaned back, terrified of the pure fury in his face.

He took a deep breath, closing his eyes and releasing all the tension from his facial muscles, returning them back to the mask of perfection. "But this is irrelevant. When I get back to where I am supposed to be, my connection to eternity will be restored and flawless. *I* will be restored. And you will be connected, too, and we have forever to—"

"Whoa, whoa, stop right there, psycho. I'm not coming with you."

He got that infuriating smile, that one that all faeries have that says they know more than you ever will and you can't even begin to function on the same plane as them but isn't it cute that you think you have any right to consider yourself a rational creature. It was a condescending head pat in smile form.

"Evelyn," he said, his golden voice trying to pull me in closer. "I love you. You'll understand. You'll want to come with me."

"No." I shook my head, trying to keep my voice even. "You don't love me, Reth. You love this idea you have of what I should be. What I am now bugs the crap out of you." He frowned, but I pressed on. "No, it's true. You don't like anything about me the way I am right now."

"But that does not matter, because you aren't what you should be. It is not your fault and merely temporary."

"*No.* I am what I should be. I'm what I want to be. And I could never be with someone or love someone who didn't love me and accept me for who I am now. Lend does that. He knows me, and he loves me how I am now, and he'll keep loving me no matter how I might change. It's not conditional on my becoming anything else." It took me a while to figure it out, and I nearly lost him because of it, but I knew that now. And I knew that what I had with Lend was worth more than anything else I had in the world. Or could possibly have in another one.

"But *you* changed *me.* I changed because of you. I could feel you, worming your way into my heart and soul, shifting things. You've no idea how aggravating it is to have to adapt to new feelings and thoughts. But of course you have no idea, changeable and temporary as you are. You cannot understand what you could be, what you should be. Your mind cannot even begin to wrap around it. When you understand, you will know, and you will choose to be with me. It won't even be a choice. It is what will be because it must be. It will be who you are."

I put my hand against his chest where I could see the quivering, still dimming brightness of his soul, rested it there. Something was different about his heart, too. It used to beat so slow, so very, very slow, but now it was racing, a rabbit heart, faster even than mine. I used my hand to push myself back a step. "You're wrong."

"I am never wrong."

"See, there you go, wrong again. Now, are you going to take me home and fix my boyfriend, or am I going to have to suck out your soul?"

He reached up and wrapped his hand around mine. "I know from experience you refuse to let in my soul. But, yes, I will fulfill the fourth condition to bind you in this contract."

He opened a door and we walked into the Paths. His steps were tentative. I thought going to the Faerie Realms would help him, but it seemed like he was getting worse. The darkness seemed more oppressive than usual, so I tried to think of other things. Things I had to look forward to. Lend. Sleeping Lend. Reth fixing sleeping Lend, because . . . why *could* Reth do it? Oh, of course.

"You are going to be in so much trouble when Cresseda finds out you were the one behind the curse. It was you, wasn't it? When you leaned down and touched his head after we got back—I can't believe I didn't put it together. You did the same thing to the werewolf in the Center."

Reth had the nerve to laugh, the silver bell sound disappearing into the void around us. "Fortunately for me you have never excelled at observation."

"Yeah? Observe this." I snaked my foot out in front of his and caught it around his ankle. He stumbled and nearly fell, and I cackled with laughter. Sure, it was immature, but when trying to get revenge on faeries you couldn't kill, the little things made all the difference.

"I do not understand you," Reth said, his voice edged with annoyance as he straightened.

"Yup. Exactly. And you never will. And if you don't fix my boyfriend the second we get to his house, I'm having Cresseda freeze you to the ground and then I'm coming after you with an iron pipe. I'll bet anything you understand that."

"Really, Evelyn."

"No, *really*, Reth. But why'd you do it? I never could have gotten him back without you, and then you go and curse him." I kept trying to be angry with him for doing this to us, but the fact remained that without Reth's help Lend would still be in the clutches of the Dark Queen. I could hold the last couple days of stress and agony against him, but knowing that there was a fix—a ridiculously easy fix—made me feel so light I wanted to laugh.

"In spite of what you may think, I am not cruel. I knew

that his death would destroy you. And you would be absolutely useless while he was still missing. So I helped you get him, and then I made sure you would be motivated to continue realizing the things you need to do."

We walked in silence for a while until he formed the door and we stepped back out into the Virginia winter sunrise, halfway between the pond and the house.

"Are you quite sure you want me to stop the glamour? It has been rather peaceful without him around," Reth said, wistfully.

"Oh, I'm sure." We walked toward the house. I knew I should yell at him more, but in just a few minutes I'd have Lend to myself, awake, and I half skipped toward the house. I glanced sideways at Reth, whose quick, shallow breaths were fogging out in front of him. "You probably thought that curse was the cleverest thing ever, didn't you?"

His lips turned down as he tried not to smile. "It was one of my better moments." I saw lights ahead of us past the trees, and for a moment I thought I was seeing souls in a whole new freaky way until I realized they were, in fact, red and blue and flashing. Police lights. Lots and lots of police lights.

YOU'D THINK THEY'D NEVER SEEN AN INVISIBLE BOY BEFORE

What the crap?" I hurried toward the flashing police lights, but Reth put a hand on my arm to slow me.

"Perhaps, for once, it would be best to evaluate the situation before charging in. This particular type of human carries weapons slightly more lethal than your beloved pink monstrosity."

"Why would the police be here though? Something must be wrong."

Reth looked exasperated. "When is something ever not wrong in your life?"

I frowned. "That's my line."

I heard someone yelling; it only took seconds to realize it was Arianna, reaming into someone with a profanity-laced tirade. I shook off Reth and ran, cutting away from the path in a straight line and breaking out of the trees onto the long driveway. Several police cars were jammed there, completely blocking the place. A SWAT truck, too, which ruled out someone having had an accident. Not that that would have been preferable, but . . .

Well, yeah, maybe it would.

I ran around the cars, then skidded to a stop. Jack was sitting on the ground in front of me and to the side of the cars, his arms behind him.

"What's going on?"

He looked up at me, a scowl marring his cherubic features. "Bloody handcuffs—made of steel, which has too much iron, which means I can't go anywhere."

"Well, yes, clearly, but what's going on?"

"Search me. Oh wait, they already did. You know, I take back everything I said about you being my only friend. I don't like you at all. No amount of fun makes up for all the pain and annoyance you introduce into my life."

"Right back at 'cha," I muttered, walking past him. I wished I had Tasey, but then again, being armed right now was probably a bad idea. I wondered why no one was watching Jack, but that was quickly answered when I walked past the corner of the unattached garage and had a view of the wraparound porch. Arianna stood there, continuing her verbal abuse, surrounded by a dozen uniformed men.

I shouldn't have found the sight amusing, but she had all of them fighting with one another. Clearly her vampire powers of compelling people were in full force, but since she could only push someone in a direction they were inclined to go anyway, the only police she could affect were those that felt some sympathy for her. Those ones were passionately arguing with the others to leave Arianna the creatively-cuss-laden-adjectives alone.

The unaffected ones, however, were utterly confused by their companions' attitudes and were pushing back. Scanning how many firearms were holstered—or in some cases already in hand—I realized this situation could get out of control very, very quickly.

I stood behind the group, unnoticed, and waved my arms to attract Arianna's attention. Her eyes widened. She quickly and furiously shook her head, then jerked her chin to motion for me to leave.

Even more confused than before, I started backing up. I'd go around and get in through the kitchen; David and Raquel had to know what was going on. Unfortunately for all of us, that was when Lend came out the front door, immediately collapsed with a thunk that made me cringe, and—perfect—went completely transparent.

The police officers stopped fighting, every eye glued on my boyfriend, now essentially invisible other than his T-shirt and flannel pajama pants.

"Okay," I said, putting my hands on my hips. "No. This is unacceptable. I don't care what the bleep is going on, we're going to get it settled immediately or I swear I will give you all to the Dark Queen and let her feed on your dreams for the rest of eternity."

Every head turned my direction, their faces a portrait of shock and disbelief.

"What, you've never seen a boy made of water before? Yawn. Go down to the pond—it'll really blow your mind."

One close to the front—a barrel-chested, middle-aged man with salt-and-pepper hair and a thick mustache—shook his head as though trying to clear it. "Are you Evelyn Green?"

"Sort of. Mostly. I mean, legally. Again, sort of."

He tried to look at me, but his eyes kept drifting back to Lend. "You're under— We're here to— Could you please come with us?"

I rolled my eyes. "No, I couldn't. You're last place in a very long line of people who want me right now. Besides, I haven't done anything."

"Actually," said a painfully tall and thin officer with a voice that struggled between tenor and bass but really sounded like a dog with something caught in its throat, "you're wanted for terrorism." He shrugged apologetically. "We're supposed to take you into NSA headquarters."

"I think you have the wrong acronym there," I said. This had Anne-Whatever Whatever written all over it. No doubt she couldn't break the barriers that the Seelie faeries and all the elementals had set up here after IPCA snatched me, so now she was sending human cronies in to do her dirty work.

The vast majority of the officers hadn't even looked up from Lend, their eyes glued as their brains tried to process something they simply couldn't accept as real.

"Look, guys, I know you mean well and you're doing your job, but it'd be better for everyone if you all got back in your cars and drove away. Pretend like this never happened. I promise I'm not going to blow anything up and the most un-American thing I've ever done is root for South Korea in speed skating during the Olympics. This whole thing falls so far out of your jurisdiction it's not even funny." I pictured the officers cuffing Reth and reading him his rights, then trying to detain Cresseda. "Okay, it's a little funny. But seriously. As far as you're all concerned, I'm just a teen girl who is really far behind on planning for the dance decorating committee. And also dating an invisible boy."

"Orders are orders," the mustachioed man said gruffly, elbowing the men around him and startling them out of their paranormal-induced stupor. "We're taking you in." He walked down the steps.

I sighed. "Don't make me call the dragon."

He laughed, and so did most of the others, but a few looked back at Lend and the blood drained from their faces.

"Look, kid, I'm with you. I think this is all a mistake, maybe even a clerical error. We'll figure it out at the station."

Arianna swore, stamping her foot. "That's *it*!" She put her fingers to her lips and let out a shrill, earsplitting whistle. A rush of wind engulfed us as the dragon in all its serpentine glory snaked out of the trees, settling onto the ground and rearing up to stare down at all of us.

I thought I'd learn a few new words, but the men were too shocked to even swear this time. The tall, skinny officer raised both hands, the gun in them trembling so badly he could barely hold it up. Arianna set her hand on his arm, making him look her in the eyes.

"Put it down," she said, her voice soft. He did as she said.

"Well, what are we going to do with them now?" I looked to Arianna for help.

"Allow me to handle this, Evie," Raquel said, hurrying out of the trees with David.

"Sorry," Arianna said. "Thought I could take care of it on my own."

"Don't worry about it." David smiled kindly at her.

"If I can have all your attention." Raquel's voice was all business. "You will please come with me, and I will answer your questions and issue new instructions." I didn't think the officers would listen to her, but I guess when you're staring at a dragon, anyone who sounds like they're calm and collected is the person to follow. "Arianna, care to assist?"

She nodded, slouching off the steps and following Raquel to the group of cars. Not taking their eyes off the dragon, who merely stood regarding them with half-lidded eyes, they all followed, tripping down the stairs and bumping into one another in their eagerness to leave.

I sat on the porch floor, pulling Lend's head into my lap and hoping he wouldn't be bruised from that fall. "Reth!" I shouted. "Reth!" Where was that blasted faerie?

After a few minutes Jack walked over, rubbing at his wrists with a sour look on his face as he casually dodged around the sentinel dragon. "I always forget how little sense of humor police officers have. Shame, really, considering how much fun they could have with their jobs."

"I'd kill for a siren and lights. Or, you know, a car and a license."

Jack sat on the steps, leaning back on his elbows. "That was a little more excitement than I usually like at dawn." He shifted a few times, all awkward, pent-up nervousness. "Evie?"

"Jack?"

"What are you going to do? I mean, with all this."

I looked out at the winterscape, absently playing with Lend's clear hair. "I'm going to try to fix it, if I can. I'm going to open a gate and send all the faeries and paranormals back where they came from."

He was quiet for a long time. I didn't ask what he was thinking; I knew how much pain he harbored, how much hate seethed inside for the faeries that stole his life away. He'd wanted me to send them to hell, and instead I was giving them—well, most of them, anyway—exactly what they wanted.

"I guess," he said, finally, "that's okay, then. Gone is gone, right?"

"Right." I smiled sadly at him. "No more faeries."

"But it makes me wonder—without faeries, what happens to those of us who depend on the Faerie Realms for our food? And what about all those new people the Unseelies have taken? Will they even be able to take care of themselves without the faeries there?"

I bit my lip, thinking. There *were* a lot of logistical problems. I was more worried about actually being able to make the dang gate in the first place, but other things needed considering. I shrugged. "I know this guy. He's a total idiot, but he's also kind of smart sometimes, and he figured out how to make faerie doors and use the Paths. Which means that he can go back and forth whenever he wants, and take anyone else back and forth. I used to think he was worthless, but, I dunno, he's kind of grown on me. I think he's up for being responsible to a whole lot of innocent people who'll need his help."

Jack looked up at me with the most open and sincere

look I'd ever seen on his face. "I will, Evie. I promise. You get the faeries out, and I'll take care of everyone they hurt."

I smiled at him, the cold soul seething in me pushed out of the way by my own warmth. "I know you will."

The dragon yawned with a tremendous clacking of its tusks and teeth. "I should have eaten one of them," it said, settling down to the ground and glaring in the direction of the police cars that were now executing three-point turns to get out of the driveway, all lights turned off.

"Sooner the better on that gate," Jack said.

For once, we were in complete and total agreement.

SWEATY MESS

Hey, can you get Reth?" I asked the dragon. It gave me a look filled with such venomous disdain I half expected fire to come from its eyeballs instead of its mouth. "Just kidding! Yeah. Totally kidding."

With a flick of its tail snapping the space right in front of my face, it ran, hopped a couple of times, and then snaked through the air back into the trees.

"Grouchy, that one. I asked it to roast some marshmallows earlier; it nearly ate me." Jack scratched his head, then stood. "Right, then, I'm going inside where it's warm."

"Stick around, though. I'm going to need all the help I

can get to figure all this out."

"That's me! Mister Helpful. Captain Dependable."

"That sounds like a brand of adult diapers."

"The nickname needs some work. Lord Wonderful? The Incredible Hunk?"

"Please, for the love, go inside."

He laughed, then clomped up the steps and into the house.

"Reth," I shouted. "Reeeeeeeeth! Reth! *Reth, Reth, Reth!* If you don't come in the next thirty seconds, I'm going to go find David's golf clubs!"

"That tone and level of voice does nothing attractive for you, my love."

I jumped, startled, but of course Reth would be behind me, leaning heavily on the porch railing.

"You," I said, glaring. "Fix it. Now."

A look of disdain on his face, he leaned over and trailed his fingers across Lend's forehead. A single whispered word, and then . . .

Nothing.

"You liar!" I shouted, standing so abruptly that Lend rolled off my lap and down a step. As he hit the first one, color bloomed through him into his usual glamour and his eyes flew open in panic.

"He was *asleep*, Evelyn." Reth's lips were pursed, but I knew he was smiling gleefully on the inside.

"Lend!" I lunged forward, knocking into him, and we

both rolled down the next two steps, landing in a heap on the gravel at the bottom. "You're *awake*!"

"Evie! I'm . . . wow, why am I so bruised?"

"Shut up," I said, grabbing his head and pulling him in for a kiss. It was freezing and we were on the ground but I didn't care, couldn't care, not when I could touch my Lend and he was awake to touch me, too. I knew I'd missed it, but it wasn't until now that it hit me just how empty and desperate it had felt to be separated from him like that.

"Maybe," he said, between tracing my neck with kisses, "we could go inside?"

"Maybe," I agreed, not getting up.

"Or maybe," Reth said, his voice dripping with disgust, "Evelyn could come with me to determine how best to fulfill her end of the deal."

Lend lifted a hand off me and held it in the air. I couldn't see what he was doing with it, but I had a good idea, and I heartily approved.

"See what I meant about the ability to focus?" Reth snapped. "You two are ridiculous." He was out of breath he was so angry. He stalked past us toward the trees, and then he collapsed in a heap on the ground.

"Reth?" I sat up, watching him, waiting for him to get up. It was a trick. Right? He was manipulating me again, or . . .

I stood up and ran to him, turning him over so I could see his face. His eyes were closed, his mouth drawn tight, and sweat was beading on his forehead.

Sweat. Faeries did not sweat.

"Something's really wrong with him!" My voice was high with panic. All the things I'd noticed—the change in his soul, his heartbeat, even the way he walked and his voice being different—I thought he was kidding when he said he wasn't dying yet.

I put my hand over his heart, letting out a relieved breath as I felt it beating, too fast by far but still steady. "Reth?"

His huge golden eyes fluttered open. "Perhaps I should have taken the couch."

A laugh choked in my throat. "You're not okay."

"No, as I told you, I am not."

"What's wrong with you?"

His eyes didn't leave mine, but they, too, were different. Before, they'd always felt like depthless pools. Now they seemed shallow, dim.

"I'm dying, Evelyn."

KIND OF A BIG DEAL

You're dying?" I shrieked.

Reth sat up and brushed off his clothes. "It's not an issue." Lend offered a hand to help him stand, which Reth ignored.

"Actually," Lend said, "dying is kind of a big deal. Especially for an immortal faerie."

"I already told you," Reth said, only looking at me. "This will be fixed when you open the gate and we go through together. My connection to eternity will be restored and this will all be a horrible memory. Now come on." He tried to project calm, but the same quivering, fraying-around-the-edges look his soul had was reflected in his face.

I stared incredulously as he stalked into the forest, pausing once to lean against a tree and catch his breath before continuing without looking back.

"Well, no pressure now. Not only does every paranormal in the world need me to open the gate so they can go home, but Reth will *die* soon if I don't."

Lend squeezed my hand reassuringly as we started walking after my fastly failing faerie. "You'll figure it out. I know you will. What was he saying about going through together?"

I willed my eyes to roll, but everything felt so serious and heavy that I couldn't muster the sarcastic energy. "He thinks I'm going to decide to go through with him." Which reminded me that Lend and I hadn't had a conversation we needed to. One I really, really didn't want to. I stopped, pulling his hand so he'd face me. "Lend, I— Your mom, she said they were going to take all the paranormals. And I know she includes you in that group. What are you . . . I mean, they're going to be gone. All of them. Forever. Every immortal creature on the earth." He'd told me he wouldn't go through, but he had to have been thinking about it. He *needed* to think about it. For a few brief seconds I was tempted to take Reth up on his offer of eternity, if only to spare Lend the agony of choosing between his two worlds.

But no. This was my home. This was who I was, and

what I loved most about loving Lend was that I didn't have to lose myself to be with him. Being with him meant I found myself. I wasn't going to try and become something entirely new.

"Not every immortal creature. I don't think they're taking vampires," Lend answered, avoiding my eyes and digging into the frozen dirt with his shoe.

"Yeah, but, Lend, you're going to live forever—you know that, right? And once they're gone, that means forever by . . ." My throat caught, trying to keep the word inside. "By yourself. Alone."

"I know," he whispered.

I squeezed his hands, bending my head until he looked me in the eyes. "Do you? I mean, do you really know? Have you thought this through? Because you're going to have to—" I squeezed my eyes shut, hating what I was saying, hating this conversation just when I got him back. "You're going to have to choose. And whatever you choose is going to be forever. I want to make sure you're thinking about it. You need to make the right choice."

"What do you think that is?" His voice was soft and vulnerable and already filled with pain.

I opened my eyes and let go of his hands, putting mine on his cheeks to frame his face. I'd missed looking into his water eyes so, so much. "I can't make it for you."

"I didn't think I'd be making this choice for years. Decades, even." He stepped back and shoved his hands in his pockets, kicking angrily at a rock on the trail. "This is all happening so fast."

"I know," I said, miserable. "But you know whatever you choose, I love you. Always. And it's important to me that you choose what is best for you. Okay?" I blinked furiously, trying to keep the tears back. I knew—I *knew*—if I asked him to stay, he would. But that wasn't something I could ask him. I had to make decisions for the rest of my life. He had to make a decision that would last for all eternity.

Dude, it sucked.

"But, Lend?" He looked up and I pulled one of his hands out of his pocket and wrapped it up in mine. "No matter what? Whatever happens? You still owe me a Christmas present."

He laughed, hugging me, and we stood there with our arms around each other for way too long and way too short. Finally I sighed. "We should get to the pond."

We reached the end of the trail that I spent so much time on I saw it every time I closed my eyes. Arianna wasn't kidding when she described the scene at the pond. A different creature inhabited every square foot. The pond was totally melted now and teeming with heads and bodies and fins and flippers. An impossibly huge, sucker-covered tentacle curled up out of the water, snatching a bird out of the air and pulling it back under.

"Holy crap, was that a kraken? How deep is the water, anyway?"

"As deep as my mom needs it to be, I think."

We walked closer to a pit glowing such a brilliant orange it hurt my eyes; when I glanced to the side, I could see it was crawling with flaming salamanders. Reth stood next to it, his perfectly square, narrow shoulders slumped. Across the pond, at the edge of the trees, the sole sylph floated miserably.

I remembered what I'd seen in the faerie dream and wondered if this sylph was all that was left of the mighty wind that betrayed the rest of the paranormals and brought them all here. No wonder it had been so desperate to find me that Jack had been able to convince it to get involved. It probably wanted to atone for what it had done.

Or it just hated being stuck in this form. Now that I knew what most of them had been before, I couldn't imagine how strange it would be to go from being limitless to being confined in a new, strange body, subjected to different rules.

I jumped back, startled, as a group of rabid pixies scrambled past, wrestling and biting and pulling each other's hair.

"They can't all be here." I squinted at the far borders. I wanted to figure this out and do it as fast as possible. As much as Reth had been terrible to me and had made me crazy, I was shocked at how deeply the idea of his being hurt affected me. He'd taken that faerie magic in my place— he'd sacrificed his buffer from this world to be with me in the first place. It wasn't that I didn't want his death on my hands. I didn't want his death at all. And to avoid that I needed to open the gate, and to open the gate I needed all the paranormals here.

Raquel walked over from where she'd been standing, talking with David, Arianna, and Cresseda. She beamed at the sight of Lend and me holding hands. "You did it, Evie! I am so happy."

I grinned, leaning my head on Lend's shoulder. "Of course. If anyone needs more beauty sleep in this relationship, it's me. Where are the rest of the paranormals?"

"Not all of them want to go, apparently. Some are so far removed that they don't remember or don't want what they had before. Most of the troll colonies are staying. A few other types are mixed. About half the selkies are choosing to stay behind. A handful of nymphs. Mostly those that can become more human when they love a human."

"What is that supposed to mean?" Lend snapped.

Raquel looked taken aback. "Simply that some are choosing to stay and others are not."

"Just because they're leaving doesn't mean they don't love people here."

I looked at him sharply, wondering if that statement applied to more than his mom. Was he talking about himself, too? Thankfully David spared Raquel having to answer Lend by joining us and making me tell them how I broke the curse. They weren't very amused by Reth's clever prank, either, but we didn't have time to dwell on it.

"When do we get this show on the road?" I tried to sound more confident than I felt. If they asked me to open the gate right now, I had no idea what I'd do, but at least I'd know one way or the other whether it'd work.

"There's a problem," he said.

People needed to stop saying that.

DUDE, FOR SERIOUS

The problem was this. Well, the problems were these:

Problem one, IPCA had managed to keep one of their containment facilities running in spite of the attempts by Seelie faeries and elementals to free whatever was there. And despite my time crunch to get them out of here and keep Reth alive, Cresseda et al. weren't going to let any gates be opened until every paranormal that had been forced through had a chance to say whether or not they wanted to leave. Most had already made the decision; turns out they'd been gathering paranormals since Cresseda first met me. I really, really tried not to be annoyed by this fact. It was still my choice.

Problem two was how to convince the Unseelie faeries that they needed to get on the take-every-paranormal-but-no-humans-back bandwagon. No one had any idea how committed they were to the idea of taking humans with them to keep using their dreams, but faeries were generally loyal to their courts.

Problem three, and this was connected to two, was how to get the people the Unseelies had kidnapped back, most especially the women pregnant with more Empty Ones. The common thought was that the faeries were feeling desperate with their threads to eternity growing thinner every day, and if we took away their only option for getting home in the near future, they'd agree to our human-free terms even if it wasn't what they had in mind.

And finally, problem four was that even if everything worked out in the best possible way, I still didn't know if I could open a gate, and, if I could, whether or not I'd still have a boyfriend on this planet afterward.

Well, number four wasn't on the Official Problems List. I wished I could talk to someone about it, but I didn't want to bring it up with Lend, and I couldn't very well call Carlee and whine about it.

Almost on cue, my cell rang in my pocket. I walked a few steps away from Lend, Arianna, Raquel, and David, who were going back and forth with ideas and strategies regarding the final IPCA holdout. Lend, unsurprisingly, shot down every suggestion of Raquel's with barely concealed derision.

"Carlee?" I answered, seeing her name on my caller ID. "I'm so sorry I haven't had a chance to call!"

"Evie?" It wasn't Carlee's voice. I frowned. "It's Carlee's mom. Have you seen her?"

"No, not since before Christmas. Why? What's wrong?"

She sounded frantic. "She's been missing since yesterday. We can't find her anywhere—she left her cell and all her things. I found a text to you where she mentioned a new boy. Do you know anything about him? We're so scared. This isn't like her."

"Oh my gosh," I said, shocked. "She wouldn't run away!"

"I know." Her voice cracked.

I shook my head, confused and worried, my brain spinning through all the possibilities. Carlee was totally happy. She got along with her mom better than any other teenager I knew. She was doing well in school and got accepted to the community college's dance program. It made no sense. "I remember the text, but we never got to talk. I have no idea who the guy was."

Carlee's mom started saying something, when I looked up and saw Arianna. What had happened to her—how she'd been changed by her then boyfriend—flashed through my mind and I couldn't breathe through the panic. But no. Not here. The vampires here were the most self-regulating, careful, anti-harming-or-turning-humans-into-vampires in existence. Carlee couldn't be a vampire.

Just when I was about to sigh with relief I saw Reth speaking with a misshapen lump of moving rocks. Beautiful Reth. Enchanting Reth. Reth who was a faerie, who any girl would fall in love with. And a faerie would count as an older guy, like Carlee described her new love interest.

"Oh no," I whispered, dread filling my stomach. I knew where Carlee was.

"Please, if you hear anything or think of anything at all, will you let us know immediately?"

"I— Of course. I'm so sorry." I hung up, numb. Carlee. My precious, beautiful, funny, completely and utterly normal friend. I could be wrong, I desperately wanted to be wrong, but deep inside I knew I wasn't. I stumbled back to the group and Lend put his arm around me, then saw my face.

"What's wrong?" he asked. "What happened?"

"Carlee's missing. I think the faeries took her."

"Are you sure?" Raquel asked.

"Pretty sure. She's not exactly the teen runaway type. It's all my fault."

Lend squeezed my shoulder. "How is it your fault?"

"I put this place on their radar. They never would have paid any attention to this town if it weren't for me. They never would have known about Carlee, or taken her. She doesn't deserve to be caught up in the middle of this."

"Who does?" Arianna asked quietly. "It's not your fault. We've all lost our innocence in one way or another because of the paranormal parts of our world."

She was wrong. I could have stopped this a long time ago. And I was tired of having to rescue the people I loved from danger that *I* put in their lives. I squared my shoulders and looked at David. "You and Raquel should lead the attack against the IPCA facility. Where is it? Iceland? Siberia?"

"Illinois," Raquel answered. "Normal, Illinois, a couple of hours outside Chicago."

I snorted. "Finally, IPCA gets a sense of humor. Arianna, can you help them with computer stuff?"

She nodded.

David had his phone out; he'd been texting furiously for the last hour. "I've got some other contacts coming in. Defectors from IPCA—people are tampering with the trackers and leaving in droves now that they've gone completely mad there; everything is shutting down without the faeries Raquel freed. We'll have all the human, werewolf, and vampire manpower we'll need."

"Awesome. And I'm assuming you'll have whatever supernatural aid you need?"

"Only a few types are up for land travel, but, yes. It won't be easy, but I think we can crack this last reserve."

I nodded. "Good. Because I'm going to the Faerie Realms, and I'm not coming back until I have Carlee and every other human with me." Reth looked up and locked eyes with me, then nodded. His eyes had dark circles under them, but he seemed a bit more energetic than he had when he collapsed earlier.

"Evie, that's much too dangerous," Raquel said. "The Seelie Court needs to be in charge of that."

"I don't trust them to be in charge of it. They don't see people as individuals. We're like sheep. There's no way I'd trust them with Carlee's life."

"I'll go with you," Lend said.

David shook his head. "You two will do no such thing."

"I know you want to keep us safe." I smiled. "But fact of the matter is we're both in this deeper than you and Raquel ever can be. That whole we're-the-adults-and-this-isn't-your-problem speech you pulled out when Vivian was rampaging doesn't apply anymore. It didn't even back then, much as I wanted it to. This needs fixing, and I am the one who is going to fix it. I'm okay with that."

Arianna nodded. "But how? What are you going to do?"

"I have some ideas. But first I need something in my stomach before I fall over. So let's go eat and plot and then save the world."

David sighed, looking thoughtful.

"What's up, Dad?" Lend asked.

"I'm trying to figure out if there's any way I can lock you two in your rooms. I don't think a simple grounding will do it."

Raquel laughed. "Good luck trying to force Evie to do anything else once she has made up her mind. She is the definition of a stubborn, headstrong teenager."

"And you love me for it."

"I do." She hugged me, the spontaneity of the gesture surprising me. Even Lend's expression softened slightly toward her.

Back at the house, David and Raquel disappeared into the office to plan. Lend watched them go, holding hands, with a troubled look on his face.

"You okay with that?" I asked.

"No. But . . . he's walking different. Springier, you know?"

I nodded, squeezing Lend's arm. "They both seem really happy."

Lend sighed heavily. Maybe he and Raquel had more in common than he thought. I slumped at the counter, exhausted after my crazy faerie dream sleep, too tired to talk more. My eyes were so dry I could hear myself blink. *Click, click, click* they went.

Lend stood staring blankly at the shelves of food. Arianna had sneaked upstairs to eat—or rather, drink—in private. "I have no idea what to make. I'm too exhausted to think."

"You have no right to be tired. And I never want to see you asleep ever again. I had enough of that for a lifetime these past few days."

"Allow me to take over," Jack said, striding into the kitchen. He nudged Lend out of the way and started pulling out a huge pile of ingredients.

"Can you even cook?"

"If Lend had let me make him an omelet earlier, that question would already be answered."

Lend sat next to me, leaning over and putting his arm under my head as a pillow against the counter. "Remind me again why we trust him now?"

"Because we need all the help we can get. And I think he really is sorry. And a lot of people are going to depend on him if all the faeries leave."

Jack furiously chopped vegetables. "Captain Dependable! Wait, we vetoed that one. The Divine Door Maker? Too much? Hmm . . . Handsome Hero, but maybe I should move away from alliteration. Something sleek. Our Lord and Master Jack."

Lend rolled his eyes and gave me a seriously-can-I-just-beat-him-to-a-pulp look. I smiled and shook my head. It didn't even feel weird to be around Jack and laughing with him anymore. I thought about the faeries, and how the last thing they wanted was to change. I, for one, had decided that I was endlessly grateful that I could change for the better and that I could let the people around me do the same.

Like Vivian. I wondered about her. The last dream we'd shared had been so different; she'd felt so far away. My stomach turned, and I hoped against hope that didn't mean she was dying. Selfish as it was of me, since she didn't really have a life at all these days, I didn't want to lose her forever, not like Lish. After we'd settled everything here, I'd figure out a way to get her out of the Center and into a proper hospital close by.

"Do you have any cheese preferences?" Jack asked.

"All cheese is good cheese," Lend said.

"True dat." I nodded solemnly.

"You did not just say 'true dat,'" Arianna said, walking into the kitchen. "Because if you think you have any ability whatsoever to pull that off, we are going to have to have a long, long talk."

"Can I at least use it ironically? Or 'dude.' Can I use 'dude?' Because I really want to be able to use 'dude.'"

"No. No, you cannot, but thank you for asking. Besides, ironic use always segues into non-ironic use, and unless you suddenly become far cooler or far more actually Californian than you are now, I simply cannot allow it."

"But on *Easton Heights*—"

"You are *not* going to bring up Carys's cousin Trevyn's multiepisode arc where he's sent there as punishment for his pot-smoking surf-bum ways, are you? Because that arc sucked, and he wasn't even very hot. Also, what's the lunatic doing?" She jerked her head toward Jack.

He flipped a gorgeous looking omelet onto a plate and placed it with a flourish in front of Lend. "I am providing insurance against frying pan boy deciding to enact all the very painful fantasies he's no doubt entertained about me for the last few weeks. An omelet this good should rule out any dismemberment vengeance."

"Have you been reading his diary?" I asked. "Because I'll bet he got really creative with the violence ideas."

"No, I only ever read yours. But let me tell you, one more exclamation mark dotted with a heart while talking about how good a kisser Lend is and I was about ready to do myself in. You're rather single-minded when it comes to adoring him."

"True dat," Arianna said, nodding.

"How come you can use 'true dat' if I can't?" I asked, rightfully outraged.

"Because I am dead, and none of the rules apply anymore."

Lend ate his omelet, refusing to answer Jack's questions about just how delicious it was on a scale from cutting off limbs to just breaking his nose. I gave Jack full points for flavor but noted the texture was slightly off, exempting him from name-calling but not from dirty looks.

Arianna lounged against the counter, and when I finished first we debated the usage rules of "dude," "true dat," and my favorite, "for serious."

"I kind of wish they'd shut up," Jack said.

"Dude, true dat," Lend answered.

Jack nodded solemnly. "For serious."

I laughed, so giddy with relief to have Lend, my Lend,

whole and well and back with me, touching me, that even this bizarre scene in the kitchen, hanging out, seemed wonderful. I was pretty sure it was the last normal I was going to have for a long, long time. Whatever happened in the next few days, things would never be the same—not for Carlee, not for Jack, not for me . . . and not for Lend.

JACK IS CLEVER, JACK IS GOOD

*W*e need a plan," I said.

"We are having far too many of those lately for my tastes," Jack said. "I vote Molotov cocktails. That one was fun."

"Much as I like lighting things on fire"—which I kind of had, more than I thought I would—"the goal here is to get everyone out safe. Not to blow them up."

Jack spun a butter knife around and around on the counter. "See, the problem with this isn't going to be the faeries. They probably won't be expecting anything because they can't imagine anyone being cleverer than them. The problem is going to be the people."

"Why?" Lend asked.

"They aren't going to want to be rescued. They don't even know they need to be."

"It's true," I said, frowning. "They looked super happy. All of them. Even the ones in the dance, but I'll have Reth send other Seelies after them." I shuddered, curling my toes. My feet still hurt, but with the faerie soul in me, it was more like an annoying fly buzzing in the next room. I noticed it, but it didn't affect me. "With everyone else, it's part of the faerie magic—when they kidnap you, you want them to." I would have happily gone with Reth back when he first started paying attention to me. It would have been a dream come true. I shuddered.

"And once you're there," Jack added, "it takes over everything. You lose who you were before. It kind of floats away from you until you can't remember and don't care."

"How did you keep ahold of yourself?" I asked Jack. "I mean, you're not exactly blissed out over faeries. What was different?"

He started tapping the knife on the granite counter, a plinking beat. "I dunno."

"There has to be something. Think."

He shifted uncomfortably, the beat going faster until it was a staccato nightmare. "I think . . . I think it was my name."

"That makes sense—repeating my name to myself is

how I kept from going under the Dark Queen's influence. But why won't the others know their names?"

"I—" Lend reached out and snatched the knife away from Jack, who glared at him but kept talking. "It's one of the first things most people lose. Because no one ever uses it, and the faeries don't care—they call you other things, give you a new name, and it sort of leeches your old one away along with all your memories. The faeries are very, very good at taking *everything*."

His big blue eyes looked haunted as he stared blankly at the countertop. I put my hand on top of his. "But how did you keep yours?"

He blinked quickly. "A song. It's the only thing I remember from before. I think my mom sang it to me; just this silly, story song about Jack the Clever Boy." He paused, then in a soft voice started singing, "Jack is clever, Jack is strong, Jack is Mommy's favorite song. Jack is sweet and Jack is good, loves his mother like he should. Jack is precious, Jack is mine, knows I love him all the time." His voice broke toward the end and he cleared his throat. "Umm, yeah. Like that. I don't remember anything else about her or my life before, but she must have sung that song to me a million times, because even in the Faerie Realms I could always hear the tune and remember the words. So I never lost my name. Then as I got older I figured out the longer I could stay away from faeries, the more I got myself back, could make my own decisions."

Even Lend looked sympathetic. How could we blame Jack for all his crazy when this was all he'd ever known, when even holding on to himself was an epic struggle?

"Okay." Lend leaned back and ran his hands through his hair the same way his dad often did. "So all we have to do is figure out the names of the hundreds of people there?"

"Yeah, that's not going to happen. The only name I know is Carlee's."

"I liked her." Jack's voice was almost wistful. "When she smiled, you always knew she meant it. I hope she's still herself."

"We'll get her back." Lend put his hand on my shoulder. I leaned my head against his skin, trying to figure out some way, any way we could make the name thing work. Jack, who apparently always had to be moving in some way, had made up for the missing knife by grabbing a half loaf of French bread and methodically ripping it into tiny pieces.

"Wait," I said, narrowing my eyes. "Why don't faeries like bread?"

"Hmm?" Jack looked up, then shrugged. "I dunno."

Lend picked up a piece, crumbling it. "My dad said he thought it was because it was the staff of life for people."

"Nasty stuff tastes like mold," Jack said. "I tried a piece once a while ago when I was still trying to force myself to eat normal food so I could stay here. It was like a shock to my whole system." He shuddered at the memory.

I sat up, an idea forming. "We can't take iron through

the Faerie Paths. Do you think we could take bread?"

"Why?" Jack asked, wrinkling his nose.

"A shock! That's what it felt like when we were stuck in the dance and Reth said my name. It was this huge jolt that got my mind off the track the faerie music had stuck it on. Maybe we can use bread to knock the people's brains off their faerie high! Get them to start thinking clearly!"

Jack scratched his head, his blond curls sticking up at a funny angle. "You know, that might actually work." He grabbed a handful of crumbs and walked over to the wall, putting his free hand against it and concentrating. The light traced out a door and opened into black. We all held our breath as he took the hand with the bread and shoved it through. It didn't stop dead like anything with iron would. He turned back to us, letting the door close, and grinned.

I jumped up, my hands in the air. "Yes!"

Lend laughed. "Okay, looks like I need to make a run to the grocery store. Do faeries hate wheat or white bread more, you think?"

"Get bread with raisins," I said. "Everyone hates raisins."

Jack was bouncing, obviously excited. "That's all we need, right?"

"We need Reth."

"No," Lend and Jack whined in unison.

"Come on, you two. Reth knows the Faerie Realms better than you do. Jack, you didn't see where the people were; it might take you a while to find them, and that's time we can't afford to lose. And Reth's getting worse; being there might give him more time."

Lend scowled, grabbing the car keys off the counter. "Fine. But I'm really getting tired of his stupid smirk and prissy clothes."

Jack nodded. "And his voice that sounds like it'd even taste good. Really, it's overkill. Best to have only a few absolutely perfect traits—for example, my hair and eyes and sparkling personality—so you don't overwhelm."

"Aww, are you guys jealous of how pretty Reth is? That's kind of adorable."

"You know I could look exactly like him," Lend said, frowning darkly.

"Please for the love of all that is good and holy, never, *ever* wear Reth. That's the stuff of nightmares."

That brightened his face a bit and he left me with a lingering kiss and a promise to be back with every loaf of bread we could carry.

"Well, go find your stupid faerie boyfriend," Jack said, lying down on top of the counter and drumming his fingers on his stomach. "I haven't filled my quota for pissing off the Dark Court yet this week."

"We are going to blow your quota sky high."

He held up a hand and I high-fived him as I walked past and out of the house toward the trail. Yet again. I should have invested in a dirt bike or something given the amount of mileage I was getting out of the path between the house and the pond.

A jumbo white van pulled up into the driveway and people piled out of it. I narrowed my eyes suspiciously when I saw that they were all werewolves. If this was another attempt by Anne-Whatever Whatever to try and get me away from the protections here, I was going to let the dragon eat each and every one of them.

"Evie?"

I did a double take. "Charlotte?"

My former tutor ran forward and threw her arms around me, beaming. She still had the same warm brown hair and warm brown eyes over her yellow wolf eyes, but the lingering sadness that had always been on her face before we got her out of the Center and reunited her with her sister was entirely gone.

"What are you doing here?"

"We're here to help David and Raquel. Some of us have scores to settle with IPCA." Her smile was still in place, but it had a hint of iron behind it. I squirmed a bit inside, knowing that because of IPCA's old eugenics policies Charlotte would never be able to have kids.

I nodded. "I'm down with that. They're inside in the office, I think."

"You coming with us?"

"Not this time. I've got a different errand to run."

"Okay." She reached up and tucked my hair behind my

ear affectionately. "Be careful. I wouldn't want anything to happen to the worst Spanish student in the history of the language."

I laughed. *"No problemo."*

By the time I found Reth, he was deep in discussion with the banshees, their discordant voices chiding him for something or other. I hated to pull him away from getting chewed out, but it had to be done. Another faerie, all spring and mint green, was with him. After briefly explaining about the location of the dancers, she left to retrieve them. I wanted to send Reth because I trusted him more, but he didn't look good. I'd keep him with me so I could keep an eye on him. He wouldn't ask for help—not from anyone— but I'd be there no matter what.

When we got back to the house, Lend was already there with several grocery bags full of bread. Reth turned his head away as though the very sight of it was distasteful. "Even the food of this world is nothing but decay."

Clearly he had never tried pizza, because honestly.

We linked hands—my ex-boyfriend, my boyfriend, and my former friend-then-enemy-then-friend and I—and walked through a door to see if maybe empty carbs were good for something after all.

BREAD BASKET CASES

Okay, yeah, this is freaky." Lend's eyes were wide as he looked around, drinking in the Faerie Realms in all their Technicolor glory. Down in the village, people bustled about, laughing and playing. The mood was like a holiday. Every day in faerie-glamoured happy land was a holiday, which made what we had to do even worse.

Reth stood straight, alert, then relaxed, his shoulders slumping. "There are no fey here at the moment. I suggest you hurry."

"What are we going to do with them once we wake them up?" Jack asked.

"Take them to a safe location protected by my queen, where we will have time to decide what to do next. Do you remember the meadow bordered by trees where you took Evelyn?"

Jack nodded.

"Sounds good to me." I shivered, though it wasn't cold. It was the perfect temperature, lazily warm, the air sweet and gentle on my tongue. This place creeped me the bleep out.

Lend handed Jack and me a loaf of bread each. Reth turned away from it. He looked pale, with faint blue shadows under his eyes. "I shall be back shortly," he said, then took a step to the side, shimmered, and disappeared. I hoped he was going to do some sort of faerie healing thing. He wasn't supposed to be weak. He was supposed to be scary and intimidating and beautiful.

"Keep your eyes out for Carlee," I said. My stomach tied in nervous knots as we walked down into the small, green valley. I didn't know which I hoped for more—that we'd find her here or that we wouldn't.

A small child skipped along a path ahead, stopping to smile when he noticed us. "Hello! Are you new?"

Jack squatted down, smiling and reaching out to ruffle the boy's head of thick brown hair. "Nope, been here for ages. Hey, I have something for you." He broke off a piece of bread and handed it to the child, who obediently put it in his mouth. His face went white with shock and then he gagged, spitting the bread out all over the ground. Huge tears rolled down his cheeks and he started wailing.

My impulse was to run forward and wrap him in a hug, but Jack beat me to it, pulling the kid in and standing up, cradling the sobbing boy to his shoulder. He patted his back soothingly, whispering words I couldn't hear and didn't think it was my place to.

I had chosen right with Jack.

He looked back at us, his eyes haunted but determined. "We've got a lot more to do. Come on."

Fortunately the kid's wails had drawn a bit of a crowd, and people were gathering around us. Their clothes were simple and beautiful, all in creams and greens and browns. Each of them looked concerned about the boy, but their concern was tempered by a happy contentment they couldn't help but glow with. We'd fix that soon enough.

"Hello!" I smiled in a way I hoped was reassuring. "We've got something for all of you. If you'll line up and take one each, and then when it's time, we'll tell you to eat it."

"What is it?" a little girl, her burnished copper hair spun into tight braids, asked. "Is it from the queen?"

"Yup. From the queen. She wants you to eat this."

I tore off pieces of the bread and put it into hand after hand after hand, Lend and I going down opposite ends toward each other to meet in the middle. The little boy's sobs were quiet, a background music to the disturbing scene. Each person smiled and thanked me as I gave them a piece, and I wondered whether or not they'd regret thanking me. Was it better to be ignorantly, blissfully, falsely happy, or to be awake and aware of the horror your life had become?

I thought back on everything that had happened to me since that night Lend broke into the Center. It felt like a lifetime ago. Since then, I'd gone from being naive, trusting, and utterly secure about my place in the world, to being tossed around on a storm, losing who I was, losing my sense of purpose, even losing *what* I was when I found out my father was a faerie.

But in the end, I was glad. I wouldn't trade what I'd learned or suffered or become for anything. It was better to know. Because when you knew, you could choose. The faeries loathed and even killed humans for using faerie names for control—yet they thought nothing of taking even the choice to decide how to *feel* from people.

I put a piece of bread into the last hand and looked up at Lend. Nodding firmly, I knew. This was right.

"Okay, go ahead and eat it!"

Everyone raised their hands in unison, and Lend and I cringed in anticipation. A few seconds later half of them were on the ground, vomiting; the other half looked like they wanted to.

"What did you do to us?" a black woman with closely cropped hair asked. "What did— Oh, dear heaven, where am I?" She put a hand to her heart and staggered back a couple of steps, looking wildly around.

"I can explain." Jack's voice was tired but clear. "Please listen."

I put my hand on Lend's arm while Jack detailed what had been done to them. "I'm going to look for Carlee, see if we missed anyone else. Stay here in case Jack needs help?"

Lend nodded, his face troubled as everyone around dealt with their reawakened awareness with varying levels of shock and dismay.

I hurried past them and into the village. A couple of stragglers were coming toward the group, so I handed them pieces of bread with the instruction to eat it when they saw the blond boy talking. I guess that was the only nice thing about people under heavy faerie sedation: they were conveniently complacent.

I looked into every building that I passed, but they were almost entirely empty, and none of the new people was the one I was looking for. I was nearly out of bread, too, so I pointed them in Jack's direction and told them to ask for something to eat. Finally I came to the end of the village, and I was sure that no one was left in it. My heart fluttered hopefully in my chest—maybe Carlee wasn't ever here. Maybe she really had run away or made some other gloriously mundane, human mistake.

Then I saw a teen girl standing on the lip of the hill at the other end of the village's narrow valley. Her long, dark brown hair floated on the gentle breeze as she stared out, away from me.

My feet felt like lead as I climbed the hill, past the gentle green and purple meadow flowers, to stand next to her. Blinking back tears I turned to face her, still hoping that maybe, maybe, maybe . . .

It was her.

"Hello." She smiled at me without recognition. "I'm waiting for my love to come back. He brought me here, and he said he'd be back. So I'm waiting for him."

I reached out and took her hand, trying my hardest not to cry. "I need you to come back to the village. We have something for you."

She kept smiling, but she looked at me more closely. She seemed different here without her usual layers and layers of mascara. Younger. So much more vulnerable. I didn't want to wake her up from this, didn't want to shatter this dream reality for her. "Do I know you?" she asked.

"Yeah, you do. Come back with me."

"Oh, I can't. I'm waiting for him. You can wait with me, if you'd like to."

I squeezed her hand. "He's not coming back, Carlee."

When I said her name, her whole body stiffened, her eyes opening wide and clearing, as though a veil over them had lifted. "Carlee," she whispered.

I nodded and waited for her to freak out, to start screaming or crying, bracing myself and getting ready to hug her or carry her back to the village, whatever it took. For a few impossibly long moments she didn't say anything, didn't move, and I wondered if the shock had broken her brain. Then her brown eyes locked on mine again, narrowing into slits.

"I'm gonna *kill* that effing creep."

I laughed, relief flooding through me, and threw my arms around her neck.

"No, seriously. I'm going to kill him! I can't believe I bought his stupid lines! I don't care how pretty he was, I mean, have you *seen* what I'm wearing?"

Laughing, I nodded into her shoulder. "So not the style."

"I know, right? I look like an extra in some fantasy movie. Some *stupid* fantasy movie."

I pulled away, searching her face. "You're going to be okay, right?"

"As soon as I figure out what's going on, sure."

"Remember that cute guy, Jack?"

"The one who never called?"

"That's the one. You and he are going to have a long chat."

Her face brightened considerably at the idea of talking with a cute boy. She really was still Carlee, and I felt about a thousand pounds lighter knowing that, regardless of what her life would be like from now on, at least she would be my Carlee.

"How does my hair look?"

"Fabulous, as always."

We started walking down the hill when Reth appeared in front of us. Carlee glared at him. "Oh, I am so done with your type!"

"He's on our side," I said.

"Evelyn, the dancers are safe, but I think you and I should attend to the others immediately."

It took me a second to realize he was talking about the pregnant girls. My previously buoyant spirits plummeted. "Okay. Carlee, Jack and Lend are over there." I pointed to where you could just see the crowd. "They'll probably need your help calming everyone down and getting you all moved somewhere safe."

"I can do that. But you and I need to have a talk, like, soon. Because this is some seriously freaky crap, you know?"

"Oh, I know." I smiled sadly at her, and she turned and ran down the hill toward everyone else. Maybe besides totally underestimating paranormals, IPCA's greatest sin was totally underestimating normal people's ability to adapt and accept everything hidden going on in their world.

I gripped the bag of the last bits of bread in one hand and took Reth's in my other. The scenery spun around us in a blur of gold and green, and suddenly we were smack in the middle of another meadow, next to the lavender stream and surrounded by girls pregnant with future little versions of me.

They blinked curiously, nonplussed by our sudden

appearance. "Hello," one girl, a brunette with a heart-shaped face who looked barely older than me, said.

"Here." I ripped off a piece of bread and shoved it into her hand. "Eat this. All of you." Lacking so much as a curious look, the other girls took pieces and put them into their mouths.

And chewed.

And swallowed.

And continued to look at me, without a single change.

POSSIBLY IMPOSSIBLE

Shut up, okay?" I snapped, rubbing my temples. Jack was still coming back and forth, bringing two people at a time, and he was nearly done. Carlee and Lend were here in the meadow of orange grass and white trees, organizing the groups of people and trying to keep everyone calm.

Reth and I were unofficially in charge of the pregnant girls, and I was about to lose it.

"But he's supposed to visit us today." A tiny blonde with tight spiral curls stamped her foot, her lips drawn in a pout. "I want to see him. He's coming to see us, he said so, and I want to see him, and if we're here he won't know where to find us!"

"We should go back right now." Another of the girls, with perfect clear skin and a healthy glow, glowered at me. "I don't want to be here. I liked where we were before. And he's coming to see us."

"Just go sit—over there! And . . . he's coming. Here. We told him you'd be here, and he's going to come visit you here, okay?"

All six of the girls nodded, some more eagerly than others. I was pretty sure Tiny Blond Terror didn't believe me, but she went with the others. There was something weird about them. Well, okay, there were tons of things weird about them. But there was a huge thing *off*. I couldn't quite put my finger on it, but I knew it would come to me.

"What are we going to do?" I asked Reth, watching as the girls arranged themselves on the ground, playing with each other's hair or lounging, staring at the aquamarine sky. "Obviously the faeries are bringing them food from the mortal realms, which explains why giving the girls bread didn't snap them out of the faerie trance."

Reth's expression clouded. He sat heavily, his legs at awkward angles like he didn't know how to sit on the ground. "I thought perhaps it would be the case, the Dark Queen keeping them here for safety but not wanting to change anything else and risk changing them and the Empty Ones, too."

"Yeah, about time she exercised some caution." One

of the Dark Queen's early experiments to make an Empty One resulted in vampires. Brilliant move, that. "We can't get them to come to their senses until we get their names."

"I doubt it will be that simple."

"Oh, because I thought tracking down the names of six anonymous girls when we have no idea where they're from would be a piece of cake."

"You do not understand the depth of the change they've gone through. The others are connected through their need for faerie food, yes, but these girls have been altered forever by loving a faerie."

I thought of my mom, what had happened to her after loving my stupid faerie father and then being abandoned by him when he didn't need her anymore. She had wasted away without him. "But their babies." My voice betrayed me by cracking. "They'll be okay if we take them away from whoever this faerie creep is, because they'll have their babies. They'll love their babies. That'll be enough." If my mom had been able to be with me, if Melinthros hadn't taken me when he abandoned her, she would have been okay. She would have had something to live for.

"Look at them, Evelyn."

I did, and for the first time it clicked for me what, exactly, was off. They didn't do anything that pregnant women did. I hadn't been around many, but some came into the diner occasionally. They couldn't go two minutes without resting a hand on their stomachs. I doubted they even knew they were doing it, but the need to touch the baby, to feel that life moving inside them, was a compulsion. I even caught a woman talking softly to her belly once.

The six girls could have had pillows under their dresses for all they cared. None of them had mentioned anything about needing to be cared for, or needing to eat or drink. The only thing I'd heard from them was whining about when they'd be able to see their faerie lover again.

"They don't care." I felt like my soul had been sucker punched. "They don't care about the babies at all, do they?"

"They cannot. They've been consumed. Even if we find their names, I doubt they will ever be any more than empty shells. Being loved by the fey is not something a human can recover from."

She wouldn't have loved me. I never would have been enough for my mother. Melinthros had truly destroyed everything about her, and I'd never been loved by either of my parents. Rage and sorrow deeper and hotter than I knew how to handle warred inside me, all the extra souls I was carrying around rising, agitated, and flowing through me.

"Would you have done that to me?" I glared down at Reth. "You wanted me to love you. Would you have destroyed me?"

He waved a hand, dismissing me with a single annoyed gesture. "I never wanted you to be mine in that way, my love. How many times must we go over this? I want to make you whole, *more* than you are. Not less. I've no interest in a human girl as a toy. It's distasteful."

I gritted my jaw. "Distasteful. Yes. That's not an understatement or anything. These girls have been destroyed. *Destroyed.* Do you understand that? Whoever they were, whoever they could have been? That's *gone.* Forever."

Reth raised an eyebrow at me from beneath his disheveled hair. "Well then, I suppose it's a good thing you are going to open the gate so we can all leave this realm. And perhaps if you had listened to me sooner and let me fill you, none of these girls would have ever come into contact with the Dark Court's machinations."

I could feel my face turning red. "Don't you *dare* try to say I'm guilty of this!"

"Were you not trying to make me guilty? I did no more harm to them than you. If I am culpable in this, you are complicit. At least I've tried to fix things, while you have dragged your heels and whined and fought me every step of the way."

"Because no one would tell me anything! You all made plans and stuck me in the middle of them without a single explanation! My whole freaking life, my entire existence is just a pawn on a stupid faerie chessboard! So you'll have to excuse me if maybe I wanted to make my own decisions rather than blindly accept the directions of the very things that have been hurting me and everyone else since they showed up on *my* planet!"

I stalked away from him to the far edge of the orange-grassed clearing, then sank to the ground and wrapped my arms around my knees.

"Evie?" Lend sat next to me and put his arm around my shoulders. "What's wrong? Did Reth do something?"

"Is this my fault?"

"What?"

"Those girls. Reth said . . . if I had listened to the faeries from the start, let Reth fill me up with his creepy burning soul, opened their stupid gate when they wanted me to, none of this would have happened. Those girls will never get better. They're as good as dead if we take away the faerie they love. And I think it's my fault."

"You can't really believe that." He pulled me closer, trying to get me to look him in the eyes, but I wouldn't.

"I didn't tell you about the werewolf, either. A security guard in the Center. He told me that one of the werewolves I let out bit him. I ruined his whole life because I was trying to help someone else. Even when I think I'm doing good, I hurt people!"

"You haven't hurt anyone."

"I have."

"You haven't. You make the best choices you can based on what you know at the time. You can't blame yourself for the choices other people make. You were right to free those werewolves. If one of them didn't take precautions at the full moon, the blame is on them, not on you. You were right to reject Reth, to wait to make a decision about opening a gate until it was *your* decision. If you had gone with the Light Court's original plan, who knows if they would have taken all the other paranormals with them? And *you* didn't make the Dark Queen a freaking psycho witch."

I snorted. "Pretty sure she came that way."

"Definitely sure she came that way. She did that to those girls. It has nothing to do with you. You've made the best choices you could."

I nodded into my knees, still not looking up. I'd made the best choices I could have. But none of them seemed to be the right ones. Maybe I wasn't cut out for this world, after all. What if by staying on the Earth I shouldn't even exist on I just screwed things up even more? And did I even want to try to stay if Lend didn't?

Then again, an eternity in that other place, the one I'd been shown in my dream . . . well, to be honest, it seemed impossibly boring. And I definitely didn't want to become this eternal creature Reth seemed to think I should be. Thinking two or three years in the future was overwhelming enough. I couldn't even figure out what I wanted to major in next year at college. I didn't want to make a choice that would last forever.

"Do you know what you're going to do?" I whispered.

He was quiet for so long I thought maybe he hadn't heard me before he finally spoke. "I want to be with you, and have my life here, but the idea of being alone, forever, after you . . ." We didn't need him to finish the sentence. After I died. It'd be the opposite of Cresseda and David. I'd be the one to leave Lend alone, but he'd be alone forever. I smiled bitterly, remembering when I tried to break up with him because I thought he'd leave me behind. It was the other way around, it had always been, which made Lend far braver than I'd been.

"Are you sure?" he asked. "About me being immortal, I mean? Because I don't feel immortal."

I turned my head toward him, able to see his soul, reflecting light like a stream of water under the brilliant summer sun. It was the most beautiful thing I'd ever seen, and I wouldn't change it for anything, not even if it would mean something could finally be easy for us. "I'm sure. And we have no idea how long I'll live."

"But really, we have no idea how long I will, either. I mean, sure, I'm immortal, but a gas pipe explosion or an asteroid or whatever could kill me tomorrow. Nobody knows when they're going to die."

"Well, some of us have a better idea than others."

He sighed. "Yeah."

We sat together, silent and melancholy on the edge of an impossible forest in an impossible place with nothing but impossible decisions to keep us company.

"So." Jack skipped over. "Everyone's settled and only one person passed out from hyperventilating. Most of them were IPCA employees—surprise, surprise—and almost everyone remembers exactly who they were and want to go home immediately, which means we're going to have to figure out logistics of feeding them soon. Plus we need to figure out what to do with all the weird pregnant girls. And you're opening the gate really soon, right?" He waited for me to say something, then poked me with his foot when I didn't move. "What's the plan?"

If I never had to make another plan for the rest of my life, it'd be too soon.

A LOT STRANGE

Carlee was with Lend, who was entertaining the kids by changing into their favorite characters from television shows. It was more than a little creepy for me to watch the boy I enjoyed making out with become some perky girl known for singing the alphabet, so I avoided that part of the meadow. Now, if he were to start acting out *Easton Heights* by being various characters, well, then I might tune in.

Carlee, as with everything else, had taken to Lend's rather unusual ability with remarkable grace.

"Are you okay?" I'd asked her when he first shifted into someone else.

She'd shrugged, eyes wide with wonder. "Not any weirder than the rest of this, right? I always knew there was, like, *something* a little strange about you two."

"More than a little."

She'd laughed and picked up a small girl who was hiccupping with tears, whispering in her ear until the girl stopped, a smile spreading over her face.

I made my way past the group of IPCA employees, who were all glowering and talking in low tones about what they would do when they got back to Earth. Most of the people were recent acquisitions of the Dark Court, but all of them were forever tied to the Faerie Realms because of the food. That sucked. I went over to where Jack was with some guy who, had he been in a suit instead of a soft, flowing peasant shirt and trousers, would have been the archetypal uptight businessman.

"This is unacceptable! Do you have any idea how many people depend on me? How much money I'm losing every minute I'm here?"

Jack's eyes had glazed over, vague and unfocused as he nodded slowly. "Mmm hmmm," he kept repeating, almost like he was humming.

"Hey," I said. "Everything okay?" Jack gave me a desperate look.

"No, everything is not okay!" Uptight Businessman shouted at me.

"Great! I need to borrow Jack, then." I grabbed Jack's

arm and pulled him away.

"Thanks. Have I mentioned lately how glad I am you didn't die?"

"Yes. But feel free to keep it up. I need to get out of here, see if David and Raquel are back." It had only been what felt like a few hours here, but time slipped funny when you were in the Faerie Realms for a while, and it could have been anywhere from a few minutes to a couple of days back home. Lend and I'd agreed that I'd go check up on what was going on there while he held down the fort here.

I needed to open that gate. This had to end. Soon.

"Sounds great to me." Jack glanced warily over his shoulder to where Uptight Businessman had started yelling at one of the pregnant girls. They'd been getting increasingly edgy, some mad and some crying uncontrollably, each desperate for their faerie love to come back. Unfortunately he picked the tiny blonde to yell at, and she turned on him, screaming obscenities before reaching up and pulling her own hair out by the roots.

"Reth!" He gave me a weary look from where he was leaning against a tree on the edge of the meadow, talking to the green Seelie faerie who had shown up a while ago as a representative of the Light Queen. A few people milled around several feet away from them, their faces shifting from anger to longing and back again. "Do something about"—I waved my hand in the general direction of, well, everyone —"that, okay? And try to get some rest. You look terrible."

His lips pursed in annoyance but before he could respond, I grabbed Jack's hand and walked with him through the door he'd just made. The empty, silent darkness of the Faerie Paths had never been so welcome.

"All those people, are they going to be okay?"

Jack shrugged. "I think so. I've got some ideas. It's not going to be easy for any of them, but we'll work something out. And anything is better than what would have happened to them."

I squeezed his hand. "You're right. And thank you." We were quiet for a bit. "Jack?"

"You know, they say when someone keeps making excuses to say your name it means they like you."

"They say that, huh?"

"They do indeed. But I want to make it very clear that, while you're acceptably pretty and moderately entertaining, it's not me. It's you."

"Color me relieved. But seriously, Jack—"

"Again with the name-dropping."

"*Shut up.* I'm trying to say that I'm proud of you. These people will owe you for what you've done for them, but they'll also depend on you for the rest of their lives. You've really stepped up. I just . . . yeah. I'm proud of you."

He raised his shoulders a couple of times, like he was

physically trying to shrug off what I'd said. Then he shook his head and sighed. "This is more awkward than that time you threw yourself at me and made me kiss you."

"I seem to recall you kissing me, followed by me hitting you. Repeatedly."

He reached over with his free hand to pat mine. "Whatever you need to tell yourself to be happy with frying pan boy. And here we are!"

We walked out of the wall into Lend's family room. It looked like we'd hit some sort of bizarre house party, with bodies packing the room and sitting on every imaginable surface. An abundance of yellow wolf eyes and shriveled corpse faces greeted me, with a few others—some trolls and a couple of dryads—mixed in.

They looked at us, surprised but not shocked, and I waved. "Hi. Anybody know where I can find Raquel or David?"

Most of them pointed, all in opposite directions. Great.

"I'll be upstairs if you need me, okay?" Jack looked exhausted, so I nodded and waved him away, picking which room to look in next at random. The kitchen was closest, so I dodged around the minglers and pushed my way in, relieved to see Raquel standing at the counter, talking with a couple of werewolves.

"You're back!" I said, squeezing in to stand next to her.

"Evie! We'll finish discussing this later," she said, nodding at the werewolves, then taking my hand to lead me through the crowds and into the empty office, where she shut the door behind us. I sank down onto the old, worn leather couch. I half expected her to sit behind the desk in our usual arrangement for debriefing, but she sat next to me instead.

"How did it go?" I asked.

"Remarkably well. IPCA was expecting a faerie assault, so for a huge group of us to walk in and calmly ask for the release of all the paranormals was something of a shock. The workers at the Normal facility didn't want to fight us or hurt humans and werewolves, so in the end we simply had to agree to let them come with us and protect them from any IPCA repercussions and they let everyone walk out."

I laughed, putting my head back against the couch and closing my eyes. "Of course, the job I don't end up doing myself would be the easy one."

"How did everything work out in the Faerie Realms?"

I told her about my last few hours, after checking to make sure we hadn't lost more time than that.

Raquel made a thoughtful noise when I finished, then brushed the hair away from my face. "How are *you* doing?"

"I honestly don't know. The girls, the ones pregnant with Empty Ones? They're never . . . they're never going to be okay. And Reth said— Well, I can't help but wonder how much of this mess, all of it, is my fault."

"None of it is your fault, honey."

I shrugged, too tired to argue or to even open my eyes. "It is, it isn't. Where can you trace the line and say here, here is where I messed up, or here, here is where the connection between myself and this event stops mattering? You can't. But I'm doing my best."

"I know you are." She sighed, an *I wish I could help you more with this* sigh, and it made me smile. "If it helps, I'm very proud of you. I know it has nothing to do with me, but watching you become the strong, smart woman I always knew you'd be is one of the greatest joys of my life."

"You're trying to make me cry on purpose, aren't you? That's just mean, Raquel."

She laughed. "But you know, no matter what, everything will be different from now on. For all of us."

"You're unemployed, for one. I think we can find you a spot at the diner, if you want. Your French fries can't possibly be worse than Grnlllll's were."

"I think I might surprise you there."

I leaned over to rest my head on her shoulder. "Are things going to get easier?"

"Sometimes it takes a little chaos for things to work themselves out. When we make it through the chaos, we can use it to shape the world around us into something better than it was before."

"I'm good at the chaos part, at least."

"And you'll be just as good at making things better on the other side. Trust me."

I sniffled and sat up. "Thanks, Raquel. Speaking of chaos, I better go see if everything is set on Cresseda's end of things. Jack's upstairs, if you and David want to go talk with him about what to do with the Faerie Realms refugees. He's going to need some help."

We parted with a hug, her scent both familiar and comforting, reminding me that family comes in a lot of different versions. I'd figure out how to take care of those pregnant girls if at all possible, and no matter what, I'd make sure their babies wouldn't slip through the cracks like Vivian and I had.

I missed Vivian. I was so incredibly tired; the desire to sleep was an ache I could feel in my entire body. I couldn't believe I hadn't dropped yet. But if I could sleep, maybe I could find Vivian and make sure she was okay.

I cringed against the cold when I walked outside, but it didn't bother me as much as it used to. Almost like I knew it was there against my skin, but it felt so temporary it didn't matter.

I really needed to dump these extra souls. The breeze played around me and I could feel the water ahead calling out. It gave me the creeps, thinking I was carrying around parts of all these creatures who had tried to hurt me. At least I could use their energy for good, something I doubt any of them had ever bothered trying to do.

At the pond my senses were assaulted by the sheer numbers of paranormals there, each of them with their own pretty, glowing soul light. I couldn't see Cresseda anywhere.

The atmosphere was even more partylike than back at the house, all the paranormals chatting and chittering and cackling, flitting from group to group, eyes wide with excitement and anticipation. Well, at least the ones that had eyes. But even the flames dancing above the salamander pit seemed to be happy.

One creature wasn't moving, though. Arianna sat on a rock to the side, watching. I picked my way along the bank over to her, careful not to draw attention to myself. I wanted to get out of here, fast, and getting into conversations with less-humanlike paranormals wasn't on my list of things to do. They weren't exactly good at brevity. Or making sense.

"Ar? Whatcha doing out here?"

"Just watching."

"You wouldn't happen to know if everything is set on this end of things, would you? Do they have everyone who wants to come?"

She nodded slowly, her eyes trained on the movements in the pond. "Yeah, they do. Cresseda declared that 'The gathering is complete, and what was altered will be set right.' Or something like that. Sounds like full speed ahead to me."

I swallowed hard, fighting nerves. "Okay. Guess I'll head back to faerie land and get everything squared away there."

"Good idea. And you might want to hurry. I was talking

to the banshees and, near as I could decipher from their mad rhyming skills, you only have until dawn tomorrow before the two worlds shift too far apart and the gate is lost forever."

"I— Wait, *what*?"

Arianna shrugged. "Apparently there's a bit more of a time crunch than we knew about."

"Well, that's just brilliant. Maybe they could have told me this? Didn't the faeries know? The Dark Queen is making new Empty Ones like she has years."

"I guess the earthbound paranormals can feel it better because they've always been here. The faeries knew time was running out, but they didn't know how soon."

I took a deep breath. "Whatever. Doesn't matter, I need to get Reth through before he dies anyway." Saying it like that made my throat stop up. He wouldn't die. I'd make this work.

"Anything I can do to help?"

"Convince the entire Dark Court to abandon their queen's plan and join Team Leave Now?"

"I was thinking more along the lines of recording tonight's *Easton Heights* rerun so that hour was freed up for you." She held up her hands at my outraged look of horror. "Kidding. Kidding. I've been helping David and Raquel set up emergency places for all the faerie land transplants and IPCA refugees who aren't leaving. We'll get everything ready here. You focus on the faerie stuff."

"Can't I be in charge of the DVR, instead?" I stood and turned around. Arianna swatted my butt as I walked away. I wanted to laugh, but it was all I could do not to hyperventilate. Everything was finally happening.

I hadn't made it very far back up the path when Reth stepped out of the woods, scaring me half to death. "Way to make an entrance," I said, my hand over my rapidly beating heart.

"You need to come with me."

"Did you know I have to open the gate *tonight*? Never mind. Don't answer. If you did know, I'll want to kick you in the nuts for not telling me, and I don't have time to do it. Good news is I'm going to save your life. We'll just get Jack from the house and then we can go."

"This isn't a matter for Jack." He took my hand and threw open a door in the middle of the air. He walked through it; I had to practically run to keep up with him, though he was breathing hard. He opened a door in the blackness and we walked through into his room. Someone was sitting on the couch with her back to us.

"Who is—"

"Hey, stupid!" Vivian squealed, jumping up and running to hug me.

YOU CAN'T BORROW
MY CLOTHES, EITHER

I stood stock-still, utterly stunned, with Vivian's long, skinny arms around me. When had I fallen asleep? I quickly ran back through my recent memories—Raquel, the path, Arianna, Reth—but they all flowed sequentially into each other. So either I was having the longest, most lucid dream ever or Reth had knocked me unconscious on the Faerie Paths.

Or Vivian was really here.

"I— You— Am I asleep?"

She laughed, backing up to arm's length and holding both hands out in a ta-da sort of gesture. "You're not asleep.

And neither am I, thank goodness for that."

"How?" I scanned her frame but couldn't see the burn-ing souls she would have inside her if she'd drained any paranormals.

"That is the question, isn't it." Reth's tone was as ill-tempered as his look. He sat on the couch and then, glaring at me as if daring me to mock him, he lay back on it, his breathing still shallow and rapid. "I plucked her body from the Center on our second visit there, lest she fall into Unseelie hands again. Imagine my surprise to return here today and find her awake."

"You woke up all on your own?" I didn't know whether to be elated or scared. I mean, sure, Vivian and I had become friends, sisters even, in the time since I stopped her from killing paranormals. But that had been in the safe confines of our dreams. Vivian out in the real world . . . "safe" was not a word that sprang to mind.

"I wouldn't say all on my own, no. And have you seen yourself? You're lit up like the Fourth of July!"

I looked down self-consciously. I'd been trying to ignore it, but I was pulsing with light. Not like when it had been concentrated in my wrist and heart from Reth, or the pale, barely there shimmer of my own soul. No, I was filled with all sorts of sparks and swirls of color if you bothered to look and could actually see.

Which Vivian, being another Empty One, could.

"Umm, yeah. I didn't want any of this, not really." Only

kind of a lie. "There have been a few . . . complications."

She lifted her eyebrows at me, a wry smile on her face. "I know a thing or two about complications."

"Yeah. So. You? Awake?"

She took my hand, hers freezing in mine, and pulled me over to the couch. "Gosh, your hands are burning up. It feels amazing. Sit down. I'm exhausted." Vivian leaned back and I noticed she was even paler than me, which was saying something. She looked winded, though all she'd done was stand for a couple of minutes. "Guess being asleep for a few months and losing the energy from hundreds of souls doesn't do wonders for your body."

"Guess not." I shifted uncomfortably, wondering if maybe she'd like to take some back so we'd be even. Added a whole new layer to the eternal problem of sisters taking each other's things.

"Still, I've got one of my own now." This time her smile wasn't vicious or hard at all, but full of wonder as she blinked languidly. She pulled down the top of the long white hospital gown she was in and we both looked at the smooth skin over her heart. There, pulsing ever so faintly, dimmer even than David's tiny candle flame of a soul, was a light.

"Viv," I said, looking up at her with tears in my eyes, "your soul."

"I know, right?" She beamed. "Guess I do have one, after all."

"But how? I mean, why now? Do you think it was building up?"

"No, I know exactly how I got it. And now I finally understand why you weren't dying when I met you, and how you kept getting brighter without taking souls from others." She reached over and tugged the neck of my shirt down to mimic her own, poking the area above my heart with one cold, bony finger. "See, right there. The others are trying to hide it, but I can see it. And it's brighter, even, than the last time I saw you."

I looked down and put my hand over my heart, wanting to hold my soul there, to cradle it. Vivian and I knew how precious they were. "It is, isn't it?" I hadn't wanted to hope, but now that she confirmed it, I agreed. I was brighter. *Me*, not just the extras.

"Yup. Because, lucky Evie, I was right. Everyone loves you. Or enough people, at least, for your little sucky Empty One soul to grow all by itself. I never had that."

I looked down, feeling guilty. Even with my bizarre life I'd always had it better than her, always had people who cared about me. "So you mean the people who loved me put it there?"

She shrugged. "Heck if I know the mechanics of it. Probably. I'm guessing you loving them helped, too."

I felt warmer than I ever had before. Because this meant that not only did Lend fill that hole inside me, but Raquel did, and David, and Arianna. And, most important of all, it meant that I had never truly lost Lish. If I had a soul because of the people who loved me and who I loved, then a huge part of it would always be hers.

"So, thanks," Vivian said.

"For what?" I looked up at her, confused.

"For being stupid enough to love your crazy, murdering lunatic of a sister and being such a pathetic dork that I couldn't help but love you, too."

"That's why you were disappearing," I said. "You were waking up."

"Because of you."

This time I was the one to wrap my arms around her in a huge hug. "I'm so glad," I said, my face buried in her hair. "But please, promise me no more killing, okay? I have way too many other things to worry about. Please be a happy thing in my life."

She laughed, pushing me away. "Ouch. You are all elbows. And no worries. I'm not about to risk my own kick-A soul to mix it with some lame vampire mess. It's too pretty." She let her head flop back against the couch and closed her eyes. "Besides which, even if I wanted to go hunt for some souls, I'm pretty sure a legless werewolf could outrun me. All your little friends are safe."

I breathed a sigh of relief, watching her face for any sign she was lying. It remained completely smooth and calm. I wasn't about to invite her to a sleepover with Arianna or anything, but I had to hope that she was sincerely changed. It was all I could do.

"What's going on that's got you so stressed? Dark Queen stuff?"

"Oh, if only that were all." I explained the entire situation to her from start to finish. At one point I thought she'd fallen asleep, but her eyebrows remained drawn over her closed eyes instead of relaxing. "So," I said after what felt like forever, "I'm going to open up the gate. Tonight, apparently."

"Wow," she said, exaggerating the lip movements to draw it out. "You have been busy, haven't you."

"Yup. What do you think? I mean, am I doing the right thing?"

She laughed and opened her eyes, her nearly colorless gray eyes meeting my own. "You're really going to ask me that? My moral compass isn't exactly known for its accuracy." Her face softened. "Seriously, Ev, I think if anyone can make the right choices in all this mess, you can. Me, I'd just try to kill all of them. Did try to kill all of them, actually. But your way seems better. And less work in the end, because you get rid of them all in one fell swoop."

I nodded, biting my lip. "It'll work, right?"

She shrugged. "You're the only one of us who's ever made a gate. But sure. I think it'll work. It's why we're here, right? At least one of us can fulfill her destiny."

"Destiny totally sucks."

"Don't I know it."

I stood up, pacing. I'd been debating what to do with her. I wanted to take her home to David's, but putting her around that many paranormal creatures didn't seem like a good idea. Best to ease her back into soul temptation. Because I couldn't deny that even I was drawn to the souls of the paranormals around me, knowing how they'd feel, how they'd fill me. How much worse would it be for Vivian, who had once carried so many?

Yeah. Far away for now. Tonight I'd make sure Raquel was in charge of her. And that Raquel had Tasey. "Reth, are there any faeries with the people we saved?"

"No," he said, his eyes closed, his thick eyelashes the same crescent as the dark circles beneath his eyes. "They are safe there alone, and all the Seelie faeries have gathered with the queen."

"And what about that meadow where we have them? Is it going to, I don't know, poof out of existence as soon as the faeries leave?"

He frowned thoughtfully. "I suppose it will remain as it is. All this will. We created it, but the matter from which it was formed was never ours. I can't see why it would cease to be since we don't do anything to keep the things we make here. Once made, they simply are."

"Are you sure?"

He opened his eyes. "Of course not."

I glared. "Well, thank you."

"Part of my queen's preparations have been gathering

food, ensuring there will be enough to sustain the duration of the lives of every mortal tied to this Realm."

"Assuming this doesn't all just wink out of existence."

"Yes, assuming that."

"Well, it's something." I'd have Jack bring over as much food as he possibly could, but I had no idea how long faerie food would stay good in the normal world. We'd have to make sure everyone was in the mortal realm tonight and hope that all this would still be here after.

"Okay." I grabbed Vivian's hand and pulled her up off the couch. "You get to go hang out with a bunch of weird, seriously screwed up humans."

"I'll fit right in, then."

"My thoughts exactly! I've got some things to do with the faeries, including somehow convincing the Dark Court to join us. You'll be safe in the meadow." And so will all the paranormals I loved. But I didn't say that part out loud.

"As long as there's a place to lie down I'm good."

We each took one of Reth's hands, Vivian sliding hers down his arm before wrapping her fingers through his. "I forgot how pretty you are," she purred.

"Have you also forgotten trying to make Evelyn drain my soul?" he asked, raising his eyebrows in a way I'd swear was flirty if Reth were the flirting type.

Vivian laughed. "Nope, I remember that part."

"And this is awkward. Let's go." I tugged on Reth's hand, and that horrible twisting thing happened, dumping us in the orange grass. Jack ran immediately over to us.

"I took Lend back home along with a ton of food and most of the calmer people. Where were you?"

I sat heavily on the ground to make everything stop spinning, hugely disappointed that Lend wasn't here to help me not freak out. I gestured to Vivian, who was already lying on her back next to me.

"Meet my sister, Vivian."

"Wait, the one you put in a coma because she wanted to kill all the paranormals?"

"Yup."

He reached down and took one of her hands in his own, bending over to kiss it. "Anyone who's personally tried to rid the world of faeries is a friend of mine."

Vivian laughed again, this throaty laugh that was so unlike mine. I liked it. "Charmed, I'm sure. Now bug off so I can sleep."

I walked away from Viv, Jack following me, and stood next to Reth, looking at the crowd. He swayed and I moved closer, nudging him with my shoulder until he leaned against me. He was lighter than I thought he'd be, for all his impossible faerie strength.

Most of the people still here had calmed down more or less, and I could see Carlee going from group to group, smiling or listening as the situation called for it. I loved her. It was super bad luck that she'd been sucked into all this but good luck for everyone else. No one could beat Carlee's infinitely perky, innately bubbly personality.

"Keep an eye on Vivian, okay?" I said to Jack. "Just . . . well, make sure she doesn't hurt anyone. You probably want to start taking everyone back right now so you'll all be safe in case the Faerie Realms get messed up. Also bring as much food as you can carry."

"That sounds promising."

I shrugged, my attention elsewhere.

Jack followed my eyes to the group of pregnant girls, sitting together away from everyone else. "They're not doing very well," he said. Most of them sat listlessly on the ground, staring into space. One was biting her arm and rocking back and forth. The blond girl was slowly and methodically ripping out her hair. My stomach turned, sick with grief for them.

"Is there anything we can do?" I asked Reth.

"Take them back to the Dark Queen and give them to her. Let the Dark Court take the new Empty Ones so they will think they can leave your world on their own terms with their human pets and reject our offer."

I closed my eyes, pressing my hands over my stomach, feeling like my own soul wanted to break into a million pieces from too many impossible decisions. "We can't."

Reth reached out and took my fingers in his own, his touch light but comforting. "I've found that sacrifice is called that for a reason. We have all lost much of what we were or could have been because of the mistakes of my

people. We'll yet lose some things to set it right. But when
you join eternity, you will not feel the sting of this life with
such intensity."

"You mean I wouldn't feel at all?"

"I feel, my love. Simply not in the same way you do. And
thank heavens for that, because you are quite an embarrass-
ment at times. Your inconsistent and flailing passions will
no longer be a concern."

Leave it to Reth to go from comforting me to insulting
me in the course of one short conversation. With one last
long look at the girls I probably wouldn't be able to save, I
tightened my hand around Reth's as he stood straight.

"Okay. Let's go convince the Unseelies I'm their only
option and get you all the bleep off my planet."

LIGHT AND DARK

Neamh. Evie. Neamh. Evie. Lend, Lend, Lend. Neamh. Evie.

"What are you doing, my love?"

I scowled at Reth for breaking my concentration. "Thinking. Shut up." The Light Queen was speechifying up on a podium made of liquid light, her radiance bathing all the faeries in a glow that was nearly overpowering. Within a few seconds of being around this much faerie glamour I was having a hard time seeing straight and found myself slack-jawed and dazed. Thus, the name equivalent of pinching myself.

I realized at some point she had stopped talking, and now every single set of faerie eyes—a few hundred of them—were trained intently on me.

"Oh, uh, hey." I waved. "What did I miss?" I whispered to Reth.

"You're supposed to tell us how to convince the Dark Court to join us."

"I— What? Seriously? I'm only here to make sure everything happens. I thought the queen would have a plan! I'm a glorified doorman. I open the gate, I close the gate. Nowhere in my job description of Empty One does it say I also manage to convince a mob of anti-Evie faeries to saunter on through the gate."

Reth smiled. "And just when she'd finished praising human ingenuity and assuring us that everything will work out according to plan."

"Yes! Plan! *Her* plan! Gosh, you guys are sucking it up all over the place. Aren't you supposed to have these things in place for centuries, or were you too busy writing pretty little poems to *describe* the plans that you never bothered actually *making* them?"

His golden eyes, now with fine lines around them, twinkled with amusement. "We had a plan, my love. I was to fill you up and you were to open a gate for us immediately. But I seem to recall you doing everything in your power to resist and change that plan. So now we've had to account for all the other creatures from our world and conform to your requirements. I think you'll find that we fey, while obviously superior in nearly every way, are not quite so adaptable as temporary creatures. If you want improvisation, you'll have to provide it yourself."

"Of course I will." I rolled my eyes, huffing. Why had I expected anything else? "Okay, fine. Do you all know any of the Unseelie names? Maybe we could force—"

"No," Reth said, cutting me off sharply.

"You don't know any?"

"It is not a matter of whether or not they are known. My queen knows every name of every soul from our world. But we will not use our brothers' and sisters' names to control them. It is not done."

I raised my eyebrows in disbelief. "So you could have stopped this—all this—at any time? Your queen could have controlled those faeries?"

"If you could stop all this by killing someone you know—anyone—would you have done it?"

"No!"

"There are some boundaries we do not cross. IPCA visited great evil on us when it ensnared us and forced us to reveal the names of other faeries. We would have sooner perished but had no choice."

"But you used my father's name!"

He sneered as though he had a bad taste in his mouth. "That creature hardly counts as fey."

"But you still broke the rule."

"I might have, yes. But there is a chasm between the Light Queen and myself that can never be crossed. You and your entire world have changed me, pulling me further and further from myself. I am not proud of it. She remains unsullied."

"Well, goody for her."

"Child?" The Light Queen's voice stilled the turbulent waves of my soul, singing calm and grace to every fiber of my being. *Neamh*. Ah, there, I was pissed off again.

I looked over the gathering of fey, all the ethereally impossible faces blending and blurring together. I didn't want to look too closely at them for fear of seeing the faerie who was my father, Melinthros. I didn't want to talk to him ever again. I didn't even want him to exist.

Putting my hands on my hips, I sighed. "Okay, here's what we're going to do. We're going to Unseelie territory, and you're all going to protect me with whatever faerie mojo you have, because I'm pretty sure the Dark Queen will not be very excited to see me. And then I'm going to talk to them."

"Talk to them?" the Light Queen asked.

"Yes," I said, trying to compose a poem on her beauty comparing her to the light of the dawn, to the rays of sunlight piercing clouds after a thunderstorm, to . . . *Evelyn*. I shook my head, trying to clear it. "Gosh, can't you at least

try to turn it down? Anyway. We're going to talk to them.
If they're anything like your court, a lot of them probably
think their queen is a freaking idiot."

The Light Queen's wide, white eyebrows rose like a
question mark.

"I mean, obviously not all these faeries agree with all
your decisions. Like the one that got them stuck here. So
we're going to tell the Unseelies that time is up and bank on
them wanting to get out, period, more than they want to
get out under the Dark Queen's terms. And then . . . we're
going to hope she decides to come rather than hanging out
here all by herself."

Yeah. This was going to go well, I could tell already.

The Light Queen inclined her head in a regal nod, holding her hand out to me.

"I'll go with Reth, thanks."

He took my hand possessively and put it in the crook
of his elbow, though I supported him more than he supported me now. With one nauseating twist we were back
in the clearing where I'd saved Lend. I had to give it to the
Dark Queen—as we suddenly popped in with a few hundred other faeries, she didn't even look surprised. My eyes
darted to her neck, but the skin was once again smooth and
unblemished. So much for my secret hope that we'd find
her wounded or dead.

But unfortunately for my grand plans to turn her faeries

against her, the only faeries in the clearing were those that had come with me. The Dark Queen's court was missing entirely.

"Sister," she said, her black hole voice passing through me like a rush of bass too loud and low to register, leaving me shaken and trembling.

"Neamh," Reth whispered in my ear, so softly only I could hear it, and I felt myself warming up again.

"Sister," the Light Queen answered. "It is time to return home."

"You have taken my things. I want them returned."

"They never belonged to you. None of this has ever belonged to us. Let us leave it all and go home, together."

The Dark Queen tilted her head to the side, a smile pulling at her violet lips. "None of this belongs to us? Have you not brought your own whelp along?" She trained her black eyes on me and I cringed, then tried to stand as straight as possible.

"I don't belong to her." I wished my voice carried power like theirs instead of sounding like a seriously scared seventeen-year-old girl.

The Dark Queen didn't respond to me, instead looking back to the Light Queen. "Do not pretend at superiority. All this was for you; I have not forgotten. If I want to go home with a prize for my ages of suffering on your behalf, it is my right."

"It is wrong."

The Dark Queen laughed, a sound so heart-shatteringly cold and beautiful I didn't realize I'd fallen to the ground and curled into a ball until Reth was kneeling beside me, again whispering my name. I stood, helping him up.

"You speak to me of wrongness when you have committed the same sins? You would control me, your other half, your equal in the eternities. You stand here with your very own Empty One after having the gall to take mine away from me? How is this any different, *Sister*?" She hissed the last word like a knife drawn across skin.

"Because I choose to be here." I narrowed my eyes and clenched my fists. "My life, my choice. You didn't give that to Vivian or to any of the new Empty Ones. But they're all lost to you now. You don't have any other options! It's now or never!"

She smiled at me, her teeth a straight, sharp white line. "And does the Empty One think it has a will of its own? How precious." I flipped her off. The gesture was meaningless here, but it sure as heck was my decision to do it.

The Dark Queen ignored it, turning back to her sister. "Do what you think best; your court will do well to pray it does not destroy them like your last whim that brought us here did. But return to me what is mine first and let me do as I desire."

"It's too late for that," I said. "If you'd ever stuck around on Earth like the other paranormals, you'd be able to feel that our worlds have moved too far apart, and whoever doesn't leave now doesn't leave *ever*, no matter how many Empty Ones you make. They won't be able to find the gate."

"Come with me," the Light Queen said, her voice filled with such sorrow and pleading I was ready to throw myself at her and beg her to take me and let me spend the rest of eternity trying to make her happy.

LEND LEND LEND EVIE EVIE EVIE.

"I will not," the Dark Queen said.

"Even if it means dwelling in this hollow land of shadows and death forever?"

"Even then." The Dark Queen's back was ramrod straight, her eyes depthless pools of rage.

"So be it. Children, did you hear? She would remain, dwindling and thinning forever, rather than give up this play at creation, and give you no choice in the matter. Will you remain also, or will you come with me?"

Out of the trees came faerie after faerie, the entirety of the Dark Court, who had apparently been listening to the whole exchange. I looked at Reth, shocked, but he just smiled. I clenched my jaw and shook my head, annoyed. They'd had a plan all along, and it hadn't involved me. I was here for show—*Hey, look! Our pet Empty One! You can hitch a ride back if you join now! Limited time offer!*

"I did warn her you were less likely to come if you thought you weren't in charge," Reth said, his voice cracked but his tone self-congratulatory.

"Did you warn her I'm highly likely to back out of the entire thing if you piss me off?"

"Perhaps you had better pay attention to what is happening."

"Perhaps you had better watch your back, stupid glowy golden faerie man whore."

He frowned at me. "That made no sense."

"Good! Now maybe I can join your club." I took a step away from him but immediately felt terrible when he swayed and looked like he was going to fall. Moving back and putting my arm around him, I saw that, sure enough, all the faeries had mixed together, slowly joining hands, leaving everyone flanking the Light Queen and no one with the Dark Queen. The Light Queen held out both hands beseechingly toward her sister.

"Please," she said.

"No." The Dark Queen smiled triumphantly at me. "She is not even filled, and I know enough of this Empty One to know she will never do what is necessary to gain enough souls."

"No," the Light Queen said. Her voice was heavy with the weight of more time and years than I could begin to imagine, and I felt my shoulders sag. "She is not filled. And this is where I will ask you, once again, to be my sister, my opposite, my equal. To join me in fixing our great and terrible wrong." She stepped forward, hands still outstretched. "Only a power as endless as the one that formed the original gate can open the new one. Neither of us is what we once were, but together we can give her the strength she will need."

The Dark Queen's eyes widened, then narrowed to glittering points. "You would have me sacrifice *myself*?"

"We will both be lost forever. But we will be lost together and set the eternities back in order." Her voice was soft and sweet, and I was sure the Dark Queen would agree. She had to. No one could resist that much love and pain and desire.

The Dark Queen cut her hand through the air between them and the sweet, yearning joy and sorrow of the Light Queen's voice dropped away like a sheet of water, leaving me gasping.

"I will never." The Dark Queen's pronouncement rang through the clearing, final and certain as death.

"I am sorry," the Light Queen said, her huge, beautiful eyes releasing a single tear. Then she leaned forward and whispered a name, a name so perfect and strange I couldn't understand it but knew immediately what I was hearing.

"Be still," the Light Queen said, and the Dark Queen ceased moving.

I felt the shock and agitation ripple through the faerie ranks around me. The Light Queen had broken their rule. Their one rule. I couldn't quite believe it, but I finally

knew I'd made a good choice working with her. She meant
to make things right, no matter what it took.

She turned to me, her smile sad. "Child, you will need
everything from both of us to open the gate. I give it freely."

My jaw dropped. "I— Wait—that's what you meant?
You want me to suck out both your souls? But that would
kill you! You can't go back to your homes if you're dead.
And besides, you promised! One of my conditions was that
I wouldn't hurt any paranormals." I'd thought she meant to
use their energy to help me. Like, both of them standing
next to me or something. Not swirling around inside me.

The Light Queen held out her hand, beckoning me
closer, and it took all my will to keep my feet firmly planted
where I was. "I promised you that no innocent creatures
would be harmed. My sister and I are not innocent in this.
A sacrifice is needed, and only with both our souls will you
have the strength to create a big enough gate for all to pass
through. It was our folly and pride that brought us here. It
will be our sacrifice and grace that will return everyone."

I stumbled forward, my brain spinning in a million different directions. "But . . . I'd have to kill you."

"It must be done, and I give you my soul willingly."

I stared into her eyes, their rainbow shades of brown
shimmering and shifting. To take her soul out of the eternities . . . it was wrong. It was too wrong. Reth I wanted
to save because he meant something to me, but the Light

Queen I wanted to save because she was and always had been and always should be. I could feel it in my very bones. "I can't destroy your soul."

"Of course you cannot destroy it, child. No one can. You will simply give it a different purpose. A nobler purpose."

"But you'll still be dead."

"Yes."

"And you're choosing that?"

"Yes."

I shook my head, overwhelmed. I could . . . maybe I could. She wanted me to. It was her choice, after all, and she knew exactly what she was doing. I was willing to potentially sacrifice myself to open this gate. I could allow her the same choice. I turned to the Dark Queen, whose black eyes regarded me with hate so powerful I took a couple of involuntary steps back.

"She doesn't choose the same thing," I said.

"I am making this choice for her."

I thought of everything the Dark Queen had done, every life she was responsible for destroying or ending, what she would have done to me if she'd had the chance. But staring at her, proud and cruel and permanent, I couldn't do it. I couldn't take that choice from her. Not even for her—especially not for her—would I lose myself that completely, would I let myself become a murderer.

"I can't do it," I whispered. "I'll drain you if that's what you want, but I won't do it to her if it's not her decision. I'm not like her."

"Well, good thing *I* can do it," Vivian said, a smile on her face as she let go of Jack's hand, darted forward, and slammed her palm against the Dark Queen's chest.

DADDY ISSUES

I lurched forward, my mind spinning with horror. I watched Vivian get brighter and brighter as the Dark Queen dimmed. "Wait, you—"

Jack grabbed my arm, and I whipped around, furiously trying to pull it away. "What are you doing? I need to stop her!"

I'd expected Jack's big blue eyes to be manic and evil, but he looked . . . calm. "Evie, this has to happen. Vivian'll do it so you don't have to."

"But it's wrong!" I jerked my arm free, only to find Reth on my other side, blocking my way. I could knock him over, the state he was in. And then I could stop Vivian, and—

"It might be wrong," Jack said, "but it's the right wrong thing to do."

Angry tears stung my eyes. I wanted to turn around and see what was happening, but I didn't want to see it if I couldn't stop it. "What about Vivian? What will this do to her? Was this her idea?" I wasn't sure I could stop her again. She'd always been stronger than me, and this time she'd be expecting an attack. And the idea of putting her into another coma killed me. Then again, I couldn't let her hurt my friends.

Jack shook his head. "No, Reth agreed that Viv and I should follow you, and if you couldn't do what needed to be done, we'd help you."

"You'd *help* me?"

"Yes." He put a hand on my shoulder. "We'd help you, like you've helped us."

"But . . ."

"It was an impossible decision for you, Evie. We made it so that you can concentrate on the things you need to do. In case you haven't noticed, your delightful sister and I are a bit more ruthless than you." He grinned, that impish, dimpled grin I knew better than I wanted to.

"But you don't know Vivian." I was scared down to my toes not only for what she could do but also at the thought of losing her to the monster she had been. "You have *no idea* what she was like before I stopped her."

A soft thud sounded behind us, and then I heard Vivian's voice, altered, both higher and lower than it had been before. "Whew! Don't you all look so pretty."

When I saw Vivian for the first time back when she attacked the Center, she'd looked like a sun goddess thrown down to earth. I turned to find her not quite so bright that I couldn't make out her features, but it would definitely have been more comfortable to look at her through a pair of sunglasses. I could barely see the thin hospital gown over her body. If she'd gotten almost as much soul from one faerie as she had from the hundreds of paranormals she'd drained, I hated to think what this taste would do to her. At her feet was the dim and infinitely lessened shell of the Dark Queen, now only a body. I jerked my eyes upward to avoid looking at her; it was too wrong to see her ended. She had been cruel and evil, but destroying her was taking something from the universe we had no right to.

"Vivian?"

She giggled, not looking at me but at the Light Queen. "That was a rush, Ev."

"Why did you do it? I thought you were different. I thought you'd found your own soul."

She had her hand half raised toward the Light Queen, who was kneeling next to the body of her sister. Vivian looked up slowly, as though she couldn't tear herself from staring at the Light Queen's soul. "Hmmm?"

"You said you weren't going to drain anyone else, because you had your own soul now. Because I love you, and you love me. What about your soul?" I wasn't mad or scared anymore, just so very, very sad. The faeries and their stupid plots had finally succeeded in destroying Vivian's soul once and for all.

"I— Oh, Evie." She jumped off the gleaming silver throne platform and walked to me, putting her hands on both my shoulders, her fingers burning my skin. "I'm sorry. I did this *because* of my soul. Because of you. I didn't want you to cross that line. The line and I are best friends by now, but you don't need to go there. You made the hard choice to free the souls I had taken, so I made the choice to take one last one. I will *not* let you spend your own soul to open a gate for these idiot faeries."

"You aren't going to . . . you know, go crazy?"

She laughed, and the sound was a little unhinged. "Oh, I'm there, stupid. But I'm not going to go crazier. I'm here to help."

I nodded numbly. "Do you think— Should you— Do you want to—" I looked helplessly toward the Light Queen. She bent and kissed the Dark Queen's cold forehead, then stood.

"I guess I can do her, too," Vivian said, but her voice was hesitant. "It's just . . . this is a lot of soul, Evie. Like, whoa, a lot. I shouldn't. I don't want to give this one up already, and I don't know if I can figure out the gate on my own. You're the only one who's ever actually used the souls' energy to make something. But I don't want . . . We need to hurry. Hurry, please?" Her confidence was quickly shifting, and I saw her hands curl into fists at her side—a gesture I knew well from when I was overwhelmed with wanting to taste souls, to make them mine.

"This is your task," the Light Queen said. "The two of you together, sisters. It is a lovely parallel, a healing balance."

She held both arms out to me, and I swallowed hard. "I don't want to."

"I know, child. But I am asking you to. You will need me to accomplish this."

"Are you sure?"

"I am."

"I'm so sorry," I whispered, putting my hand on her chest, hating my stupid, empty shell of a body for being able to take her out of eternity. I steeled myself to ask the channel to open, but instead of having to pull it out, her soul rushed forward, a torrent of light and heat and time and agelessness and regret and hope, swirling and filling me until I was full from my toes to my head, and then filling me even more, not stopping, more and more warmth and energy and light and burning, and I never wanted it to end, I wanted to be connected to this, to feel this forever, just like I knew the soul could. I could feel myself stretching, changing, becoming more than I had been before, being taken out of the tiny stream flow of my time and thrust into the tidal oceans of immortality.

"Thank you," she whispered, snapping me back to reality as the last of her soul drained out into me and her eyes changed from the color of life to plain brown, then went dim and cold forever.

"Hey look! We match!"

I turned to Vivian, feeling fast and slow and warm and cold, like everything that had ever happened and ever would happen was happening right now, like nothing mattered and everything mattered and I was at the center of it all—

"You are totally tripping, aren't you?" Vivian asked.

I shook my head, looking down at my bare arms that glowed brilliant blue-white. A hand settled on my arm, and though the touch registered I didn't feel it the same way I knew I should, that I knew I had. It was simply there. I looked up at Reth, seeing straight through to his quickly fading soul and knowing him in a way I never could have. Surpassing him. Finally understanding what he wanted us to be, together.

"Say your name." His eyes were serious and oddly sad. Why was he sad? I was eternal now. The girl I'd been, capricious and angry and scared, tossed and turned on the currents and whims of time, that girl was gone. I stood straighter, flexing my fingers, luxuriating in the power that infused my whole body, burning away what had been before, purifying me.

"Say your name," Reth said again, his voice insistent.

I narrowed my eyes, then formed the word; it felt foreign and strange on my tongue, the lip movements forced. "Evie."

"No, your real name."

"Neamh." I gasped and closed my eyes, breathing deep to hold on to the flare of my own soul, lost amid the power of the Light Queen's. "Oh, gosh, Neamh, Neamh, Neamh. Me." And Lend. The image of him popped up in my brain, the memory of his touch, his laugh, the way he made me feel. I clung to it, our relationship as much a part of me as my own soul.

"You okay, baby sister?" Vivian asked, putting her arm around me. It didn't burn anymore—it felt the same as my skin. "I should have figured it'd affect you more since you've never built up a tolerance. They can take over pretty fast."

"I'm good. I think. I know who I am, at least." It hadn't stopped the other feelings, but I could separate from them. I could feel the weight of the faeries' stares on me, and I wondered how they felt about what I'd done. I dared to look out at them, and was met with equal parts sadness and peace in their faces. I hoped we'd be able to pull this off; otherwise I doubted they'd be so chill with the fact that we'd ended the lives of their queens. "Okay. We need to get to the pond and make this bleeping gate." Not only were we almost out of time, but I wasn't sure how long I could keep the Light Queen's soul from overwhelming mine and making these changes permanent.

Vivian leaned close, so close I could see her real eyes underneath the brilliant light of the soul inside her. "We could maybe keep them? Just you and me, forever?"

"Vivian," I said, despairing.

"Kidding! Totally kidding." I sincerely doubted it, but she took my hand. "Let's make a gate!"

Reth took my other hand, and I moved his hand into the crook of my elbow, letting him put all his weight on me. Jack took Vivian's, then immediately let it go with a hiss. "Ouch!" he said, shaking his burned hand. "I'll go get all the people left in the meadow to Lend's house and then meet you. Don't start until I'm there, though. If this place implodes or something while I'm in it, I'll be very upset." He disappeared, and the entire clearing around us lit up as door after door was opened, and all the faeries left behind their carefully crafted world.

"Evelyn," a voice that felt familiar said. I turned to see a faerie whose soul was ragged and dim, tarnished among the pristine brilliance of the others. Worse even than Reth's. I didn't know that soul. "I can't go back unless you tell me I can."

I frowned, and then I realized how I knew the voice. My faerie father. The one I'd banished to the Faerie Realms forever. The part of me that held onto my soul had an instant and harsh desire to leave him here. He'd be alone and lost until the end of time—the same way he left my mother and then me. He deserved it.

But I was better than he was. More proof that he had no claim to the soul I'd made in spite of him. "Melinthros, you may enter the mortal realms for the sole purpose of leaving through the gate." He stood straighter, but I hadn't finished yet. "And while there you absolutely cannot have any carbonation whatsoever."

Okay, maybe I was a bit petty after all. But the way his shoulders slumped back down as he stumbled off was highly gratifying.

"That was good of you, Evelyn," Reth said. I shrugged and, for the last time ever, we walked through a door and into the darkness, my own light filling my vision so not even the Faerie Paths could darken it.

WE'RE NOT DAWN YET

The night was clear and sharp in a way only winter nights with a bright moon can be, every leaf and twig and rock brought into colorless contrast by the pale white light. Or maybe I could see them all for the same reason I could sense the borders of this world pressing in all around, hinting and dancing at the paths and possibilities of other realities.

"Evie!"

Lend's voice rang through me, a welcome reminder of who I really was. I smiled and turned around, nearly knocked over when he ran into me and grabbed me up in a hug. "I was so worried! You should have taken me with you. I—" He stopped dead, his arms tightening around me even more as he looked over my shoulder. "Umm, you do know Vivian's here, right?"

"Oh, is she? I hadn't noticed." He looked at me, scared, then rolled his eyes when he saw my smile. "It's okay. She's here to help me."

"That's me, helpful Vivian. And, flaming souls, Ev, your boyfriend is beautiful."

I smiled even bigger, soaking up this way of seeing him, his soul blue like reflected light off rippling water, alive and shimmering and dancing, his and his alone. Unlike the last time I'd been overwhelmed with other souls inside me, I wasn't even a little bit tempted to take his.

"What is it?" Lend asked, noticing my stare as he wrapped his scarf around my neck. I was far, far from cold right now, but it was sweet of him. "And why is your voice different?"

"You really are beautiful. And I really want to kiss your brains out. But I've got to make a gate and save the world and stuff first."

"Kiss my brains out after?"

I bit my lip. "Are you going to . . . will there be an after?"

"Hurry, please," Reth said.

Lend ignored him and pulled me in closer, his lips touching my ear. "The only world for me is the one you're in. Let's make the best life we can here and not worry about what comes after. I want to grow old with you."

"Really? We'll get rocking chairs and be all cute and wrinkly!"

"You'll be wrinkly. I'll just pretend to be."

I punched him lightly in the stomach, but closed my eyes, my own soul once again singing out louder than the others in me. "Best plan I've heard this week. And, trust me, I've heard a lot."

"I love you forever, Evie."

I pulled back and kissed him, all the energy and light in me springing up in joy and passion and happiness. "I love you forever, too, my Lend."

"Wow, your lips are really hot. Literally and metaphorically. But mostly literally."

I laughed, stepping back from him. "Yeah, comes with the bursting-with-eternal-souls territory."

Reth collapsed to the ground next to me, his breathing shallow and frantic. "Lend?" I said, my immortal voice still managing panic.

Lend reached down and picked Reth up, carrying him to the edge of the gathering. I turned to the group, suddenly aware of our very, very large audience, a collection of souls in every color of the rainbow (as well as some definitely not in the rainbow I knew) and the bodies that held them standing, waiting, watching. It was a good thing David's property was on the edge of a state forest, because there were a *lot* of paranormals here.

I took a deep breath, my eyes trained on Reth's chest to make sure it was still moving. To my relief he lifted his head and pushed out of Lend's grasp with a disgusted sound, choosing to sit on the ground instead. He was still okay. But for how long . . .

"We've got to do this *now*." I lifted up my hand, and—

"Stop," a woman shouted. Everyone turned to see someone in a power suit and sensible pumps stomping out of the trees toward me. It was not Raquel. Raquel was running after her, swearing rapidly in Spanish and trying to grab Anne-Whatever Whatever.

"Wow, you are so not invited," I said. She was a lot less threatening now that I could see straight through to her soul, a pale, quivering, barely there thing.

"Stupid girl, you have no idea what you're doing!"

"Really? Because I'm pretty sure *you* have no idea what I'm doing."

She stood directly in front of me, huffing with exertion and anger. Lend loomed protectively beside me, but I wasn't exactly worried she'd whip out a Taser and try to take me in. All her faerie cronies were on my side now, and I didn't see a single paranormal or even another human backing her up.

"What do you think will happen to IPCA if you take all these creatures out of the world?"

"Hmm. I believe the answer falls somewhere under the categories of Don't Know and Don't Care. Take your pick."

"Oh? You don't care? You may think you're helping by banishing this group, but how many vampires and were-wolves are leaving? Hmm?"

I looked around. The only vampire I could see was Ari-anna, standing next to David, and a couple of werewolves who had come out of the woods after Raquel. I shrugged. "They don't belong in that other world."

"They don't belong in ours, either, but here they are! How exactly do you propose IPCA continue to keep people safe from paranormal menaces that will still be alive and well among us when you take away the faerie magic we depend on?"

I remembered the werewolf guard who had been turned against his will. And there was poor Arianna, innocent of anything other than falling for the wrong boy. As bad as IPCA had been—and, whoo boy, it had its bad points—it did fill a necessary role in the world to address problems that the average person had no idea existed.

"But you're doing it wrong." I frowned. "I mean, you're all about capture and control. Look at my friend." I pointed to Arianna, easy for me to pick out of the dark-ness next to mortal Raquel and David. "She's never hurt anyone in her life. She's done nothing but try to make the best out of the crap hand she's been dealt. In fact, she and David have devoted their lives to doing what IPCA should have been doing all along: helping and guiding the people who need it most instead of automatically treating them like criminals and killers."

"Evie, if I may?" Raquel stepped forward, regarding Anne-Whatever Whatever with cool, professional detachment. "I'm afraid your brief and disastrous reign as head of IPCA has come to an end. As has IPCA as a functioning international body. Which is why I've already set in motion everything necessary to form the United Paranormal Aid and Rehabilitation Group. Each geographical area will act with cooperative autonomy, and the focus will shift from containment to education and aid, with minimal policing only when necessary." Only Raquel could talk like an official memo. I glanced at Lend, shocked to see him smiling at Raquel.

"You have no right!" Anne sputtered.

"Oh, I think you'll find your most powerful contacts immediately came out of an inexplicable fog once the Unseelie faeries stopped working with you. They want answers. I have them. So while you have been running around, desperately trying to grasp at power, the rest of us have been finding solutions."

"I won't let this happen! I'll—" Her shrill voice cut off, although her mouth kept moving. I turned to Reth, who raised an eyebrow at me from his seat on the ground.

"I am not going to miss humanity," he said.

I laughed. "Humanity's not going to miss you, either."

Raquel smiled, then motioned to the werewolves, who were only too happy to come and bodily haul away a now rapidly flailing Anne-Whatever Whatever.

"Will she get her voice back when you leave?" I asked Reth.

"I may have accidentally made that permanent."

"Well darn. Too late now!"

Raquel moved to give me a hug but then jerked back. "You're burning up!"

"Yup. So I'm told."

"I want you to know how proud I am. You're doing the right thing, and I don't want you to worry about what's going to happen after. We'll figure it out." She looked back at David and beamed, as happy as I'd ever seen her.

"I have no doubt of that. Although I do have one serious concern."

"Yes?"

"UPARG? It doesn't roll off the tongue in quite the same way IPCA did."

Raquel heaved a *why must you joke at inappropriate times* sigh, then lifted her chin haughtily. "Well, maybe we won't invite you to be a part of it, then."

I laughed. "Please, by all means, leave me out. I think it's high time I retire."

"Even if we issue you your own custom companion Taser for Tasey?"

I pursed my lips thoughtfully. "We'll talk when I'm done here."

"Umm, Evie?" Vivian said behind me, her voice

strained. "This is . . . really not a good place for me to be right now. We need to hurry."

I turned to her, worried. If I could feel the pull of the souls, how much worse must it be for her? "Okay, we're only waiting on—"

"Hey-oh." Jack skipped up next to Arianna with Carlee. They were holding hands, and I had a sneaking suspicion it wasn't because they'd just come out of the Faerie Paths. He waved and shouted, "All clear on our front! Also, to my fabulous faerie friends, good-bye and good riddance!" He let go of Carlee's hand, turned around, and dropped his pants.

Jack's brilliantly white, moonlit mooning of the unearthly crowd was strangely beautiful. Lend was less amused, rolling his eyes and muttering, "My mom's *right there*. Can't we send Jack, too?"

"Not today. Raquel, go to the house and take everyone not going through the gate with you. I don't know what's going to happen, and I want you all where I know you'll be safe." She nodded and ran back to the others, who waved and, when Jack had pulled up his pants, disappeared back toward the house. "Vivian? You ready?"

She nodded, but she seemed distinctly nervous.

"Okay," I said, looking up to find the gate in the stars. I lifted a hand, only to have it jerked violently down.

"What are you doing?" Reth hissed.

"I'm making the gate!"

"Not that one." His eyes were wide with—fear?

"Why are you so scared of that gate?"

He looked to the side, deliberately avoiding staring at the stars. "Because that is . . . that is another part of eternity. It's not ours."

I frowned. "But I sent the other souls there."

"Yes, and without bodies they were ready to go there. But I am not, nor will I ever be."

I couldn't help smiling. "Ooh, poor little Reth, are you scared of what happens after you die?"

His voice and face were shockingly sincere, his skin pallid and his lips nearly blue. "More than anything. I have no desire to discover that realm of eternity. None of us do, which is why we need that gate. Myself most desperately. Now, please."

I looked back up at the stars, trying to figure out if I was scared of that gate or not. And, strangely enough, I discovered I wasn't. It was like Lend and I had talked about—no one could say when they were going to die. You did the best with the time you had, filled it with people and things you loved, and hoped that whatever came after was as good or better. I was finally okay with this whole finite mortality thing.

"Alright, you big pansy. I'll figure out the other one."

Frowning, I tried to sense the area around me, knowing that beyond the surface of the world were other worlds, the distance between almost paper-thin. But I didn't know what I was looking for, didn't know how to find it. I turned to Vivian, but she shrugged.

I closed my eyes. The only things I knew about why Empty Ones worked the way we did was that we had room for extra souls because we started out with less, and that we could make gates because of our innately human sense of home. But my home was *here*. How on earth was I supposed to find another one?

"The gate needs to be opened and closed before dawn," Cresseda said, a hint of strain flowing through her voice.

"YES. THANKS FOR THAT. VERY HELPFUL RIGHT NOW." I glared at her, but a splash drew my attention to another part of the pond, where I saw the head of the fossegrim I'd partially drained watching me, his murky eyes narrowed, whether in hatred or anticipation I couldn't tell. Then I looked up and saw the sylph nervously swooping around, and an idea clicked. I was still holding on as tightly as I could to my own soul, and my own soul belonged right here. But the others . . .

Taking a deep breath, I released control, letting the other souls well up and overwhelm me, changing and shifting my senses, making this world feel cold and old, the dirt and decay clogging my sinuses, the very air hastening my death even as it prolonged my life. I shuddered, knowing that I didn't belong here, this wasn't my world. My world was—

There. Just beyond my fingertips. I could even feel the rough edges of the tear that had brought them here, nearly healed, almost past the point where it could receive them back.

I blindly held out a hand and felt Vivian take it, squeezing reassuringly. "Here," I whispered, guiding her hand forward. "Their home. Can you feel it?"

"I . . . yeah, I think I can. I definitely can. It feels— Oh, Evie, I want to go there." Her voice was low with longing.

"Let's open the gate, then." We pushed against the air together, and I willed everything in me, all the souls there that belonged elsewhere, to push through.

Then the world exploded.

MISS YOU FAERIE MUCH

Light and sound and wind filled everything, momentarily blinding me in a massive sensory overload. Gradually my eyes adjusted as they stared through a hole in the night, into the shifting world of light and motion that was the paranormals' home. My hair whipped past my face, stinging my eyes, pulled forward with the rushing wind into this strange, eternal land.

Vivian staggered back, and I looked at her, pale and winded and without any soul other than her own again. She was already shivering violently, only the threadbare hospital gown around her. I still had some souls left from the others I had drained, and it took every ounce of them to push the edges of the gate back until it felt stable, though it still pulled with an insistent intensity I feared would only get stronger.

"Okay," I shouted, finally feeling like myself again, except more tired and heavier, like gravity wanted me back with a vengeance and was trying to pull me down to the ground. "We did it. Oh my gosh, we actually did it!" I laughed, nearly hysterical with exhaustion and wonder, collapsing against Vivian. We wrapped our arms around each other to stay steady, my scarf ripped from around my neck and sent flying into the other world.

Lend came and put his arm around my free side, staring wide-eyed through the gate. "It's beautiful," he said, and fear twisted inside my stomach. What if it called him through? What if he realized that's what he wanted?

"And," he said, his voice changing, "kind of freaky, too, right?"

I let out a breath, relieved. "Totally freaky. It doesn't feel right, you know?"

"Yeah."

I couldn't explain it, because it wasn't that the feeling I got when I looked through was bad, it was just . . . foreign. So impossibly foreign it was like I didn't have an emotion that could express it. It made me feel less and more than I was, like who I was or thought I was didn't matter at all.

I happened to like mattering.

I turned to the crowds of paranormals. "Well, get going! Dawn waits for no paranormal!"

They didn't need a second prompting, rushing forward and with bursts of light leaving our world for theirs. As they went through I could see their forms shifting, become less physical and more pure spirit, everything bigger than it had been here, everything brighter, everything more beautiful. Dryads became swirls of green light, dancing along the ground; Grnlllll ran past me with a wink of her beady black eyes and flashed, changing in the light to something grand and wonderful, everything good and pure about earth and stone as she disappeared into the ground.

Three unicorns trotted past me with glowing salamanders on their backs, and I held my breath against the stench. But as soon as they crossed the threshold everything small and repulsive about them burst free, and they became the unicorns of my dreams, more a vision of light and motion and power than a simple horse, pounding away free, while the salamanders turned into living flame, curling and twirling on the wind.

They were going through so fast now I couldn't keep track, couldn't notice everyone, although the dragon paused long enough to incline its head at me in a way that still looked disapproving, before going through and exploding into a thousand writhing, dancing dragons even larger than it had been here. I saw Donna run through with several other selkies, her face a mixture of joy and sadness. Kari would never go through with her.

The tree spirits wound their way through, and again, Nona wasn't with them, her spirit forever lost to that realm. On the other side they sank into the ground, spreading out and away, covering Grnlllll's rich earth with trees and flowers and growing things too perfect and strange and wild for this Earth.

And then a rush of water flowed past us, carrying the countless water elementals with it, straight through into their home. I was wet up to my calves but it didn't matter, not now. I watched light after light as souls passed through in a torrent to the other side, but my attention was brought back to our own cold Virginia predawn when the last of the water rose up in front of us.

Cresseda, beautiful and lit from the inside by her own soul, smiled at Lend and held out her hand. "Come, my son. Join with the water and discover your true nature. Be with us always."

Lend made a noise somewhere between a choke and a sob. "I— Mom— I can't. This is my true nature. This is who I choose to be. I'm sorry."

Her features contorted in confusion, then reset themselves into a peaceful smile. "When I brought you into this world, I thought I could set your path. I see now that by naming you Lend it was not to your father I was giving a temporary gift. It was to myself. Are you certain?"

He squeezed my shoulder, and I wrapped my arm around

his waist, anchoring him here with every ounce of love I possibly could. "I'm certain. I love you, Mom."

"And I love you, my beautiful boy. Be well." With a massive splash and rush of water, she disappeared down and through the gate. Lend let out a gentle sigh next to me, and I took my other arm from around Vivian and wrapped him up in a hug.

"I'm going to miss her." His heartbreak echoed through his voice.

"I know." I didn't know what else to say. He'd been given an impossible choice between two worlds, both of which he belonged in. I was ecstatic he'd chosen mine, even though I couldn't imagine how much pain it must be costing him.

With an extra burst of wind, the sylph flew past us, giving me a dirty look with its strange lightning eyes. When it went through, the wind kicked up a notch, becoming a gale. We had to lean away from the gate to stay standing.

With a jolt I realized that all the paranormals had gone through except the faeries. In a line they went by, their orderly passing a somber dance to music I couldn't hear. Part of me was unavoidably sad to see them go. I knew that much of the magic of this world was leaving with them, and, whatever else they were, they were wonderful in the fullest sense of the word. I tried to pick out faeries that I knew—crazy, broken Fehl, Melinthros, or any of the other faeries I'd had to use, particularly the midnight or Goose

Down Hair faerie, but this many together wove a pattern of light and beauty that blended from one faerie to another and made my eyes tired.

In the end it didn't matter, really, about individual faeries anymore, about fights I'd had with them, feelings I'd harbored for them. Their time here was over. I had no good-byes for any of them. I'd given them more than they deserved.

"Evie." I looked up to see Arianna standing in front of me.

"What?" I said, having to shout to be heard over the whipping wind. It stole my words, flinging them away from us and through the gate.

"I'm going," she said, and even though I could barely hear her, the words hit me with a shock.

"You're— Where? Where are you going?"

She nodded toward the gate, staring at it with eyes so weary and mournful they made me want to cry.

"You can't! You don't belong there!"

She stepped closer, smiling at me. "I don't belong here, not really. I haven't for a long time."

"But you have no idea what going through there will do to you!"

She shrugged. "I'm willing to find out. I'm tired, Evie. I don't want this life, not like this, not here."

"But—" I struggled for words, trying to think of some

way to talk her out of it. "But what about me? What about us? We're your friends! We love you! And your games! What about your—"

She put her hand over my mouth. "Look at me, Evie." Her smooth, pale-skinned glamour seemed so thin over her corpse's face. "Tell me I belong here."

"I . . . I want you here."

She leaned in and hugged me. "I know. Thanks. I love you, too. And for the record, Cheyenne and Landon are soul mates and if they don't end up together, I want you to find a poltergeist to haunt the *Easton Heights* writers."

I sniffled, hiccupping a laugh. "Okay."

She pulled back, smiling at me, then reaching out to ruffle Lend's hair. "Take care of each other, you two obnoxious kids."

Then, throwing her shoulders back and staring straight forward, she walked through the gate. I watched, dreading seeing her turn into dust or something, but gasped in relief and joy as her ruined, unnaturally preserved body blossomed into something new, something strong and proud and undeniably alive.

She turned back, just once, and although she was nearly unrecognizable, I could see our Arianna in her smile that managed to maintain its trademark ironic twist.

"I'm going to miss her," I said.

"What?" Lend shouted.

"I said, I'm going to miss her!"

"I can't hear you! I'm going to miss her!"

I shook my head, smiling. A few last faeries were going through when I realized that Reth was still standing nearby, his frame visibly shaking.

I gestured to the gate, but he stood there, frowning at me, then motioned me to him. Disentangling myself from Lend, I walked over, having to pull my hair out of my mouth three times.

"You should go!" I shouted. "You're the only one left and you look terrible and it's almost dawn!"

"I want to go through with you. I want to be there when you become what you should be."

"Reth." I shook my head. "I'm not going through!"

His eyebrows rose in confusion. "You're not going through."

"No! I'm not going through!"

"Of course you are going through. This is what everything has been about, escaping this wretched planet. Together."

"You can go!"

He reached out and cupped the side of my face with his palm that, once again, felt warm to my now extra-soul-free body. Feverish, actually, and I could feel his pulse racing through it. "You are the only thing I have ever cared for besides myself. I cannot leave you here."

I—oh, bleep, I actually felt sorry for him. And a part of

me wished that I could give him what he wanted, because even now, even dying he was so beautiful that the remnants of the girl I was when I loved him wanted to do nothing but make him happy.

But I wasn't that girl anymore. And I didn't want to become a different girl so I could be with him. I wanted to be with the boy who loved Evie, not the faerie who loved the potential for Neamh.

I put my hand over his and smiled, then shook my head. "I'm sorry, Reth. I'm not coming. This is my home."

His eyebrows came together and formed a line that had never been there before on his smooth, perfect forehead. "You are really choosing to stay."

"I am."

His frown deepened. "I do not understand."

I grinned, shrugging. "Isn't that what you hate about me? Flighty, unpredictable, squirmy human emotions? Even though you're a total jerk, and I hate you more than I like you, I can accept that you always thought you were doing the right things for me. You can't make these choices for me though, because you don't really know me and you never could."

"But I love you."

I pulled his hand away from my face and patted it. I'd seen the pregnant girls in the meadow. I knew what it meant to give everything in yourself to a faerie. "Faerie love is something I can live without. And I think you'll find that I'm something you can live without, too."

Reth narrowed his eyes and looked from me to the gate and back again.

"Don't even think about it," I said, suddenly scared. "If you so much as take a step to drag me through, I will drain your soul and send it through the gate in the stars you're so scared of. And you know you can't fight me right now."

His lip jutted out petulantly, then he sighed. "I really will miss you, my love. If nothing else you were always entertaining."

I smiled. "I think I might miss you, too. So few things left in this world to terrorize me and look pretty while doing it. Now get out of here and enjoy your eternity." He glanced calculatingly at the gate once again, and I raised my hand in warning. "I can drain faster than you can run."

He looked torn, then leaned forward and pressed his smooth lips against mine in a whisper of a kiss. I staggered back, putting my fingers to my lips and still feeling his heat there.

"Perhaps if I had done that earlier you would be coming with me now." He smiled at me, that enigmatic faerie smile that I realized with a pang I really would miss, then turned and walked, stooped and unsteady, through the gate.

"Good-bye, Reth," I whispered, letting the wind carry my words through the gate and wondering if he heard them on the other side. Something tight around my heart released as he grew taller and brighter, healed, his features smoothing until they were so much less human than they had ever been. He turned his head ever so briefly in my direction, smiled, and then ran on dancing feet to join the rest of his brothers and sisters.

I smiled back, happy and relieved that at least this time I'd managed to save someone I cared about, even if it meant losing him forever. I was strangely glad I had known him. And non-strangely glad he was gone forever. High time to have an easy life. I turned and ran back into Lend's arms, burying my face in his shoulder with a smile as I breathed him in.

"We did it!" I shouted, looking up at Vivian and smiling. "That's everyone! We're done! We can do anything we want now!"

Her teeth chattering, she smiled back, but hers looked oddly more like a grimace. "Umm, Evie?"

"Yeah?"

"Shouldn't the gate be closing now?" she screamed, her voice already hoarse from competing with the wind.

I looked at it, edges as strong as ever, but the gale picking up speed. Leaves and small branches spun past us and through the gate, one smacking my cheek and leaving a stinging welt in its wake. And still the gate stood, permanent and strong and greedy, pulling for more life to come through, just as it had done when everyone in that world had been forced through into ours.

Well, bleep.

NEVER FOREVER

Vivian was screaming something, but I couldn't hear her over the shrieking wind. We all stumbled farther from the gate and into the trees, where we could lean against their trunks to escape the pull.

Gasping for breath, Lend looked at me, his face open with fear. "What now?"

"Yeah, what now?" Vivian asked.

"How am I supposed to know?" I shouted. "I've never done this before! The gate before sucked the souls through and that was that! I didn't have to do anything!"

"How did they close it when they got pulled through to our world?" Lend asked.

I closed my eyes, trying to remember the dream. "The sylph! The one who whipped up enough energy to open it! It closed when the sylph got pulled through to this side."

"So it got closed from this side?"

"I think so!"

"Maybe it can only be closed from . . ." he stopped.

"The other side," Vivian finished.

"Oh no," I whispered. "Oh no, oh no, oh no."

Lend looked stricken. "No, it's okay. It'll be okay." He was talking fast, like his tongue was trying to sort through his thoughts and pick something useful out of them. "We can . . . we can both go through. We'll still be together."

"But I don't want that life!"

"I know, neither do I. But we can't let that gate destroy this world!"

"No, we can't. Okay. We'll still be together." I sniffled, letting out a choking laugh. "And at least I won't have to decorate that stupid dance, right? And it won't matter which college I get into." This time my laugh was definitely more a sob.

Lend leaned forward and smashed his lips against my forehead, and I closed my eyes, letting myself rest against him. We'd fought so hard to stay here together, and now we'd have to give it up.

It sucked. It gave new meaning to the word suck, really. They'd have to change the definition after this ultimate suck to beat all suck.

"Evie, do you have any left?" Vivian asked.

"What?" I pulled my face away from Lend and looked at her.

"Any souls. Do you have any left?" She was staring intently at my chest.

"I . . . no." My heart sank even further. The only soul I had left was my own. I would be making an even bigger sacrifice than I thought. "Maybe we could leave it open?"

A small sapling, ripped from the ground by its roots, flew past us toward the gate.

"I think we can safely assume it's only going to get worse," Vivian said, her tone flat.

I nodded and nodded and nodded again, like the motion could buoy me up for what had to be done. "Okay. We'll be okay. I'll go through and use . . . use my own soul to close the gate."

"You can't!" Lend said.

I shrugged, putting on a brave smile. "It'll be okay. They can probably fix me. I mean, Reth was able to put soul into me on this side. He should be able to do it on the other side, right?"

I looked from Vivian to Lend for reassurance, but neither of them had any to give. I needed them to be brave for me, to tell me it was going to work out. I'd come so far to get this bright, happy soul of my own, to figure out who I was and how to love and let myself be loved. I didn't want to give it up, and I needed to know it would be okay.

"Lie to me!" I shouted. "Tell me it's going to be okay!"

Lend shook his head. "There's no way I'm letting you use your own soul to close the gate." He stood straighter. "Use mine."

"What?"

"Take mine! I have more than you do anyway, right? It only makes sense."

"But who knows what that would do to you on the other side! You would be mortal! We'd have no idea how long you'd live, how it would change you."

He smiled bravely, shrugging. "I never asked to last forever. I'm not interested in immortality; *you* are the life I chose."

"Oh, will you two shut up?" Vivian stomped over to us, her white-blond hair whipped up into a bizarre halo around her head and her cotton gown barely staying on. "'Let me sacrifice myself!' 'No, let *me* sacrifice *myself*!' 'I love you more than the eternities!' 'No, *I* love *you* more than the eternities!'" She was pale, her huge, manic eyes wide. Maybe having and then losing the Dark Queen's soul really had tipped her over the edge. "This one's all me."

She pushed Lend away from me and slammed her palm against his chest. I screamed, clawing at them, but he looked her in the eyes, then nodded, a small smile on his lips. "Okay," he said.

"What are you doing?" I tried to pull her arm away from him, but she shoved me to the ground with her free arm and pushed her foot against my chest so I couldn't get up.

I watched in horror as the light I could see from Lend got dimmer and dimmer, his glamour fading in and out. He grimaced in pain but didn't move. Vivian closed her eyes, throwing her head back from the rush.

"Vivian!" I shouted.

Her eyes opened, and she came back to herself, snapping her hand away from Lend's chest. He collapsed against a tree, hand over his heart as he panted. He quickly shifted through a variety of glamours before dropping them all and looking down at his water skin, then putting his head back in relief that everything seemed normal. Well, as normal as he ever was. I jumped up, touching his face, his chest, trying to see how much she'd taken, see whether or not he'd be okay.

"It's fine, Evie. I'll be fine." Lend gave me a pained smile, putting his normal glamour back on. I could still see his soul, but it was a faint hint now, like mine.

"How could you do that?" I screamed as I spun around to Vivian who now glowed with Lend's own soul's light. "How could you take that from him? Do you hate me that much?"

"No! It's the best gift I can ever give you. You gave me everything, Evie. You gave me the soul I never deserved to have. So I'm giving you and Lend the life you deserve together."

"I—" My jaw dropped as I realized she hadn't been attacking Lend at all. "You're going through."

She bared her teeth at me in her crazy, off-kilter smile. "In case you hadn't noticed, the only thing I have on this planet is you. If you left, where would I be?"

"But you don't want to live with the faeries forever!"

She laughed. "I dunno, an eternity of pissing them off and being a thorn in their sides? I can live with that. Plus I can keep your vampire friend company, right?"

I shook my head. "You don't have to. I can still do this."

"No, you can't. But will you walk me there?" She held out her hand and I took it in mine.

Lend struggled to stand upright but I waved him away. "I'll be back," I said, my voice breaking because, thanks to Vivian, it was true. He nodded in understanding as Vivian and I braced ourselves and stepped out of the shelter of the trees, tripping forward with the wind shoving us toward the gate.

We barely managed to stop directly in front of it. "Are you sure?" I shouted.

Vivian nodded. We hugged, clinging to each other, and she put her lips to my ear to shout, "I'll see you in your dreams, okay, stupid?"

I nodded, even my tears being whipped away and through the gate. Vivian stepped back and let herself be pulled through to the other side.

The light was so bright it hurt my eyes, but I didn't look away, wouldn't look away. She jolted like an electric current had run through her body, then opened her pale gray eyes. But they weren't the empty pale gray they'd always been. They were shining and bright and bold. It was like she'd been when she was full of souls, but this time there wasn't the emptiness she couldn't get rid of no matter how hard she tried. This time it was all her, as she should be, happy and full and complete. She smiled at me, and I mouthed the only words I could say, as pathetic and inadequate as they were.

"Thank you. I love you."

She smiled, then held up her hand, her face going still with concentration. But it wasn't working, nothing was happening, and Lend's sacrifice would be for nothing. I put my hands to my mouth in horror. Then the edges of the gate went fuzzy, the remains of Virginia night curling in around them, eating at the light until it started collapsing in on itself.

Vivian met my eyes for the last time, and she winked. And then, with an ear-rupturing silent pop like all the air pressure in the world had changed, the gate connecting us closed forever.

I didn't realize I was sitting on the frozen ground until Lend collapsed next to me and put his arm around my shoulders.

"She did it," I whispered, the silence nearly as deafening as the wind had been but so empty it made me ache. If I didn't have Lend here, I didn't know what I'd do. It was almost like I *had* sent my soul through the gate. So much of who I had been—the people who had defined me, even the work that I'd lived for—was gone now. I felt small, and cold, and a little bit lost.

"*We* did it." Lend smoothed my wind-tossed hair away from my face.

"It's really over, isn't it?"

He laughed and pulled me into his lap. "That's the beauty of it all. Nothing's over. It's just a new start."

"Re-forming after the chaos," I said, remembering Raquel's words. "Choosing what we'll do with how things are now, who we'll be in this new world where the only magic left is what we make ourselves."

"Exactly. So who do you want to be?"

I smiled, resting my head against his chest. "I'm not sure yet, but I'm looking forward to finding out."

ACKNOWLEDGMENTS

Parting is such sweet sorrow. Or, you know, sometimes it just plain sucks.

To Noah, for being my own piece of eternity in a broken world. To Elena and Jonah, for bringing endless light and joy into my life. To my parents, for always believing in me. To my siblings, for being my friends down to their DNA. To my in-laws, all eleventy-billion of them, for loving and supporting me (especially when that support is babysitting). To my friends, who are many, for putting up with me both in real life and online.

To Natalie Whipple, who started this journey with me and without whom I never would have made it past the starting line. To Stephanie Perkins, who keeps me company in humorous insanity and understands everything, always, just the way I need her to. To everyone else who has read any of these books in any of their forms—especially Shannon Messenger and Scott Tracey, for racing me through an impossible draft—thank you. So, so very much.

To Michelle Wolfson, my fabulous, tiny, spitfire of an agent, for being my partner in all this and the engineer of my dreams. To Erica Sussman, my brilliant and insightful and ever adored editor, for choosing Evie. Heigh ho!

To my team of mild-mannered Superhero Alter Egos at HarperTeen: Christina Colangelo, Casey McIntyre, Tyler Infinger, Lauren Flower, Megan Sugrue, Alison Donalty, Michelle Taormina, Jessica Berg, and everyone else whose tireless efforts give Evie the prettiest covers and the best copyediting and marketing and publicity, and get her from my head to your bookshelf (or e-reader, I'm not picky).

To Evie for being a bright voice in my head, even through dark times. To all the music that helped me slip into that voice, as always Snow Patrol but especially Florence + the Machine, whose haunting weaving of fantasy into music fed this entire book. To dreams and stories and wonder, and all the writers and musicians and artists who have fed my inner dreamer through the years.

To you, my readers, without whom none of this would matter. Thank you for embracing Evie in all her pink-loving exuberance. Thank you for reading. I bleeping love all of you.

The end.

DON'T MISS A SINGLE PAGE OF THE *NEW YORK TIMES* BESTSELLING PARANORMALCY TRILOGY!